We hope you enjoy this book.
Please return or renew it by the due date.
You can renew it at **www.norfolk.gov.uk/libraries**
or by using our free library app. Otherwise you can
phone **0344 800 8020** - please have your library
card and pin ready.
You can sign up for email reminders too.

10/20		

NORFOLK COUNTY COUNCIL
LIBRARY AND INFORMATION SERVICE

D1424985

29 08436 522

Loris Owen likes mysteries, enigmas, conundrums, puzzles and synonyms. She roamed around the world a bit before moving to Kent where she runs a 'mowl' sanctuary and spends her days hunting for interesting combinations of words. *The Ten Riddles of Eartha Quicksmith* is her first novel.

The Ten RIDDLES of Eartha Quicksmith

LORIS OWEN

Firefly

First published in 2020
by Firefly Press
25 Gabalfa Road, Llandaff North, Cardiff, CF14 2JJ
www.fireflypress.co.uk

A CIP catalogue record of this book is available
from the British Library.

ISBN 978-1-913102-31-9
ebook ISBN 978-1-913102-32-6

This book has been published with the support of
the Welsh Books Council.

Typeset by Elaine Sharples

Printed and bound by CPI Group UK

To Liam:
half Steampunk, half Theo and half mowl.
For all the pages you turned,
and times you believed in me.

See the ordinary as extraordinary,
the familiar as strange

Novalis

Quicksmiths
College of Strange Energy

1 - Skycrackle Tower
2 - Music Rooms
3 - Sixth Year Block
4 - Atlas House
5 - Hall of Maps
6 - Clock Tower
7 - Botanical Gardens
8 - Fifth Year Block
9 - Fourth Year Block
10 - Celestial Hall
11 - The Buttery
12 - Portrait Gallery
13 - Second Year Block
14 - Confucius Courtyard
15 - Garden of Giant Leapfrogs

16 - Aristotle's Theatre
17 - Playing Fields
18 - The Library
19 - Workshops
20 - Singing Mill

21 - Labs
22 - Quantum Quarter
23 - Storage Rooms
24 - Professors' Block
25 - Ptolemy Courtyard

26 - Porter House
27 - The Hive
28 - First Year Block
29 - Q10
30 - Third Year Block

Chapter One

The Coin

Someone's watching me.

Kip looked down from his favourite hideout halfway up the Chess Nut Tree. A couple of Saturday joggers and dog walkers went by, but they all had their eyes on the ground.

He returned to his homework, which was balanced on the flattest part of the Halfway Branch. But he'd written only a few lines when that unmistakable feeling of being watched came back, stronger this time.

There was definitely no one looking up at him. As usual, Ashleigh had disappeared with her squawking friends right after dropping him off. And Chess Club didn't start for twenty minutes.

Who is it? he wondered.

Kip shifted his weight to scan the park behind him, then pulled back instinctively. Silently hovering between the bare branches, and swaying ever so

1

slightly, was a flat, oval drone. It was white and metallic and about the size of Kip's hand. Two fat antennae stuck up from the front, and at the top of each antenna was a bright, emerald light that turned the nearby branches a ghostly green.

After a few seconds, Kip said, 'Hello?'

The drone did not respond. Kip noticed with a sense of unease that it was expanding and contracting gently.

Looks like it's breathing.

Like a floating, futuristic beetle, the drone moved closer, weaving slowly through the branches. It stopped just as Kip could see his forehead and short-cropped brown hair reflected in its gleaming side, distorted like your face when you look into the back of a spoon.

'What do you want?' he challenged.

The reflection of his own eyes looked back – a mixture of glittery brown and light grey, as if copper and iron had half melted together.

Kip tried waving a hand cautiously in front of the green antennae tips and, at last, the drone did something. With a quiet *whirr-click*, a tray slid out from its underbelly.

In the tray was an envelope, and below the first-class stamp there was something handwritten in dark-red ink.

To Kip Bramley

Kip picked up the envelope. It could be a prank. He checked thoroughly in every direction: still no suspects in sight. Carefully, he pulled open the glued-down flap so it came away without ripping.

Instead of a letter inside, Kip found a fifty-pence coin. He held the envelope upside down and gave it a gentle shake. Nothing else fell out.

'What…?'

But his question faded away as he looked up. The drone had gone.

A few people were setting up their chessboards on the tables underneath the tree. Voices drifted up through the branches stripped clean by winter.

'Spring is finally here.'

'Can't believe it's warm enough to have Chess Club outside already.'

Kip put the coin back in the envelope, zipped it safely into his rucksack and began to climb down. It wouldn't be long before everyone else arrived – young and old, tall and small – all brought together by their love of the game.

After Chess Club, Ashleigh was waiting. To earn her wage, she had to collect Kip and take him home to Eelstowe housing estate. As usual, she dumped him at the front door of his flat like she was a bored delivery girl with something much better to do.

'Be right back,' she said, tapping at her phone.

It was often hard to tell if she was talking to him, or saying her texts out loud.

Kip let himself in, sat down at the small kitchen table and took the envelope out of his rucksack.

Who would send me fifty pence? In a drone? he thought.

It couldn't be a mistake. There was his name in dark-red letters on the envelope. Kip ran his fingers around the seven edges of the coin. Weren't they usually silver? But this one was gold. Something else was different, Kip was certain, but he couldn't quite work out what it was.

I should find another one. To compare them.

He emptied the contents of the chipped mug that held all the spare change. Fortunately, there was a shiny fifty-pence piece hiding among the pennies. Kip put the silver and gold fifties next to each other.

On the tails side of the silver coin was a lion. But the gold coin had a strange candle with a flame at both ends. When he turned the coins over, the silver one had a portrait of the Queen, with her name and the year written in an arc above her. The gold coin had the Queen too, but instead of her name there were three words:

CHANGE YOUR WORLD

There was a jangling of keys outside, and Kip hastily returned the gold coin to its envelope as the front door opened.

4

The Pointers

The Pointers lived a few doors down and Mr Pointer was employed by the council to do repairs on the sixty or so flats in their building. Ashleigh, their daughter, had finished school last year. Now she sold second-hand vinyl records online to make money. Almost as soon as the Bramleys had moved in she had been hired by Kip's dad, Theo. Her job: to hang around when Theo was working late shifts or overtime, which was most days.

'Does she have to? She's so annoying,' Kip had complained after a few weeks. 'And I'm too old to have someone looking after me.'

Theo had picked up the family photograph on the windowsill and stroked the glass with his thumb.

'I worry about you, that's all...'

As his dad had blinked away tears and hugged Kip tightly, Kip had felt his own eyes prickling.

'Sorry. I know, Dad. It's OK, Ashleigh's not that bad really.'

A hand waved in front of Kip's face, interrupting his thoughts.

'Hello Kipper,' crooned Ashleigh.

She leaned against the fridge, loudly picking food out of her teeth and holding another reminder from the electricity company for Mr T. Bramley to pay the bill, written in big, shouty letters.

'It's Kip,' he said for the two-hundredth time.

But Ashleigh was already yelling at someone behind her.

'Dad. DAD – you coming?'

She turned back to Kip and looked at her phone instead of at him.

'Your sink's blocked.'

A lanky, grey-haired man carrying a rusty toolbox creaked slowly into the kitchen after Ashleigh. Close behind him was a large woman wearing rubber gloves and waving a duster.

'You been washing noodles down the plughole again, Kip?' said Mrs Pointer. 'Course you have.'

She prodded Mr Pointer with a yellow finger.

'Tony, it's noodles. Check for noodles.'

Mr Pointer grunted and Mrs Pointer scanned the kitchen for anything of interest. Her greedy eyes noticed the envelope in Kip's hands.

'What's that? A party invite? Course it is. See Ashleigh, he's making new friends already. Didn't I say he would?'

Ashleigh looked up from her phone.

'Wassat?'

'Who's it from, dear?' said Mrs Pointer.

Kip slipped the envelope behind his back and inched away.

'Exactly ... a party invite. From ... um ... 'scuse me for a moment.'

'Must be a girl…' Mrs Pointer's voice trailed from the kitchen.

On his way to hide the envelope, Kip glanced at the menu on the worn-out corkboard in the hallway and smiled. Theo Bramley was a chef and every week he made up a daft theme. He was a genius with food, turning everyday supermarket ingredients into fiendishly realistic creations.

Last month had ended with *Supervillain Banquets*, and March had begun with *Disgustible Dining*. The last couple of days had already included some of Theo's finest creations ever.

Thursday

Dinner:

Tentacle-and-beak surprise with extra ooze

Twice-boiled drain toad on peppered slug tracks

Pickled zombie skin in slime mould trifle

Friday

Dinner:

Find-the-eyeball soup

Runny sock cheese with wet dog armpits

Lice pudding in four-sneeze sauce

They were going to be hard to beat, but today's menu looked promising.

Saturday
Lunch:
Coughed-up hairballs and bedbug couscous
Chefs fingernails in bin-juice jelly
Dinner:
Bellyflap mushrooms on furry green toast
Elephant earwax stir-fry
with thousand-year-old cabbage
Bath-scum ice cream with grated frostbite

In the kitchen Ashleigh and Mrs Pointer started arguing about something and Kip hurried on to his bedroom. Above him, a small white butterfly crawled across the white-hot bulb of the hallway light. Had Kip looked up, he might have wondered why the heat wasn't frying the insect's delicate wings into two flapping crisps.

Pinky

Once the envelope was stowed safely between two pages of a big blue notebook, Kip put the book inside Pinky's lair. This was a tall, metal storage rack from a used-furniture shop, which Kip and his dad had adapted, adding wire mesh to make a secure hutch with lots of roaming room. One of Kip's happiest memories was creating a paradise for Pinky inside: apple tree branches, rope swings, toys, and comfy hiding places packed with shredded old clothes. A board tied to the mesh proclaimed 'DANGER' in pink paint.

'Pinky, guard this with your life! Don't let anyone near it!'

Pinky was curled up in her favourite napping nook – a half coconut shell Theo had saved from work. Two chocolate-drop eyes peered out from under a scrap of Kip's outgrown pyjamas. Beneath them, a small smudge of a nose twitched at the centre of a spray of long, dainty whiskers.

This was her way of saying, 'I am Pinky – security guard – licensed to kill – message received.'

'However bad Ledhill Academy gets,' Kip said, 'you were worth it, Pinky.'

His mobile beeped and Kip grabbed it eagerly: it might be a message from his best friend, Hal. It had been weeks since he'd heard anything.

We're short-staffed again : (*Back before dinner. Don't forget your homework. Sorry, Dad.*

Doubly disappointed, Kip left the phone on the bed and wandered back to find that Mrs Pointer had put his plate of coughed-up hairballs on the fold-out dining table. Now she was dusting two photographs on the chipped windowsill.

'This is such a good one,' she said, holding up the plain wooden frame. 'What's the joke?'

'No joke, really,' said Kip. 'You just had to be there.'

It had been taken in one of those photo booths that

prints out a strip of four different snapshots. Theo and Kip were pulling uglier and uglier faces in each picture, except the last one where they had both collapsed in laughter.

'And this, so beautiful, such a beautiful family.'

She dabbed a faded golden frame with her stained duster.

Theo had his arm round the shoulders of a girl with braces on her teeth and her hair done up in twisty buns – Kip's older sister Suzie. That photo sometimes seemed more real than his memories of her, memories that came and went like the sun trying to break through thick clouds: her zebra-stripe slippers; falling off her BMX; the garden den she built from old sheets. Theo's other arm was around a pretty woman with light brown hair just like Kip's. Rosalind Bramley – or Rose as everyone called her. On her knee was a toddler as chubby as a dough ball – mini-Kip. The sun was shining behind them so their faces weren't very clear, but you could tell they were all smiling.

'So tragic,' Mrs Pointer muttered, as if Kip wasn't even there. 'Isn't it just like a story from the news?'

Kip pretended to blow on his lunch a lot and made sure his mouth was always full so he didn't have to say anything.

'Falling in love at the museum,' mumbled Mrs Pointer. 'So romantic. Meets the handsome chef at

10

the Valentine's Day chocolate fountain. Then happy families … but such heartbreak…'

Sometimes when Kip was thinking about his mum, he found himself twisting the piece of quartz crystal that hung on a thin leather cord around his neck. When he looked at it, tuning everything else out was easy, even Mrs Pointer's babbling.

All those years ago, after the lightning struck, Theo had found Rose and five-year-old Kip on the path from their old house to the sea, and she had been clutching this fragment of quartz tightly. Although unconscious, Rose hadn't relaxed her grip. It was only later, in the hospital, that she had woken and called Kip over. With great effort, she had pressed it into his hand and spoken a single word: 'keep'. With all the bad stuff that was happening, everyone except Kip had been much too busy to give it more than a fleeting glance at the time.

To Kip, the forking pale-blue icicle was both beautiful and terrible. There was a shape inside that only appeared in the right light and it was there as he stared down now – an amber wave trapped forever in the moment of breaking. Every so often, staring at it was like trying to remember something.

'And how is your mother doing, dear?' asked Mrs Pointer, suddenly standing right next to Kip.

'OK I s'pose,' said Kip, shifting uncomfortably. 'The same…'

The bedbug couscous had now cooled down enough to finish in a few bites. Kip took his plate back to the kitchen, grabbed his bowl of bin-juice jelly and an orange, and excused himself to do his homework.

Both bedrooms were tiny but Theo had given Kip the larger one, so there was just enough space for a small desk next to Pinky's lair. Kip squeezed past the wardrobe and put down his bowl.

Inside the lair, Pinky's face emerged from the coconut cradle. Kip's lunchtime was only halfway through her usual ten hours of sleep, but her delicate nose snuffled alertly in the direction of the jelly. Then the tiny flying squirrel darted out of the half-coconut and scampered up the wire mesh until she was hanging upside down from the hutch roof in line with Kip's ear. She somehow clung to the wire expertly while she scratched under her chin with one back paw, and blinked sleepily.

'Come on then, Furball,' said Kip, opening the lair door to let Pinky out. 'You can have some orange. But no jelly.'

Pinky's daily routine usually went something like this:

04:00 – 05:30 rope climbing; ladder scurrying; search for secret nut stash
05:30 – 06:30 rockstar rehearsal with toy cymbal/bell; investigate different sleeping options
06:30 – 07:00 bedtime snack and cuddles

07:00 – 17:30 hide away from bright sunlight in one of the following a) scarf hammock b) sock nest c) coconut cradle d) Kip's pocket or under Kip's shirt; sleep, squeaking occasionally; forget location of secret nut stash; get up for mid-sleep fruit snack
17:30 – 18:00 chirruping and waking-up cuddles
18:00 – 21:00 breakfast; play Find-the-Raisin; curtain climbing and gliding practice; more breakfast; watch Kip go to sleep
21:00 – 04:00 guard Kip

As Pinky nibbled on her orange slice, Kip took the big blue notebook and shook the coin out of its envelope on to the bed. The boy and the squirrel stared at the heptagon of shiny metal.

'Look Pinky. Someone's sent me a weird fifty pence. But why? It's not like I collect coins.'

Pinky dropped the orange and tried to flip the coin over as if the answers to Kip's questions might scuttle out from underneath.

'And what about that drone? I agree – it doesn't make any sense.'

Frowning, Kip opened the notebook. On the front were these words:

Book of Squirls Part 13

Sometimes, when Kip was thinking really hard about

something, the space behind his closed eyes would fill up with irresistible patterns: squirls. It was a childish word now for a boy his age, but he didn't care; it was the name his dad had given them.

'Your drawings are halfway between squiggles and swirls,' he had said. 'Squirls.'

Kip flicked through the pages. He had been drawing squirls for as long as he could remember, but had never really found the exact words to explain what they were. To him they felt alive, with veins of light instead of blood, and sometimes it even seemed as if he shared the same pulse.

Pinky yawned and crawled up Kip's arm to snuggle in the crook of his elbow. He stroked her silky brown back gently with one finger and she closed her eyes and sighed a tiny sigh.

Kip reached across to the desk for a pen and closed his eyes too. But not to sleep. It wasn't long before a squirl shimmered and rippled into focus from the far distance. As Kip drew, it felt like he was sailing along its waves and rolling down its bright corkscrews. And when he was lost in a squirl like this the hours could sail and roll away like minutes...

'Knock knock?'

The door opened a crack, then widened and Theo Bramley entered the room. He was a short, broad-shouldered man with a kind face and a neat salt-and-pepper beard.

'Sorry I'm so late,' he said. 'But the good news is our weekend starts … now!'

At the sound of Theo's voice, Pinky woke with an excited chirp. Kip jumped up to get a hug that smelled of freshly baked bread, and Theo rubbed the soft bristle of Kip's hair with his knuckles. They sat back on the bed and Pinky ping-ponged between her two favourite people in a blur of brown and white fur until Theo produced a sweet potato treat from his shirt pocket. Pinky took it delicately with her teeth and began to eat, nibbling and squeaking at the same time.

Theo stood up to straighten the duvet and Kip's mobile slid off the bed.

'Anything from Hal today?' asked Theo gently, putting it on the desk.

Months ago, when Theo had quit his old job, they had moved to London and ended up at this flat on the estate. That had meant a new school for Kip – Ledhill Community Academy – and leaving his best friend Hal behind.

At first, Kip and Hal had texted and called all the time, and had visited at weekends whenever they could. But then, disaster had struck: Hal moved to Australia with his family. As the weeks passed, Hal's replies took longer and longer to come back and Kip felt more and more alone.

'I guess he's busy,' said Kip.

'Well, I'm sure you'll always be close. But he's

started a whole new life on the other side of the world. He'll need to make new friends there.'

Theo looked down at the half-drawn pattern in the Book of Squirls.

'Things getting any easier at Ledhill?'

Kip tried to put on a brave face. He didn't want his dad to worry.

There were three groups in his class. First there was the sporty group, but Kip didn't like the way they shoved each other for fun and picked on the kids who weren't good at PE. Kip didn't belong in the clever group either: they talked noisily about how brilliant they were, did sums out loud and boasted about how many awards they'd won. And the cool kids just made fun of everything everyone said and mocked anyone who dared to do well in class.

Then there was The Snibbug.

Kip's form teacher – and the dreaded Head of Science – was Miss Gubbins. But when Kip said her name backwards it seemed to suit her much better.

The questions The Snibbug asked made Kip wonder if she thought all children were stupid. She actually even called her students 'dense' or 'dull-skulled' if they didn't get something right first time. Most infuriatingly of all, she swallowed yawns when Kip was answering her questions.

Kip's 'it's-fine' face didn't fool his dad.

'Perhaps I should talk to Miss Gubbins?' he suggested.

'No, it's OK,' said Kip hurriedly. 'I don't think that's a good idea.'

'Maybe you could invite a friend to come to the climbing wall with us?' Theo said.

Kip said nothing. There was no one he could call a friend, never mind a best friend.

'Let's give it to the end of term and see if things get better.'

Kip nodded. But he knew it would feel like forever until the holidays.

'Look what I found,' he said, changing the subject.

Won't mention the drone. Probably just a bored, rich kid. Don't want Dad to overreact and cancel Chess Club or something.

Theo took the gold coin.

'Hmmm,' he said. 'That's unusual. Heads: it's leprechaun gold and gives you three wishes. Tails: it's for the drinks machine at MI5's secret headquarters.'

He flipped the coin.

'Heads it is.'

Six chimes spilled out from the clock in the hallway.

'Better get dinner on,' said Theo, giving Kip the coin back. 'Don't know about you, but I could eat an elephant.'

'Think we've only got elephant earwax,' Kip replied, trying to keep a straight face. 'Double helping?'

17

The Vending Machine

Like all the best Sundays the next day was full of promise. Kip and his dad wallowed in the morning and lazed through lunch. But as always, the afternoon ran into the evening too fast and another Monday came stomping up to crush the short-lived weekend under its heel.

Kip usually sat at the back of the classroom, trying not to get volunteered for anything. On this dull Monday morning, he felt occasionally for the cold, smooth coin in his pocket, to check it was still there.

When school finished there was no one to say goodbye to, and he hurried to the gate where Ashleigh was waiting. He passed Olly Gorton, the boy from his class who had made it his mission in life to be as unfriendly to Kip as possible. Olly was always boasting about his hunting knife, as if he liked the idea of making other kids uneasy.

Don't turn around, Kip thought. *Don't ask me who Ashleigh is.*

Kip's back arched involuntarily as he thought about the Claw Chair. For the last few weeks, someone had kept swapping his chair for the spare one with the sharp nail that stuck out. He had suspected Olly and challenged him in front of everyone. It didn't turn into a fight but after that someone drew the outline of a knife in pink glitter pen on his desk. And the Claw Chair kept on turning up.

Kip tapped Ashleigh on the shoulder and walked on ahead as fast as he could.

'Where's the fire?' Ashleigh complained, unable to text and keep up with Kip's get-away-from-school pace at the same time. 'Wait! I have to buy tomatoes.'

Kip stayed outside the grocer's, watching an ant carrying a breadcrumb. He followed it round the corner of the building and came across a gum-vending machine on top of a thick black pole.

They must have put this up over the weekend, he thought.

The upper half of the machine was clear and, instead of gum, Kip could see a pile of plastic eggs inside. The bottom half was made of steel, into which these words were stamped:

CHANGE YOUR WORLD

Kip took the gold coin out of his pocket and looked at the letters around the Queen's head.

Knew I'd read that somewhere before.

There were so many things he wanted to change in his world, but only one really mattered. His fingers felt around the shape of the crystal pendant hidden safely out of sight under his shirt as always.

There was only one option. The coin rattled down inside the machine and a few seconds later a plastic

19

egg dropped into the collection drawer. As he picked it up, Kip felt his heart pick up a beat too.

The plastic egg screwed open easily and inside Kip found two things: an oblong pin badge with a protective peel-off cover, and a piece of folded paper.

Really? A stupid badge? What a scam.

He put the badge in his pocket and unfolded the paper, hoping for something more promising. The last thing he was expecting was a wordsearch.

The theme was 'Types of Energy'. Twelve letters had been ringed with dark-red ink, making a diamond in the grid. In a blank space under the wordsearch someone had scribbled something, also in red ink. Kip recognised the handwriting from the envelope.

You already have the other half.

Questions poured from his head like the overflow from a hydroelectric dam.

Other half of what? How can this possibly be meant for me? Who knew I would put the coin in that machine? And get that exact egg?

Kip took the badge out of his pocket. On closer inspection, it looked broken – there was no pin at the back to attach it to his clothes. The cover peeled away easily, revealing a honeycomb-patterned red candle. At each end of the candle was a white flame and in each flame was a golden eye.

The image on the coin!

Things were looking less and less accidental. It was hard to believe, but someone had planned this. Someone was trying to get a message to him.

The shop doorbell tringed as Ashleigh came out.

'Wassat?' she muttered, glancing at the badge.

'Just a stupid free gift,' said Kip, putting it back in his pocket.

It wasn't long to wait until he was back in his bedroom, away from prying eyes. Everything was peaceful: it was an hour until sunset and Pinky was still sleeping in her scarf hammock. Silently, Kip placed the drone envelope, the candle badge and the wordsearch on his desk.

First, he picked up the wordsearch and looked at the letters that had been circled.

q i k m t s n i e y u o

Kip spent ages thinking about those twelve letters. He read them backwards. He looked at them upside down and in the bathroom mirror, in case they spelt out something back to front.

'Anagrams!' he whispered suddenly.

But when he tried jumbling up the letters into something that made sense, this was the best Kip could do:

I quit monkeys

Mini sky quote

My quiet oinks

This isn't going anywhere, he thought. *Try something else.*

On the desk, still awaiting inspection, were the candle badge and the envelope. He picked up the badge first. There was a slider on the side, which he pushed up and down – but it didn't do anything – so he turned his attention to the envelope.

It was made of ordinary paper, but that didn't mean it couldn't be hiding something. None of the letters in his name were bold, underlined or highlighted. And there were no hidden flaps. Kip dabbed it with lemon juice from the kitchen, in case something was written in invisible ink. But all that did was make it smell of lemons.

There was a rattle in the lair, and Kip looked up to see Pinky gnawing the edge of her cuttlefish bone.

'What am I missing, Pinky?' he asked.

Kip opened the lair door and held up the badge, the wordsearch and the envelope. Pinky bounded over, extended one paw uncertainly and sniffed at the envelope.

Clock Face

'You're right,' Kip said. 'It's definitely the envelope. But why?'

He looked at the stamp in case there was a postmark showing where the envelope had been sent from. And then excitement sparked between his ribs as he realised.

'I've got it, Pinky! Why would you put a stamp on a letter delivered by drone?'

The stamp looked innocently stamp-like – small and square and smooth.

'Maybe it folds out?'

But it was just as thin and flat as a stamp should be.

The picture on the stamp was of a red brick clock tower with a yellow face. Outside in the hallway, the Bramleys' clock ticked encouragingly.

The time might be a clue? Kip thought.

But the yellow clock face on the stamp was blank, with no hands or numbers to mark off the hours. Kip stared at it so long that his eyes started crossing.

'Anyone home?' Theo's voice drifted in from the hallway.

Kip shoved the candle badge and the wordsearch in the envelope, hid it under his pillow and ran out to greet his dad. By the time dinner was finished and they had played an hour of Find-the-Raisin with Pinky, Kip's eyes wouldn't stay open and he fell gratefully into bed.

Late that night, when the dark was at its darkest, Kip woke up from a dream that promptly faded. With a surge of excitement, he remembered the unsolved

23

mystery and lifted the corner of the pillow. Now, in the still of night, there was something different about the envelope. A faint, yellow glow was radiating from the corner where the stamp was.

Instantly awake, Kip opened the curtain. He didn't want to hurt Pinky's sensitive nocturnal eyes with sudden bright light, and the streetlight that seeped in was just enough to see by. From the highest platform in her lair, she watched curiously as Kip dived under his bed for a box of old, abandoned toys. After an impatient hunt, he held up a chipped magnifying glass like the prized trophy of a lost civilisation.

Staring down into the ghostly circle of the magnifying glass was like looking into a shadowy well, with the stamp floating at the bottom. And there, around the stamp's clock face, glowing in the dark, were twelve tiny letters instead of numbers.

By the soft light of the moon and the streetlight leaking through the window, Kip copied these luminous letters on to a piece of paper.

u c s i h i v t s o c m

Twelve letters, he thought.

Somewhere in the toy box was a torch. It still worked, and soon Kip was examining the wordsearch. There were exactly twelve letters there too, ringed in red.

q i k m t s n i e y u o

Underneath them was the unsolved clue: 'You already have the other half.'

One by one, he wrote down the letters from the wordsearch, slotting them in between the letters he had already copied from the stamp. The two halves of the puzzle fitted together perfectly.

'Quicksmiths...' he whispered.

'...invites...'

Pinky chittered softly, sensing something important.

'...you com.'

Quicksmithsinvitesyou.com? A website. And an invitation?

Kip waited impatiently for his ancient, second-hand laptop to start up, while anticipation drummed like fingers on his ribcage.

When the website finally loaded, there was hardly anything on it. Just the candle symbol again, an address, a date and a time, and his name.

88a Helix Avenue, London
March 20th
Kip Bramley
Appointment time 09:30

Underneath, there were two download buttons which linked to a chess puzzle and a series of large emojis.

'Not exactly answers, Pinky. And nearly two weeks until March the twentieth.'

As Kip closed the laptop lid, his eyes started to shut down too, so he climbed back into bed. Pinky kept watch silently, making sure that her human was safe and all was well. From her vantage point in the third-floor flat she looked down at the tops of the streetlamps, clinging on to the night and refusing to give up their light. A white butterfly circled one of them energetically. The little flying squirrel watched it with interest until the orange glow of dawn began to spread across the sky like Kip's favourite breakfast marmalade.

Chapter Two

The Snibbug

Oh, how The Snibbug loved the sound of her own voice! That was why she had become a teacher, Kip decided, so she could hear herself telling other people what to do every day of every term of every year.

Kip closed his eyes and thought about the website.

What's Quicksmiths? Who's sending me puzzles? And how do they even know I like puzzles?

In this space that no one else could come to, the space within his closed eyes, endless questions and endless possibilities stretched out in all directions, like restless squirls.

'Mister Bramley!'

The Snibbug's voice was as deep as an ogre's because of all the cigarettes she chainsmoked at Chimney Corner outside the staff room.

'Are you sleeping in class?'

'Sorry, Miss Sni … Gubbins. No, I was just listening.'

'Well, your eyelids aren't broken, are they? You can listen with them open,' she croaked, and the whole class laughed.

'In fact,' she continued, 'seeing as you're awake now, you can come up to the whiteboard and draw us a cell structure.'

Kip dragged his feet to the front of the class and picked up a marker pen while The Snibbug read aloud from a textbook. Once he had drawn the cell membrane and started on the nucleus, his attention wandered. It was impossible not to think about Quicksmiths and the two puzzles from the website.

Distantly, he heard the class erupt into laughter again and wondered what The Snibbug had said. But it wasn't The Snibbug.

'Miss! Miss!' he heard Olly Gorton yell. 'Kip's drawing worms again.'

'Kip Arthur Bramley!' The Snibbug barked coldly, and Kip jumped and cringed at the same time.

He looked at the whiteboard in dismay. The cell structure he had been drawing had been taken over by a squirl – the long sweep of a spiral breaking out into smaller and smaller spirals.

'I've lost track of the times you've disrupted this class in just a few months. This will have to go in your report. Jennifer, please come up and correct the drawing.'

Kip went back to his desk, wishing he could crawl

inside a cupboard and never come out. Every day on his way to school, he imagined something happening out of the blue so that he would never have to hear The Snibbug's ogreish voice ever again. But every day, he didn't *have* to join the Earth's army because of an alien attack, and a meteor had *not* squashed her car while she was driving to work. Monday to Friday, he found himself trying not to get into trouble just for being himself.

Circuitous Rambler

BRIIIIIIING!

The final bell. And not just the final bell of any old day, but the final bell of Friday. Things got better when Kip saw his dad waiting at the school gate instead of Ashleigh.

'Surprise!' said Theo. 'I've got the evening off. Boys' night!'

'Bad kung-fu movies?' asked Kip. 'Back-to-back?'

'And dinner in our pyjamas.'

Kip grinned. This was exactly what he needed after another painful week at Ledhill.

'Time with Dad' topped the list of Kip's five favourite things, the things that always cheered him up. These were the others:

Pinky
Puzzles
Climbing
Chess Club

Kip tried to drag out that evening with his dad as long as he could, and Pinky helped by entertaining them with her best acrobatics. But it had to come to an end eventually. He fell asleep full of food and laughs and that warm feeling of weekend freedom.

That feeling was still with him when he woke the next day and got himself ready. Mrs Olah's Chess Club met every Saturday morning – usually at the nearby community centre. But the good weather had lasted so the club was meeting outside again.

The number 16 bus dropped them outside Leafields Park and Ashleigh followed Kip right up to the Chess Nut Tree.

'Back at twelve,' she said, smiling at something on her phone.

Chess Club didn't start for a while, so Kip tightened his rucksack and took a running jump to land high on the trunk. In his old gym class he'd come first in climbing for two years straight, and now he scrambled effortlessly among the first leaves of spring like a lemur in a tracksuit.

'Seen any more drones?' Kip asked the tree, as he pulled himself up to the Halfway Branch.

Over the last few months, he had smoothed out the bark on this wide, almost horizontal branch with an old kitchen knife. His jumper made a comfortable cushion against the trunk and he settled down and opened his rucksack. Pressed inside the Book of Squirls was the envelope containing the candle badge, and two pieces of folded paper – the puzzles he had printed from the website.

Kip unfolded one of these printouts. Just four images on the page.

'There should be a confused emoji too,' he muttered.

The second printout was much more promising.

Black Castle A2
White Bishop B7
Black Knight C6
Black Prawn D5
Black King E7
White Castle H4

Someone had been careless, typing prawn instead of pawn. But a little spelling mistake wasn't going to get in Kip's way. He'd packed his old magnetic chessboard, which he now opened out on the flattest part of the branch. Like many chessboards, this one had numbers running down each side...

8

7

6

5

4

3

2

1

… and letters running across the top and bottom.

A   B   C   D   E   F   G   H

Kip took the six chess pieces listed in the puzzle and arranged them in the right places on the board. Resting his elbows on his knees, he stared at the scene of war beneath him. In no time at all, Kip was in another world, eyes dancing as he imagined different strategies.

Something brushed against his face. Deep in thought, he was only half aware of raising a hand. A few seconds later, he felt it again.

When Kip looked up, a butterfly did a loop-the-loop right in front of his face. It looked like an ordinary cabbage white but, still, he was pleasantly surprised when it decided to land on his arm. When it stopped moving, he could see a faint pattern on its wings.

Forgetting about the chess puzzle, he slowly raised his arm so as not to scare it away. Now he could see silver threads shimmering across its white, wafery wings that reminded him a little bit of electrical circuits.

I've never seen a pattern like that, he thought. *You must be rare.*

Just then a bicycle bell rang below and the butterfly launched back into its chaotic flutter. Kip stood carefully, holding on to a woody knurl growing from the trunk. As he tried to catch the butterfly, it melted away into the white background of the cloudy sky.

You need a name. Electronic Flash? Silver-Veined Dither? Circuitous Rambler?

'Circuitous Rambler,' he said out loud. 'Definitely.'

'Are you up there, Kip?' a frail voice floated up from below.

Kip looked down from the Halfway Branch. Mrs Olah was wearing a huge brown-spotted sun hat, which looked like a giant mushroom had settled on her head for its Easter holiday. You could tell she had once been very beautiful; and these days she'd easily win a Miss Wrinkly Universe competition. When he had first met her, Kip had never guessed that this tiny, scatter-brained old lady who ran the club was a brilliant chess Grandmaster.

Being careful not to cause a freak rain of chess pieces down below, Kip packed everything back into his rucksack.

'I'm here, Mrs Olah,' he called down. 'Just a minute.'
The puzzles would have to wait.

Undersea Emporium

The light swilling through the gap under the curtains
prised open Kip's eyes shortly after dawn. A sea of
excitement sloshed around in his stomach when he
remembered that another week had passed and today
was the day he'd been waiting for.

The water heater started up with a creaky groan as
Theo turned the shower on. A little while later, Kip
heard his dad going round the flat, opening the
windows to let in the fresh, spring air.

Kip lay in bed considering his plan. When he had
checked the address on the Quicksmiths website he
had found that it was very close to Leafields Park, so
it might be possible to slip away from Chess Club for
an hour or so by himself.

'We can't tell Dad just yet,' he said quietly to Pinky.
'He'll only worry.'

The blanket over the coconut bed rustled and two
large, chocolate-drop eyes looked out.

This is actually happening, Kip thought.

Sensing Kip's excitement, Pinky jumped out of the
half-coconut and scrabbled round and round in her
nest of old socks.

'This is actually happening, Pinky,' he said.

34

Adventure was out there somewhere, waiting for him, revving its engine.

Once Ashleigh had dropped him off at Chess Club, Kip noticed something small and white and fluttery, glinting in the sun like a piece of foil resisting the breeze.

'Circuitous Rambler?' he said in surprise.

For a second Kip thought it was going to come over to him but it hither-thithered out of view behind a bench.

At the chess tables, Mrs Olah and Aakash were just setting up.

Aakash Gurung had previously taught art at Ledhill. Before that he had travelled all over the world in the army. He always wore a brimless hat, and a smart grey suit, and had a neat handkerchief triangle in his top pocket. Apparently, before retiring he'd been everyone's favourite teacher.

'Drawn anything good lately, Kip?' he asked as he lined up the pieces.

'About six pages this week,' Kip replied. 'There's one that looks a bit like a fingerprint. But I didn't bring my Book of Squirls today.'

'Who's playing first?' said Mrs Olah, looking up from the board.

'Actually,' said Kip, 'there's an appointment thing at nine-thirty I need to go to. It's not far,' he pointed, 'just the other side of the gate really.'

Before Mrs Olah could reply, Aakash stood up.

'As it happens, I need to go to the shops too. If Mrs Olah can spare me for a bit, I'll come with you.'

As they walked further away from the chess tables, things gradually became quieter, until there was hardly anyone around. It wasn't long before Kip spotted the street sign.

'It's down there. I'll be OK,' he said, hoping he wasn't going to have to explain everything instead of getting on with his quest. He needn't have worried.

'You have Mrs Olah's number in your phone, don't you?' said Aakash. 'Call us if you have any problems.'

There were a few shops on Helix Avenue but most had 'closed' signs in the windows. It was as if the whole street were still asleep.

Number 88 was a jeweller's with metal shutters over the windows. After the jeweller's there was an aquarium shop called *Undersea Emporium*. It was open but there was no number on the door. The next building along, 90 Helix Avenue, was a house with net curtains in the window.

At the end of the street, Aakash came out of a newsagent's and waved. Kip waved back and checked the address again.

'88a Helix Avenue.'

He hesitated at the aquarium shop door.

I can ask for directions inside, he thought, and went in.

The shop was bathed in a calm, yellow light that came from hundreds of illuminated fish tanks stacked in long rows. Kip sniffed. There was a smell of spicy seaweed.

Next to the door was a desk where the shopkeeper sat reading a magazine. The picture on the front showed a man with a huge, bushy moustache. The shopkeeper was holding the magazine up so that it looked like the face on the cover was his.

'Um,' Kip said. 'Is this 88a?'

The magazine twitched down an inch, revealing two big woolly, black eyebrows.

'It is,' came a rough voice from behind the magazine.

'Do you know if Quicksmiths is near here?' Kip tried again.

The magazine was very slowly lowered. Two hawkish eyes inspected Kip carefully.

'This is *Undersea Emporium*,' said the voice that belonged to the eyes.

The man put the magazine on the desk. If Kip hadn't been on a mission, he might have laughed to see that the man's moustache was exactly like the one on the cover of the magazine, and wider than both his eyebrows added together.

'The map brought me here,' said Kip, not giving up.

The prickly shopkeeper took Kip's printed-out map. He squinted at it and turned it around a few times.

'So it did,' he said, going back to his magazine.

'What about this?' said Kip, remembering the candle pin badge.

He held it up for the bushy-browed man.

'Looks like you got it in an old Christmas cracker,' said the man.

He seemed to enjoy this idea and, as he laughed to himself, he actually said the words 'heh, heh, heh'.

Getting Warmer

As Kip put the badge back in his shirt pocket, a troubling thought hit him. What if there was another Helix Avenue somewhere else in London and he'd somehow looked up the wrong one? He took out his mobile and checked the time. Nine o'clock. There might still be a chance if it wasn't too far away.

The man took a pipe off the desk and put it in his mouth. He didn't put tobacco in it or light it, but just chewed it thoughtfully as he read. Kip opened his mouth to ask another question and closed it again sharply as he spotted something on the desk, next to a white bowler hat.

It was a square paperweight with a Q-shaped twist of glitter inside.

'What's that, then?' Kip asked, watching the shopkeeper's response carefully.

'Haven't you ever seen a paperweight before?' the man answered with a slight scowl, not looking up.

If the man knew something, anything, about Quicksmiths, he wasn't giving it away that easily.

'I meant … never mind,' said Kip. 'I think I'll just look around if that's OK.'

'Feel free! It's a shop,' said the man gruffly. 'That's what people do in shops.'

There were eight aisles, each designated by a letter. Kip looked down the nearest one, hoping for another clue to tell him he was in the right place, but saw nothing of immediate interest. Choosing an aisle at random, he walked along and read the some of the signs on the tanks.

C3 Neon Tetras
C4 Guppies
C9 Mosquito Fish
C12 White Cloud Mountain Minnow

At the bottom of each tank were different ornaments – castles, mermaids, barrels, shipwrecks. Each had its own special combination of plants too. There were beds of pea-green moss, thin brown fronds and waving leaves that looked like bright yellow parsley.

Swimming around these plants were the peacocks of the sea: squads of darting fish with blue splashes on their bellies; clouds of silver fish with tails the colour of sunrises; black fish with wafting frills that looked like a carnival of ninjas.

Each tank also had a light switch on the side. They

seemed to have small logos that were hard to make out in the watery gloom. Kip took out his phone and unlocked it to get some extra light. And then his excitement returned like a boomerang, as the logo became clear: a two-flamed candle.

Kip flicked the switch. The light inside the tank turned from yellow to red but nothing else happened. He flicked it back and then moved on.

Hung on the wall at the back of the shop was a clock: it was already 9:12. Kip's insides wriggled with worry.

I'll make a bad impression if I'm late.

There had to be some answers in the puzzle printouts. The emojis still refused to make any sense, so Kip turned to the chess instructions.

Black Castle A2, White Bishop B7, Black Knight C6, Black Prawn D5, Black King E7, White Castle H4.

An idea jumped out at him. What if the shop floor were patterned like a chessboard? But when he looked down, his idea quickly melted away. It was just a regular floor-coloured floor.

A few steps down the next aisle Kip stopped at a tank, although he didn't know why at first. The fish were shy and were all hiding in the caves of a rock stack. He flicked the switch several times.

Red, yellow, red, yellow, red.

And then he saw it. At the bottom of the tank, half hidden by a forest of threadlike ferns, was a large decorative prawn. A Black Prawn.

Kip looked at the sign for the tank, not daring to breathe.

D5.

He checked the printout and galloped gleefully to the next aisle. At the seventh tank, he stopped. There, on a bed of white sand, was a head statue like the ones from Easter Island. Only this one was wearing a black crown.

Black King E7.

There was no stopping him after that, and soon he had located all the tanks in the chess puzzle.

But I can't reach inside them, he thought. *The tanks have covers and some of them are too high up. Plus, I don't have any sort of net.*

As he placed his hand against the glass of the white castle tank, a flash of inspiration hit him.

The switches!

One by one, he turned the six tanks red. When the last switch was flicked, Kip heard a squeaky, mechanical sound at the back of the shop, and half-ran-half-walked towards it.

Sitting innocently in the corner of the wall was a photo booth. It had definitely not been there before.

'Fish don't need passports,' he murmured.

Kip peered past the tanks at the shopkeeper, who seemed completely absorbed in his magazine, as if he had forgotten there was anyone else in the shop at all.

The photo booth had a stripy red-and-yellow

curtain, which Kip closed quietly once he was inside. As he sat down on the stool, there was a sudden intense warmth in his shirt pocket. When he pulled out the badge, its two flames were glowing softly. It was impossible to resist a quick celebration spin on the stool as he realised what the badge was telling him: *you're getting warmer!*

There was no keypad or payment slot, just a big black button. Kip pressed it and looked into the mirrored screen for the photo. A camera eye flashed at the top of the screen, then there was a pause, and three more flashes. When the camera had finished, Kip waited. Nothing happened. He poked his head outside and looked in the photo collection tray. It was empty.

Being in the photo booth reminded Kip of his birthday last year and the strip of snapshots on their windowsill.

We made faces, he thought excitedly.

He looked at the remaining puzzle printout. Four emojis. Four different expressions. Kip prepared himself and pressed the button again, making the right face for each camera flash.

He looked sad.

He smiled.

He frowned.

He looked amazed.

A mechanism somewhere inside the booth sprang

to life so forcefully that the stool started to shake. Kip leapt up in alarm but the noises stopped as suddenly as they had started. After a few seconds of silence, there was a long *hisssss*.

A door in the side of the photo booth swung outwards an inch and Kip felt a gust of pine-scented air on his face. Visible through the crack was a streak of blue sky, green grass and a grey, gravel path.

That's impossible.

He pulled back the curtain of the booth slightly and peeped out. The shopkeeper was still reading his magazine. So Kip picked up his rucksack, pushed the door and went through.

Q

Meanwhile, at the back of the aquarium, there was a small white flutter. As the butterfly approached, the empty photo booth gave a final clunk and a strip of photos fell down into the collection tray. The four faces of Kip looked out from the machine, the ink still drying.

Sad Kip.
Happy Kip.
Angry Kip.
Amazed Kip.

Chapter Three

The Garden of Giant Leapfrogs

What's happening?

There was a weird feeling in Kip's throat, like wanting to sneeze and be sick at the same time. Something he could only describe as a faint frothiness warmed the centre of his chest. Everything had gone fuzzy. He blinked a couple of times and then screwed his eyes up tight until the strange feeling faded away.

And ... open!

The world came back into focus and Kip looked around in disbelief. Just a second ago he had been in the photo booth of *Undersea Emporium*. And now he was here, standing on an ornamental wooden bridge on a neatly mown lawn. A magpie croaked and pecked at the grass.

Leading away from the bridge was a gravel path and, not really having a better plan, Kip began to follow it. As he walked, he saw it was one of many paths which ended at an iron gate on the far side of the garden. A man stood there, shielding his eyes against the sun. A giant word floated in an arc over the man's head, clear even from a distance:

Quicksmiths

Hovering below it were four slightly less giant words:

College of Strange Energy

At first it looked as if the man had a beard, but as Kip approached he realised that his jaw and cheeks were tattooed with inky indigo brambles. Resting on the bridge of his sturdy nose were some glittery triangular spectacles, completely out of place above the fearsome facepaint. A second pair of red glasses was pushed up on the man's forehead, and pinned to his shirt was a candle badge, just like the one in Kip's pocket.

The tattooed man held out his arms in welcome.

'Well done!' he proclaimed, stepping forward and shaking a very confused Kip warmly by the hand. 'Well done, Kip. You've made it in! I knew you would!'

'But … how…?' Kip tried to get the right question out. 'Who are you…?'

'I'm Professor Motukōmuhumuhu Kānekeneke.'

The man and the boy stared at each other for a second, while Kip wondered how he was ever going

45

to remember that name. The Professor's dark eyes were cheerful and intelligent, with just a sprinkle of mischief.

'Everyone calls me Professor Mo,' he chuckled.

Kip looked up at the letters above them. He still couldn't quite believe all this. Pinching yourself to check if you're dreaming was surely something no one ever really did. Still, he put his hand in his pocket and dug his fingernails into the skin of his palm. That felt real enough.

'So this is Quicksmiths?' he said.

Professor Mo nodded, and beamed.

'But how did I get here from the shop?' asked Kip.

'You just travelled through a wormhole,' said Professor Mo.

Kip breathed deeply and looked around again. All he saw was a calm, country garden and a couple of magpies.

But now he was looking closely there *was* something odd about those garden paths – they didn't seem to go anywhere. One went straight into the trunk of a tree. Another ended in a mossy stairway of three steps that stopped in mid-air. And one was a spiral that curled tighter and tighter into its own centre.

'This is the Garden of Giant Leapfrogs,' said Professor Mo, answering Kip's unspoken question. 'A wormhole hub that allows you to take shortcuts from one place to another. You're one of our first visitors this morning; candidates from all over the world will be arriving here throughout the day.'

'Shortcut? So we're nowhere near Helix Avenue?' said Kip, his mind racing.

'Distance is but an illusion,' said Professor Mo mysteriously, raising one eyebrow.

'Then where *are* we exactly?'

'We're actually on an island of sorts – but not the type you're used to,' said Professor Mo. 'Quicksmiths is built in this place and no other, because at this spot a number of very important streams of energy cross.'

Strange Energy

Kip looked back up at the floating words.

'Strange Energy?'

Professor Mo took the pair of red glasses off his forehead, pinched a square of green silk out of his shirt pocket and cleaned the lenses.

'Precisely. Now listen carefully, Kip. Billions of years ago, our Universe changed in a way we are still trying to understand. It became born, if you like. As it took its first breath, time too began to uncurl, or at least time as we know it.'

Swapping his glittery spectacles for the red ones, the Professor carried on excitedly, as if he were only just discovering something for the first time himself.

'With this first breath came a nameless, shapeless

force of unimaginable power. And that force cracked apart into hundreds and hundreds of energies. Some of the energies that were flung out you know very well and they do not seem like mysteries to you. Light. Heat. Microwaves. But there are many deeper and rarer energies. Strange Energies.'

The Professor reached up and touched the 'S' of 'Strange' in the pearly words that hung above them. The giant letter began to spin around, sparking like a Catherine wheel. As he spoke again, these sparks rained down and left a warm tingle on Kip's arms and face.

'People are like bulbs lighting up as all these hundreds of energies pass through us and around us. When we are born, we are close to our Universe. We experience the world as it truly is. That's why babies always look as if they know something we don't. Sadly, as we grow older, most of us lose this gift. But you and I, well, we're lucky. We can still *feel* the Strange Energies.'

'*Feel* energy?' said Kip.

'We hear and see Strange Energies of course. But we can also feel them like raindrops on our skin, or the beat of a drum in our chest. Oh, wait until you see what Quicksmiths can offer you. A life of Strange Energy shines so much brighter, Kip!'

While Kip was still thinking about that, Professor Mo swept him through the iron gate and towards a black stone building draped with green moss and drizzled with white lichen. Above it rose the shapes of other, taller buildings; and rising even above those buildings was a soaring tower of white glass.

They entered a courtyard overlooked by rows of crooked windows in the black-stoned walls.

'This is Celestial Hall – one of the four main buildings here at Quicksmiths,' said Professor Mo. 'And we are in Confucius Courtyard. Now, before we do anything else, we must get you registered.'

At the centre of the courtyard was a mighty oak tree. Waiting for them there was a woman dressed in a black jumpsuit. She had high, wide cheekbones and her charcoal hair was cropped short with a long fringe. Kip had never seen eyes like hers before – dark and shaped like sidelong apple seeds.

'Kip, this is the Head of Security, Tamara Okpik.'

'Very pleased to meet you, Mister Bramley,' said Tamara.

Kip looked at her suspiciously. *Mis*-ter Bramley was what The Snibbug liked to call him when he was in trouble, though it sounded a lot nicer when Tamara Okpik said it.

'Next, if you agree,' said Professor Mo, 'we have to give you a Scrambleguard.'

'Visitors, students and professors,' added Tamara, 'must consent to keep the secrets of Quicksmiths safe. Some bad eggs – really evil eggs – have tried to steal our technology before now: technology that the world out there isn't ready for yet. The Scrambleguard makes sure there are no information leaks, not even by mistake.'

Okpik took an eyedrop bottle out of her jacket pocket and gave it a good shake. The liquid inside looked milky.

'You'll still be able to talk about the Open Day and everyone you meet,' Professor Mo said, seeing Kip's hesitation. 'But not about the nitty-gritty of Strange Energy, and the confidential aspects of Quicksmiths. Not now, nor in the future.'

'The Scrambleguard also has a second function,' said Tamara. 'If you don't enrol at Quicksmiths today, it will jumble up any memories of how you got here, making all this seem like a pleasant but distant dream.'

'If you join today but later decide to leave, it would also activate,' said Professor Mo. 'Same thing if you're ever voted out.'

'Voted out?'

'Yes,' said the Professor. 'There aren't many rules here, but if one does get broken by a student or a teacher the whole college holds a vote on whether to let them stay.'

The subject of memory always put Kip on high alert. It made it hard not to think about his mum.

'Can a Scrambleguard unscramble memories as well as scramble them?' he asked.

'It doesn't quite work like that unfortunately,' replied Tamara.

She unscrewed the bottle top.

'Here, I'll do myself first, so you can see it's safe.'

Kip watched as she demonstrated and then held back his head and waited. Strangely, it felt more like a puff of air than a drop of water.

'Best to wear your Candle too,' she said, pointing to the badge on her jumpsuit.

Following her instructions, Kip pushed up the slider on his own badge and pressed it on to his shirt. It stuck to the material firmly, as if it had been glued. Professor Mo nodded a thanks to Tamara and led Kip away, towards an archway in the wall of the courtyard.

'Your Candle unlocks all the wormhole tunnels that connect Quicksmiths with the rest of the world,' said Professor Mo. 'It also logs you into GENI…'

'What's GENI?' asked Kip.

'Oh, silly me! Why don't you ask her yourself?' said Professor Mo. 'Just say, "Question GENI" and then ask away. Have a try while we walk.'

For a split second, Kip wondered what would happen if he turned out to be sleepwalking. Would his dad find him in the hallway at home, mumbling to himself? If this was a dream though, he wanted it to go on forever, so he did as the Professor suggested.

'Question GENI: who are you?'

A woman's voice came out of nowhere, as cool as cucumber ice cream.

'I am GENI, Giant Enigmatic Nebulous Intelligence. I am a Strange Supercomputer.'

'Where are you?' said Kip, looking around the courtyard. 'Where's your voice coming from?'

'I exist in electron clouds. My voice travels along hyperdark highways,' said GENI. 'My nerve network spreads out beneath your feet like the roots of the old oak.'

'Are you made of Strange Energy then?'

'I could not exist without it.'

Now that Kip had started to get some answers he needed more and more. It was like realising he had been thirsty for a very long time, only he hadn't known it. And now he had found this deep, full well, he couldn't stop drinking.

'Why did *I* get an invitation?' he asked.

'You came to the attention of one of our talent scouts,' replied GENI. 'Ambassador A.'

It couldn't be Ashleigh, surely.

'Aakash?'

'That's right,' said Professor Mo.

Kip chewed his lip and thought for a bit.

'But why all the puzzles?'

'Ah, the puzzle of the puzzles!' said Professor Mo. 'GENI, shall we explain together, if you would like to begin?'

'Of course,' said GENI. 'Your body, Kip, is made of trillions of cells. Some of those cells are specialised to allow you to sense energy. You have rod and cone cells in your eyes that let you see light. Nerve cells in your skin that let you feel heat. We call them receptor cells. And scattered throughout your body are Strange Energy receptors called quixars.'

'Quixars,' repeated Kip slowly.

'They help us experience the world in a different way,' said Professor Mo. 'Close your eyes and rub them. Gently now. Those patterns you see? That's quixars picking up on Strange Energy all around you.'

Kip rubbed his eyes and watched the prickles of light turn into rivers of squirls.

'"What's that got to do with puzzles?" you're thinking,' the Professor said. 'Well, at Quicksmiths we realised many years ago that large concentrations of quixars can be found in the puzzle-solving centres of the brain.'

'So if you're good at puzzles you can see and feel Strange Energy?' Kip asked.

'In a high percentage of cases,' said Professor Mo. 'And this special gift will take you to the hidden spaces of reality. Let you do things you never thought possible.'

'You have just the right kind of mind to fit in at Quicksmiths,' added GENI. 'Everyone here is like you.'

Kip nodded, feeling like an astronaut taking his first steps on a new planet.

'That's why the talent scouts go to chess clubs?'

'It's one of the places we look. Chess players love a good puzzle. And they almost always have plenty of quixars upstairs.' Professor Mo tapped his head as they reached the archway. 'Now there's just one more thing you should know. That notebook of yours, Kip – it's not just full of ordinary doodles. We believe they show that you are strongly connected to one of the Strange Energies. Only it's a little too early to say which one.'

The Professor took a pair of enormous tartan sunglasses from his pocket and began to wipe them, waiting for the meaning of his words to sink in.

'But drawing always seems to get me into trouble,' Kip said.

'A terrible injustice! That will never happen here,' said Professor Mo. 'You must keep drawing until it comes out of your ears. Don't you see, Kip? We *want* you to be yourself here!'

A school where he could be himself? Kip felt his mouth make a smile. But this smile still wasn't quite sure it was safe to come out completely.

Just in front of the archway was a large, marble statue. Kip looked up at the stern eyes and haughty smile and stopped in his tracks.

Looks like a Mister Snibbug.

'Sir Solomon Grittleshank,' he read out loud from the statue's plinth.

Please don't be a teacher here, Kip thought.

'Is he a teacher here?' he asked.

'Sir Grittleshank?' said Professor Mo. 'Good Lord no, he's been dead for nearly four hundred years. Ah, right on time! Kip, this is Leela – she's a Second Year, one of our student hosts today.'

Open Day

The girl who approached had a lighthearted look in her eyes and a slightly lopsided grin over a sharp pixie chin. Her black hair was cut in a bob at shoulder length and there was a pattern of gold, turquoise and green peacock eyespots all over it. It looked as if the eyespots weren't just on the surface either – they went all the way through.

'Leela Lee,' she said. 'Just found out about Strange Energy? Believe me, that's *nothing* – Quicksmiths is THE best thing that will ever happen to you – better than winning a lifetime's supply of ice-cream cake – the type of ice-cream cake you like of course – something else if you don't like ice-cream cake – but who doesn't like ice-cream cake – AND a butler made of ice-cream cake who follows you around all day, handing you ice-cream cake – no, even better, puppies – handing you puppies...'

She paused for breath, not quite long enough for Kip to get a word in.

'... *ice-cream-cake* puppies,' she said, decisively.

Kip stared at her, not sure if she'd stopped yet. He had never heard anyone talk so fast in his life; nor met anyone who used their hands so much when they spoke.

'Do you like my hair by the way?' said Leela. 'You don't have to stare, you can just ask, you know.'

Kip wasn't sure what to say.

'She's finished,' said Professor Mo.

'Um, what did you do to it?' asked Kip.

Leela's smile gave Kip a feeling that her reply wasn't going to be sensible. She cupped a hand on either side of her mouth and whispered loudly.

'*Eye* added a *spot* of Strange Energy.'

Professor Mo and Leela took Kip through an arched corridor into the next courtyard. It was much larger than the first one, and carpeted with lush grass. At the very centre was a tall clock tower of red brick, just like the one on the stamp. It had four faces – looking north, south, east and west – and each face showed a different time.

Dotted at intervals throughout the courtyard were about twenty square tents made of white silk. Among the tents were countless flying objects: glowing globes of every size and colour, spinning discs within discs, and floating pyramids with eyes.

Kip's own eyes wanted to look everywhere at once, but settled on watching a girl and a boy chasing a bird-sized dragonfly.

'GENI likes to make drones,' explained Leela. 'It's her hobby.'

'Can computers have hobbies?' asked Kip.

'You're forgetting she's "super" and "strange",' Leela said. 'Anyway, welcome to the Quicksmiths Open Day! Expect everything, and assume nothing.'

As if to prove her right, a burst of dark-pink fireworks exploded silently against the clear blue sky. The sparkles didn't fade away but hung in the air, spelling out a word in giant, cloud-high letters.

B A N G !

Kip spun around slowly, looking at all the tents and the children wandering among them. It was as if a red filter had been pulled across the whole scene.

'Everything's gone red,' he said, looking at Leela and Professor Mo for an answer. 'And everything … tastes red.'

He wiggled his tongue around in his mouth while he tried to work out what was happening.

'Cherry? That's an amazing trick. How d'you do it?'

'No trick,' said Leela. 'That was a Cherry Bomb firework. Make the most of it – it only lasts a few minutes.'

57

'We won't have time to see everything,' said the Professor, 'so we'll let you choose. Whatever takes your fancy.'

They walked among the tents and Kip read some of the signs out loud.

THOUGHTWAVES
TIMEYARN
SLIPSTREAM

Eventually he stopped outside WORMHOLES just as the effect of the strange firework was fading. As he looked around for an entrance, a pole-thin person wearing a crash helmet and safety goggles ran *through* the white silk as if it weren't there, nearly knocking them all over.

'He's got four arms!' Kip couldn't help shouting.

'That's Professor Steampunk,' said Leela. 'He's the Head of Strange Invention. And he teaches First Year Wormhole Technology.'

'Careful!' shouted Professor Steampunk. 'Runaway wormhole – stay out of range!'

Leela pulled Kip back as Steampunk was chased behind the tent by a purple shimmer in the air. As it sped over the lawn it attracted blades of grass and daisies, which gave away the shape of a whirling cone.

Professor Steampunk completed a lap of the tent and ran around the back again, the tails of his white lab coat flapping. The shimmering wormhole closed in behind him, like one hyperactive whirlwind after another. Leela started giggling and Kip knew it was safe to let out the laughter he had been holding in.

'Wormholes are purple?' he asked.

'Not exactly,' said Leela. 'We add dye so we can see where they are.'

'It's very useful,' panted Steampunk as he dashed past them again, 'especially when they've gone rogue.'

Steampunk circled back around the tent and emerged again, chasing the wormhole and brandishing a small, aluminium-coloured briefcase.

'What happens if it catches him?' Kip asked.

Professor Mo replaced the red spectacles he was wearing with the tartan sunglasses.

'Oh, that one only goes to…'

But Kip never heard the end of the Professor's sentence. There was that sneezesickness again and he found himself standing at the iron gate they had passed through only ten minutes before. Dazed, he walked back to Confucius Courtyard, where the two professors and Leela came running to meet him.

'Sorry about that,' Steampunk said, trying to catch his breath. 'Not to worry – I've got it locked up now.' All in the same moment, he patted the briefcase, smoothed down his crumpled lab coat, pushed his safety goggles up on his forehead and took off his crash helmet. The compressed hair underneath sprang up in white, feathery crests.

'Those cheeky wormholes don't half put up a chase,' he said. 'I'm going to have to make myself some extra legs…'

'Professor Steampunk, I was telling you about Kip?' said Professor Mo. 'Kip, Professor Steampunk has been called Professor Steampunk for so long, everyone has forgotten what his real name is.'

'Including me!' said Steampunk, shaking hands with Kip, Leela and Professor Mo all together.

He gave the briefcase and crash helmet to Leela, took a small alarm clock out of his pocket and then five more, and started juggling as he led the way back to Clock Tower Courtyard.

'I bet you're wondering if his extra arms are real?' said Leela, trying on the crash helmet. 'Some people are too shy to ask, aren't they Professor Steampunk?'

'Oh indubitably. I'm VERY shy myself.'

'So, *are* they real?' Kip asked.

'Well, it depends what you mean by "real",' replied Steampunk, not even looking at his juggling. 'I waved goodbye to my original arms years ago. When I was a younger man, most of my experiments ended in explosions.'

He leaned closer to Kip as if he were telling him classified information.

'These four scratching sticks are all bionic. Powered by Strange Energy. A *handy* little invention of my own. Now, would you like to guess how wormholes work?'

Kip nodded.

'Um … teleportation?'

'No, no, no. Teleporting is sooooo old-fangled,' said Steampunk. 'Only old-age pensioners teleport.'

'Wormholes bend space-time back on itself,' said Leela. 'Like the Universe is chasing its own tail. Isn't that right, Professor?'

'That's close enough,' said Steampunk. 'Energy is matter and matter is energy and when energy takes a shortcut, so can we!'

As they neared one of the tents, a splash of something cool and fresh poured through the white silk, straight at Kip. Expecting to be completely drenched, he ducked and shielded his face with his hands. Only he wasn't soaked at all. He felt a bit foolish until he saw a passer-by do exactly the same thing.

'That's the Slipstream,' laughed Leela, as if reading his thoughts. 'You'd better get used to it – now you're at Quicksmiths you'll start tuning in more. Strange Energy is absolutely everywhere.'

The clocks Steampunk was juggling all started beeping at the same time.

'Thank you, Professor Steampunk,' said Professor Mo. 'Perfect timing. Come on, Kip, we have an appointment to keep.'

Steampunk put the alarm clocks back in one pocket, and took out a teapot and two teacups from another. His spare hand waved goodbye enthusiastically.

'I shall reserve a seat of honour for you in my class next term,' he called out. 'Quicksmiths needs you!'

'Don't be shy!' said Leela, waving too. 'Come back soon! You won't regret it. Next term will be mega – Miss Twiss is going to read the Letter!'

'Thanks,' said Kip. 'Bye!'

'What does she mean by that?' he asked, following Professor Mo.

'Ah, the Letter,' said the Professor. 'It's been waiting for four centuries. Everyone is beside themselves with excitement. You'll find out soon enough.'

All teachers should be like this, Kip thought. *And all schools.*

It was the place for him, no doubt about that. Here was a welcome like he'd never felt before, something that a teacher like The Snibbug couldn't possibly understand. But before he could be glad for too long, Kip's face turned serious again. No one had mentioned fees yet.

Change Your World

They walked away from the tents, back towards the mossy walls of Celestial Hall. There was a figure waiting for them, and as they approached Kip saw that she was much older than Professor Mo. Her trouser suit was dark red with a golden trim. Neat enough to be a hat, her hair was a shaped into a steel-grey beehive. And her mouth was twisted in a wistful smile, as if something unseen was exerting an enormous force of gravity on her.

'Congratulations, Bramley!' she said.

She said the words, only she didn't: her lips didn't move.

'Good work getting here, we've been most impressed by your progress.'

It was the sort of voice that might read the script for the very best kind of nature documentary.

It has to be her talking, Kip thought. *But how?*

'Kip, this is Miss Twiss,' said Professor Mo. 'Professor-in-Charge of Quicksmiths.'

'You're probably wondering how you can hear me,' said Miss Twiss. 'My mouth and my voice box were damaged when I had an illness, long ago. But under my hair is a Thoughtwave Lens, an extension of my physical brain that projects my thoughts directly into your skull. I'm throwing my mind just as ventriloquists throw their voices. Don't worry, it's only one-way, so I can't tell what you're thinking.'

Kip nodded, not quite sure what to say. Miss Twiss gave him a long, magnetic look, as if she were studying the secret hieroglyphics of his face. He tried his best not to be troubled by her motionless expression. It was hard to tell if she was really smiling or not. But after a few moments he saw that, despite her slightly sad appearance, her eyes were warm and lively.

'It's time to discuss your scholarship,' Miss Twiss said finally. 'A scholarship means that we want you to join Quicksmiths so much that we will take care of everything – we'll buy your equipment and pay your way. And at the end of your education, you won't owe us a thing.'

Kip couldn't remember feeling as happy as this in his whole life, and the smile at his lips felt safe to come out properly at last. His front teeth wouldn't stay in his mouth, and poked out to see what all the grinning was about.

'If you join us,' said Miss Twiss, 'you will learn secrets of the Universe that you would never otherwise have a chance to know. Secrets that will make your mind do cartwheels and your imagination do flickflacks.'

Just as she said the word 'imagination', the sun emerged from behind a perfect, fluffy cloud. A streak of light fell across the dark stone of Celestial Hall, illuminating a wall full of silver inscriptions in hundreds of languages. Some of them Kip recognised and others were just collections of pictures, or dots and lines. He looked for the English writing and found it almost straight away, just at eye level.

Change Your World

'Our college motto,' explained Miss Twiss.

They stood and looked at the wall for a while, letting Kip find his own meaning in the words.

'At Quicksmiths,' Miss Twiss continued, 'you will be treated not as a child, but as an exceptional human mind – a mind that can achieve greatness.'

The sunlight teased out strands of green like miniature northern lights in the mist-grey eyes of the Professor-in-Charge.

'In fact,' added Professor Mo, 'it is our hope that your achievements will be far greater than our own.'

'And now,' said Miss Twiss. 'It is decision time. Will you join us?'

Kip gazed back at Clock Tower Courtyard. Over by the wormhole tent, Professor Steampunk was arm wrestling himself. A cloud-shaped drone drifted above the Professor and started to snow. With a shrill whistle, a geyser of green smoke blew the top of a tent off.

Maybe I really can change my world, he thought, looking at the college motto again.

There could only be one answer.

'When do I start?'

Professor Mo clapped his hands and Miss Twiss's eyes creased into deep and cheerful wrinkles.

'But wait, what about my dad?' said Kip, crashing back down to earth. 'He has to say "yes" too.'

'Absolutely, you should talk to your dad,' said the Professor. 'And so should we. We'll need to discuss your scholarship. And boarding arrangements.'

'Boarding? Oh no, you don't understand,' said Kip, feeling his mouth flatten out as the smile faded. 'My big sister went missing. It was nearly seven years ago but Dad still won't let me do anything by myself. I don't know if he'd ever let me go to a boarding school, doesn't matter if it's free.'

'That's completely reasonable,' said Miss Twiss. 'He wants to keep you safe.'

'Let us talk to him, and explain how important this is,' said Professor Mo. 'We'll see if we can come to some sort of agreement.'

Miss Twiss said goodbye and Professor Mo walked Kip back to the Garden of Giant Leapfrogs. Approaching from this side, Kip noticed that each path had a numbered signboard. They stopped at 88a.

'Your shortcut home – the path back to Helix Avenue,' said Professor Mo.

He held out his hand and Kip shook it, before turning and crunching along the gravel to the humpbacked bridge.

'See you next term!' called the Professor.

Kip stepped on to the bridge and there was a moment of sneezesickness. For a few seconds his eyesight blurred and all he could see was a shadow play of geometric shapes. When his vision came back into focus, he was standing in the photo booth of *Undersea Emporium*.

He only just made it back to the chess tables in time to meet Ashleigh. Aakash looked over expectantly and Kip gave him a big thumbs-up.

When he arrived home, Kip went straight to his room where Pinky was nesting in a wad of cotton wool just inside the lair door. He swooshed her out on the cotton cloud, and landed her gently on a pile of books on the floor before lying down next to her on his stomach. She stretched out her tiny paws as Kip talked at a million miles an hour.

He tried to say: 'Professor Mo told me all about Strange Energy, which shattered apart at the beginning of time, and I went through a wormhole – two wormholes – and I met a Strange Supercomputer called GENI and Professor Steampunk has four arms and it's all just ... incredifying!'

But Kip had forgotten about the Scrambleguard, and what came out was this:

'In the markets of Dar-es-Salaam goat-sized fleas nibble at the king's knee tusks while the Bald Princess sells monobrows made from yeti hair...'

When he heard those odd words coming out of his own mouth Kip laughed so hard he couldn't finish the sentence. But it didn't matter. Pinky understood Kip perfectly. She shuffled around on her cotton cloud and her flat, feathery tail dangled down over the side of the book pile, pointing to the *Encyclopaedia of Amazing Things*.

'You're right,' said Kip. 'It is full of amazing things. You have to see it to believe it – even then you don't believe it. And they want *us* to go there.'

Chapter Four

St Antony's

Kip and his dad sat in the stationary car, saying nothing. A few leaves escaped from a nearby willow tree and landed on the windscreen. Theo stared straight ahead, his hands still on the steering wheel, while Kip tried in vain to put back a loose petal on a small bunch of white daffodils he was holding.

Suddenly, Theo leaned back and slapped his hands on his knees. Father looked at son, and that look said everything.

'Today might be the day,' Theo added hopefully.

Kip tried not to slam the car door as he got out. But it always sounded much too loud in the quiet car park of St Antony's, the care home where his mum had lived since they had moved.

'At least it's better here than the old place,' said Kip, and his dad nodded.

Rain was forecast for the afternoon, but it was dry

for now. The gardens were full of the residents and their visitors, resting on plastic chairs or walking in twos and threes. But Kip's mum was alone in the sitting room, staring out across the flowerbeds. The curtains were flung wide, letting the weak sunshine in. Pollen and dust floated in the air like gentle drifts of sun snow.

Kip sat down next to her and his dad stood beside him, one hand on Kip's shoulder. They might have been posing for a portrait, the three of them.

'Mum, I brought you these,' said Kip.

He gave her the bunch of daffodils. Her face brightened and she held them up to the light, admiring them as if she had never seen a daffodil before.

'That's so very kind,' she said eventually.

As Rose looked at him, something in Kip's heart flickered like a flame in a storm lantern.

'Your mother must be so proud. What a well-brought-up young man.'

'Mum…' said Kip.

'Where is your mother?' interrupted Rose, looking around. 'I'd love to meet her. She must be *terribly* nice.'

'Rose…' Theo started to say, but he choked on the rest of the sentence.

She put down the flowers, stood up and walked towards a full-length mirror on the wall. Halfway there, she paused and looked around as if she had lost her way. Turning slowly, she began to walk back to her chair but, seeing Theo and Kip, she stopped in her tracks.

'I'm looking for my daughter,' she said, her eyes starting to fill with panic. 'Have you seen my Suzanna?'

Kip bit his lip hard. Every time they came to visit his mum, the awful memories returned. Helplessly, he found his mind being pulled into the past.

Suzanna had been about the same age that Kip was now when it happened. The Bramleys had lived in a former coastguard's cottage right at the end of a stretch of rugged, grassy cliffs freshened by salt spray and the wind. Theo had come home that day to find the front door wide open and the house empty. He ran out to look for his family, only to discover Rose left unconscious by the lightning strike, lying on the sea path where the charred grass was still smoking. Five-year-old Kip was stumbling towards her from the shadow of the old ruined lighthouse, dazed but otherwise unharmed. As for Suzanna … after weeks of searching all they ever found of her was a zebra-striped slipper, soaked with seawater on the wave-smashed rocks at the bottom of the cliff.

At the hospital, Rose's doctor had invited them into a spotless office, where Kip couldn't stop staring at this strange man's fake tan and blinding white teeth. The conversation was burned into Kip's mind like the after-effect of a bright light, despite his young age at the time.

'Lightning strikes can cause unique brain injuries,' Doctor Whiteteeth had explained.

'What sort of injuries?' Theo had asked.

Kip had never forgotten how his dad's voice shook.

'It isn't just forgetfulness. There's a strange distraction to it, as if she isn't sure what's real.'

'How do we fix it?'

'This is a most unusual situation. A recovery is unlikely,' said Doctor Whiteteeth, closing Rose's file firmly. 'The best we can do is make her comfortable.'

The best they could do was make her comfortable. Just like every visit.

The nurse came to give Rose her medication. Kip glanced at the pill bottle. The logo was familiar – a large 'G' and a small 's'. And now he recognised the word underneath it as well: Grittleshank.

It was surprising to see a reminder of Quicksmiths in the outside world and he stared at it for a few moments, relishing the rush of his delicious secret. Gradually, though, his dad's voice came into focus.

'Rosie…' he was saying. 'Rosie, it's just us now. You and me – Theo – and Kip.'

'Theo…' she repeated. 'Kip…' She paused. 'But everyone's outside,' she said bemusedly, 'in the garden. Won't Suzie be there?'

Kip took his mum's hand. It was like they were

searching for her in a vast fog. Every now and then she called out to them and they ran to her voice. But when they got there, it was just an echo.

'Maybe we should go outside then, darling?' said Theo. 'Get some fresh air?'

Theo opened a window and a cool gust disturbed the room. With it, Kip felt the secret he had been carrying blow away, leaving behind a cold, detached decision.

That evening after he and his dad had eaten they watched something stupid on TV, curled up together on the sofa. Neither of them felt much like talking, but something was burning in Kip's chest and he had to say it.

'I'm not going to go, Dad.'

Theo put his mug down on the coffee table.

'I'm not going to go,' Kip repeated. 'To Quicksmiths. I can't leave Mum. What if she's going to remember me one day soon? And I'm not around for it to happen? So then it *never* happens? I can't go.'

Theo breathed out heavily through his nose, turned off the TV and faced his son.

'Kip, I didn't think I was going to say yes when that professor came and told me about the scholarship. Letting you go off to boarding school, well, it just seemed too risky. But I had to get over myself – this isn't about me. It's about you. You're clever. Much cleverer than I am. Clever enough to know that this might be the biggest opportunity you will ever have in your whole life. It's like the spotlight has stopped on you right now, just for a moment, and when that moment has passed it will be gone forever.'

'But what about Mum?' said Kip.

He picked up a cushion from the sofa and poked a finger through the thinning material at the corner.

'Your new teacher told me this is the best school in the world,' continued his dad. 'It's so good, they keep it quiet, so they can pick the children who really deserve to go there. And we don't even have to pay. What's to stop you becoming a brilliant doctor while you're there, the greatest there's ever been, and coming back to fix Mum?'

Coming back to fix Mum? Kip hadn't even thought of that, although it was so obvious. Gratitude flowed out of him and formed itself into a hug that curled tightly around his dad as if it would never let go.

Stretch Limo

Just a few short weeks later, on a chilly Monday morning, Kip and Theo waited in the car park of Eelstowe Estate. Pinky was awake and alert inside a small travel box on the pavement. Sensing adventure, her whole body was trembling with excitement.

At five-thirty sharp a white limousine pulled up – long and sleek like the ones that celebrities ride in. Its sides were decorated with a candle-flame pattern and the engine purred gently.

'Your car is self-driving *and* a limo?' said Theo, hopping around excitedly on the kerb. 'Pretty good start!'

He rolled Pinky's lair on its castors over to the wide door of the limo, which swung up as he approached. Kip and his dad pushed and slid the tall metal hutch until it was propped up on the sofa seats inside. The big scuffed suitcase with the broken handle went in after it, followed by Kip's rucksack, and Pinky in her travel box.

Father and son faced each other on the pavement.

'Well, this is it,' said Theo, and he opened his arms wide.

The hug smelled of fresh coffee and lemon laundry, and Kip breathed it in deeply.

'I'll miss you,' said Kip.

'I'll miss you too. Just six weeks to half-term.'

Saying goodbye to his dad felt like being torn down the middle. One half of Kip still wanted to stay here inside the hug, hoping for the day his mum would start to get better. But as he got into the car, the other half grew stronger. It longed to burst up through the sunroof and howl at the quiet street as they sped towards the new world of Quicksmiths.

Kip leaned out of the limo's window as the car accelerated away. He kept waving until his dad had

Q

disappeared and waved a bit longer for good luck. When he pulled back inside, the blacked-out glass rolled up behind him.

The lavish interior of the limo had several tempting compartments. While Kip explored, Pinky scrabbled around in her travel box helpfully.

'Look,' said Kip. 'There's a mini-fridge with snacks and drinks. There's even some Brussels sprouts for you!'

'Hello Kip,' said a welcoming voice. 'It's good to see you again. And this must be Pinky.'

'GENI?!' said Kip. 'Of course – you must be driving the car.'

'I drive the entire Quicksmiths fleet of limousines,' said GENI.

'At the same time?'

'Yes,' said GENI. 'That is not a difficult task for a Strange Supercomputer.'

As they were talking, Kip spotted something crawling up the inside of the window.

'Pinky, we have a stowaway – there's a Circuitous Rambler in the car! GENI, do you know what species of butterfly this is?'

'That's your Mothball,' said GENI.

'My what-what?'

'Mothballs are drones, made by myself. We use them to track progress or make sure someone's safe. Everyone at Quicksmiths has one.'

75

'I knew there was something special about it,' said Kip. 'You'd better not try and eat it, Pinky.'

'There's nothing to worry about,' said GENI. 'Pinky will get tired out long before she can catch a Mothball.'

Kip looked down the length of the limo; the lair was taking up most of the other seats.

'So, where next? Are we going to pick up some more passengers?' he asked doubtfully.

'*We* aren't,' said GENI. '*I* am.'

Kip had no idea what that meant.

'I can see you are confused,' said GENI. 'Let me explain. This is a stretch limo.'

'I think I knew that,' said Kip.

'But this is no ordinary stretch limo. It's a Timestretch Limo. That means it stretches seconds into hours so that I can travel in a heartbeat to collect each person individually. Once I have dropped you off, your luggage will be unloaded and this limo will go to the Faroe Islands. Right now, I am dispatching cars from the fleet to Portugal and Algeria.'

'So, when a stretch limo stretches out seconds, it's like hardly any time has passed at all?'

'Yes, Kip. Time is elastic.'

The limo by itself was impressive, thought Kip. *But Dad's head would fall off if he could hear this.*

'Do you have any more questions?' asked GENI.

'Just one really: how long 'til we get there?'

'We are already here, Kip. We've been here the whole time we were talking.'

The door swung open with a quiet click.

'Your luggage will be sent to your room later,' said GENI. 'If you aren't sure where to go, then follow your Ballmoth.'

'I thought it was called a Mothball?' said Kip.

'It is,' she said. 'But it can also turn into a Ballmoth – you choose. Just remember this: Mothballs follow you and you follow Ballmoths. You can ask them to take you to anywhere or anyone. Goodbye Kip, we'll talk again soon, I'm sure.'

Clutching his rucksack and Pinky's travel box, Kip got out of the limo in a daze and looked up.

Up: because the sky was busier than migration season. Only instead of birds it was full of children gliding on colourful, flat discs about the size of open umbrellas. There were even treetop traffic lights in the very busy areas.

'What are they, Pinky?' he asked.

'More importantly, how fast do they go?' said a black-haired boy as he rolled past in a wheelchair.

Kip wondered where he had come from and turned around to see GENI's limos delivering their passengers like phantoms in fast forward. As each second passed, they appeared at different drop-off points in the car park and more new arrivals hopped out. Fluttering white Mothballs filled the air, like petals falling from a cherry tree.

What did GENI say? Ballmoth? You choose?

'Ballmoth,' he muttered aloud. 'Ballmoth.'

As soon as the word left Kip's mouth, his Mothball's wings began to flap so fast they became a white blur. Its head and tail disappeared and, in a blink, Kip found himself looking at a moth-sized ball of glowing white light. Uncertain of what she had just seen, Pinky ran in circles inside the travel box.

The Ballmoth hovered in the air about a metre off the ground and three pearly words appeared above it:

FOLLOW ME KIP

Kip looked around. About half the students seemed to be following one of these glowing globes – some confidently and others obviously for the first time. The black-haired boy was using his baseball cap to try and trap his Ballmoth, which skipped about in front of him.

Dreaming doesn't even come close to this, Kip thought. *Not even close.*

As the Ballmoth led Kip alongside the black-stone building from the Open Day, the words above the sphere of white light merged and reformed:

CELESTIAL HALL

They approached a smaller, sunflower-yellow building, and the pearly words changed again:

FIRST YEAR BLOCK

Kip counted three doors and then the Ballmoth stopped at a fourth. Behind it was a corridor and a staircase taken over entirely by a group of boys and girls talking loudly.

Albert

Kip squeezed past them and followed the Ballmoth up three flights of stairs until it came to a stop outside room Q10. Behind the door was an L-shaped attic room that was about ten times the size of Kip's bedroom at home. Some wooden bunk beds with sturdy wooden steps were pushed up against one wall. Next to the bunk beds was a bookcase, half full of books.

A loud thump came from the other side of the room, so Kip walked around the corner and came to two desks with comfy-looking swivel chairs.

'Hello?' he said.

One of the desks looked as if the world's cleverest bird were building a nest on it – it was a jumble of pens, pencils, erasers, paper clips, two calculators, crumpled-up paper, and sticky notes. The other desk was completely bare.

'Hellooooo?' a voice replied.

A rustling came from underneath the messy desk and a boy about Kip's age emerged. As he straightened up, his eyes came to the same level as Kip's, but his hair made him seem at least a head taller. It looked as if all the ideas inside his brain had exploded in a wiry, black starburst.

'I'm Albert Masvingo,' said the boy.

'Kip Bramley,' said Kip.

'Well then, welcome to Albert and Kip's room,' said Albert, 'because we're roomies! Hope you don't mind – I chose a desk already.'

Kip put down his rucksack and Pinky's travel box.

'A desk's a desk,' he said. 'Where are you from?'

'I'm Zimbabwean,' said Albert. 'And Irish. Zimbwish.'

'Not Irbabwean?'

'Either way,' laughed Albert. 'What about you? Where are you from?'

'I live in London,' said Kip. 'But I'm not from there.'

Albert held out a jar of peanut brittle. Kip took a piece and Albert shook the jar so Kip would take some more. Pinky's travel box rattled in reply and Albert bent down to look inside. Two vigilant eyes studied him back.

'Is that a hovering hamster? No wait, an abseiling chinchilla? Oh, how could I be so stupid … it's a flying squirrel!'

Kip grinned, impressed.

'Most people wouldn't recognise a flyer.'

'My brother did a biology project on them last year. Is this one of those ones that glow in ultraviolet light?'

'You do know your flyers! Bright pink. That's why we called her Pinky.'

Albert turned to Kip.

'Can I hold her?'

'She can be a bit shy at first,' Kip said.

'I'll be careful,' Albert said.

It was hard not to be protective of Pinky – especially after what had nearly happened to her. But now, when Albert scratched at the side of the travel box, Pinky scratched back. So Kip took Pinky out, gave her to Albert, and watched carefully. After all, Pinky was his best goodguyometer. Once Pinky had given Albert a thorough sniffing and decided he was definitely a friend, she rolled on her back and stuck out all four paws. This opened out the cape of soft skin between her arms and legs so she looked like a miniature furry manta ray.

'She's awesomic!' said Albert, tickling her sugar-white underbelly. 'Where did she come from?'

'It's a long story,' said Kip.

'Pleeeeeeeease,' said Albert. 'It has to be at least as interesting as she is.'

'OK, you win,' said Kip. 'Before we moved to London, Dad worked in a really posh restaurant. For people who have so much money they don't know what to do with it. Basically, you could bring whatever you wanted and the chefs would cook it for you.'

'Anything at all?'

'Well,' said Kip, 'I saw some weird things there. But one day a woman in a snakeskin dress gave Dad a padlocked picnic basket. She said she wanted an omelette for a special breakfast the next day and gave Dad a key for the basket.'

'What was inside?' asked Albert.

Kip looked at Pinky.

'No!'

'Dad thought she might be an endangered species, and brought her home. She was really tame so we knew she hadn't just been caught from the wild. "You can't cook her," I said. But Dad said that if he didn't, he'd have to quit. And if he had to quit, he'd have to find a new job and we might have to move house.'

'That's a pretty big decision.'

'It was,' said Kip. 'We agreed that it didn't matter where we lived. But it was life or death for Pinky. Even if Dad refused to turn her into an omelette, we couldn't hand her back because she was still going to end up in a frying pan. And, although she wasn't technically ours to take, that was that. Dad quit the next day. He found a job in London and we moved to the estate.'

'Wow,' said Albert, looking at Pinky and then at Kip. 'Wow.'

'So whenever I have a bad day and come home to see Pinky,' Kip finished, 'all my problems don't seem that terrible after all. I mean at least no one's trying to eat me!'

'That's an amazing story. Pinky's the luckiest glowflyer in the world,' said Albert.

'I'm the lucky one,' said Kip. 'And good word by the way: glowflyer.'

Albert put Pinky on his desk, where she skipped about happily, exploring the clutter. Balling up a piece of paper, Albert sat down and then threw it to Kip. Back and forth it went while they spoke.

'So do you know why you're here?'

'I think it's something to do with the drawings I do,' said Kip, a bit embarrassed. 'They're connected to Strange Energy. Maybe. But Professor Mo said it's too early to say. What about you?'

'I'm a bit rubbish at chemistry and German and all that stuff, but I sort of get Time,' said Albert.

'Like the Stretch Limo?' asked Kip.

'I loooooooove that car!' said Albert. 'GENI told me there's a Strange Energy called Timeyarn. It sort of distorts Time.'

'What, like time warps?' said Kip.

'Sort of. You know, Time is always doing crazy things. Slowing down and speeding up and sometimes getting stuck. But we've got no way of measuring it properly. The closest thing we have is a clock. It lets us see Time the same way a windmill lets us see the wind. But that's still a bit misleading. I got suspended last term for stealing clocks, just couldn't help myself. Built a megaclock with a hundred and seven faces on the school roof.'

He took a phone out of his pocket and showed Kip a picture. It looked like something out of a bad science fiction film – a lumpy cone of clock faces and digital displays with coat hangers sticking out of it.

'What does it do?'

'I was trying to prove there was a timeloop, right there on the roof,' said Albert.

'Seriously?' Kip said. 'How did you know?'

'I just knew,' said Albert.

The paper ball went back and forth a few more times.

'So, what do you draw?' Albert asked, batting the ball up towards the ceiling.

Kip hesitated and then took the Book of Squirls out of his rucksack. Pencil and ink threads curled across the pages, like the path of a book beetle working its way through a maze.

Albert looked over curiously.

'Is that what it's like to be inside your head?'

'Kind of. The pictures sort of happen when I'm thinking about something really hard. Sometimes I see them when I rub my eyes – you know the patterns you get. If I can't draw them for whatever reason, it's like not being able to scratch an itch.'

'Sweeeet,' said Albert.

'It's not that exciting,' said Kip, closing the book. 'Not like timeloops.'

There was a knock at the door. It was a porter delivering Kip's luggage, who turned out to be the grumpy aquarium shopkeeper with the big moustache. He was wearing a white bowler hat that looked a bit too small for his head. Printed in black letters around the rim was his name: **Bagsworth**.

Huffing and puffing, he unloaded Kip's suitcase and Pinky's lair off a hovering platform, muttering something about *don't know why you kids need all this useless stuff anyway*. After plonking a thick paper bag by the door, Bagsworth left without another word.

Kip opened the bag and saw it contained a selection of nuts, some fruit and vegetables, and a hard-boiled egg – a feast for a flying squirrel. But, after all this excitement, Pinky was more interested in bed than food. As soon as Kip opened the lair door, she headed straight for her scarf hammock.

Albert was already mostly unpacked so he helped by stacking books on the bookcase. Then he found a hook on the wall for Kip's calendar, which had a red circle around today's date. Each day since the Open Day had been carefully crossed off, and the number of days in the countdown adjusted.

'I did the same thing,' he laughed, pointing to another calendar on the wall.

They had almost finished putting Kip's things away when their Ballmoths came to life with a new message.

BREAKFAST YUM...YUM...YUM

'What Strange Energy do you think they're made of?' asked Albert, trying to grab one of the Ballmoths. 'It's like trying to catch a fish.'

'I wonder what happens when two meet?' said Kip. 'Do they explode, or combine into one bigger energy ball?'

'Let's find out!' Albert said, already walking towards the bunk beds to put some distance between them.

He raced back towards Kip, who jumped to meet him. Although their Ballmoths swerved at the last second, Albert and Kip collided in a crash of arms and legs.

'That was dumb,' said Kip, rubbing his forehead and his elbow at the same time.

'Ballmoths – one. Albert and Kip – zero,' said Albert, limping out of the door.

Plasma Slug

From room Q10 they followed the Ballmoths along an old, uneven corridor that spiralled down to the ground, where it widened out. There was a stream of human traffic going in both directions.

'Ballmoths are like guide dogs,' said Albert. 'Look, if you stop they come back for you.'

'It's like there's an invisible lead,' agreed Kip. 'It's about … OW!'

Kip stopped in surprise as a shooting pain travelled up his body. He looked down to find a mysterious sticky blob – the colour of mouldy potatoes – had clamped itself heavily around his trouser leg, and he shook it off in a panic. It hit the wall forcefully and clung there, twitching inside a sickly-green cloud of something that looked to Kip like slimy gas.

An older boy stomped furiously through the crowd towards them. Everyone looked away and walked on fast.

The boy swore loudly and bent down to inspect the blob. A wide, puffy face with eyes like raisins turned up slowly to stare at Kip. Although his smile stretched nearly from ear to ear, he wasn't really smiling. Kip was sure he recognised the face, but couldn't work out where from.

'You've broken my Plasma Slug!' said the boy, through gritted teeth.

'Sorry,' said Kip automatically.

A girl with cruel eyes stepped out of the crowd. She had hair that was cut very short on one side and grew past her shoulder on the other, and she was wearing a sharktooth necklace.

'You weren't looking where you were going,' she said.

'I *was*,' said Kip. 'It just came out of nowhere.'

'Are you disagreeing with me?' said the wide-mouthed boy.

When he straightened up to his full height, he was taller and wider than a fridge-freezer.

'It *did* come out of nowhere,' repeated Kip.

'Maybe you should just shut your wormhole,' said the girl with the sharktooth necklace, poking Kip hard on the shoulder. 'And show Thag some respect.'

'Let's give him a chance,' said Thag, smiling-but-not-smiling again. 'How's about you pick it up?'

Kip looked at the dense, mottled slug-blob. It was about the size of a shoe and had four pairs of greasy-looking feelers. An electric arc rippled between several of them.

'No way,' he said.

'It's your fault,' said Albert angrily. 'Not Kip's.'

Thag grabbed Kip's collar and began to push him down towards the floor. Kip was strong for his age, but Thag was much older and Kip found his face getting forced closer and closer to the Plasma Slug. Albert tried to hook the back of Thag's knee and trip him up. But the cruel-eyed girl shoved Albert against the wall.

'Fighting already?' said a voice. 'And we haven't even had our first lesson.'

The voice bobbed lightly into their heads, but it had all the authority of a vast, unbreakable iceberg. Kip's

88

attacker froze instantly. Bent over double, all Kip could see was the gold hem on some dark-red trousers.

Thag ruffled Kip's hair in a friendly, big brother kind of way and let him go.

'Just teasing the newbies, that's all, Miss Twiss,' he said.

'It doesn't look like teasing,' she said and turned to Kip. 'Is it teasing?'

Kip said nothing. Not because Thag glared as if he wanted to rip out Kip's tongue, but because he didn't want someone else fighting his fights for him.

'I see,' said Twiss, turning back to Thag. 'Pythagoras Grittleshank. I won't say this again. It doesn't matter if you're the fifteenth great-grandson of Sir Solomon Grittleshank himself…'

Kip groaned inwardly.

Grittleshank? he thought. *The company? Some relation to that famous statue guy? And I've managed to get in a fight with him on the first day.*

'…you are in the Upper Sixth now,' Miss Twiss continued. 'Act like it. Respect the other students and the rules of Quicksmiths. Instruction GENI: four hours' community service for Pythagoras!'

Thag's Candle badge glowed and made a "you lose" sad trombone sound.

'Now, get to breakfast all of you! An empty stomach will only produce empty thoughts.'

The girl with the sharktooth necklace had already

melted into the crowd. Thag walked off after her, casting an evil stare behind him. Kip and Albert hurried after their Ballmoths, putting as much distance as possible between them and the enemy.

'What's his problem?' muttered Kip.

'His problem is he *looks* like a thag,' said Albert. 'Whatever that is.'

The Buttery

Breakfast was at a place called the Buttery on the ground floor of Celestial Hall. The Buttery was bright and warm and full of queues, although there were so many food stations that none of the queues were very long. It was noisy too, very noisy for the number of people in here, Kip thought.

Following Albert, Kip took a tray and joined the queue for the hot buffet.

'What's on the menu today?' asked a student with thin, rectangular glasses and rusty-gold hair.

Kip thought he looked old enough to be a sixth-former and eyed him warily after the encounter with Thag. But there was something magnetically nice about him. For a start, he had a fistbump or a wave for nearly everyone who walked past. Large, light-brown freckles covered his face and arms. In fact, it looked a lot like he'd been painting a ceiling with freckle-coloured paint. On his T-shirt were these words:

I like your energy.

On the other side of the counter a short, stout man with a barrel chest buzzed around. He wore an apron and a chef's hat, like Theo Bramley did, and Kip was an instant fan. A twinge of homesickness plucked at him, and he hoped his dad was doing all right on his own.

The chef swept his hands through the air over the displays and spoke with a deep voice like an opera singer's.

'A better question might be, "What isn't on the menu?"'

'Oh, you spoil us, Chef Garibaldi!' said the freckle-painted sixth-former, with a radiant smile. 'This isn't breakfast, it's a break-*feast*!'

'I'll have a Morning Shepherd's Pie, please,' said Kip, when it was his turn and he realised how hungry he was.

Albert went for Baked Bean Breakfast Pizza and once they had their food they stood around with their trays, trying to work out what to do next. There were just four picnic tables, and they were all completely full.

'There's nowhere to sit,' said Albert. 'Do we go back to our room?'

'Nowhere to sit? But there are plenty of tables!' replied a voice.

Kip turned to see Professor Steampunk, the four-armed wormhole wrangler from the Open Day.

'Over there,' said Steampunk, balancing a muffin on top of a tower of hash browns stacked on a fried egg.

'Where?' Kip said.

Steampunk pointed vaguely, busy filling his pockets with more muffins.

'That's a wall,' said Albert.

'Of course it's a wall, otherwise all the weather would be coming in, wouldn't it?' said Professor Steampunk. 'Follow me!'

Kip and Albert watched as Steampunk walked past the four picnic tables, and up to the wall. The paint looked smudged and dirty and out of place in the sparkling clean room. And then Kip realised why.

Professor Steampunk put one foot on the wall and then the other foot, and, without pausing, marched upwards, sticking out from the side of the room. Kip and Albert lifted their heads and their mouths opened wordlessly. The four walls of the Buttery stretched up and up and up towards a tiny glass ceiling in the distance. And each wall was full of busy picnic tables, clinging like colonies of giant wooden insects.

'Come on then,' Albert said to Kip. 'Guess we should follow him.'

Although all the logic in his brain told him not to, Kip copied Professor Steampunk and put one foot on the wall, followed by the other. And then, just like that, the wall wasn't a wall any more: it was a floor.

They walked past thirty or so tables all full of children and clatter and chatter. The used-to-be-a-ceiling-but-now-a-window ahead of them got larger as they walked towards it. And, even though it was grey outside, the room was filled with bright daylight.

'How is this even possible?' asked Kip, looking back along the tables.

'And why is our food not sliding off our plates?' Albert wondered.

'This is Quicksmiths, remember?' Professor Steampunk shouted from his table, waving four half-eaten muffins around. 'Your perspective has changed, that's all!'

Chapter Five

The Mowl

'Did you expect Quicksmiths to be like … this?' asked Kip, stabbing a breakfast pea that was trying not to be eaten.

'No way, it's much better than I expected,' replied Albert, through a mouthful of two-inch pizza topping. 'Even the baked beans are more beany here.'

They both stopped mid-bite when Leela walked up to their table, pulled up a chair and sat down. Her mouth started moving and words were coming out, but Kip had no idea what she was saying. All he could do was stare at what she had brought with her. For, sitting on a gauntlet that went all the way up to her shoulder, was the weirdest *thing* he had ever seen.

'What. Is. That?' said Albert slowly, uncurling his forefinger into a point.

'What?' said Leela innocently. 'Do I have something on my face?'

'Er, no,' said Albert. 'Actually, you have something on your shoulder. And, er, hello: *what is it*?'

It stood about as high as Kip's fork and was made up entirely of black feathers and wispy fur and enormous orange eyes with long eyelashes. Its chubby body wasn't quite a square and wasn't quite a circle, and the creature seemed to have no neck at all.

'Oh, that's just the mowl,' said Leela, as if she got asked that all the time, which she probably did.

'Mowl?' echoed Kip and Albert together.

'Yes. Mowl,' she said, as though that explained everything they would ever need to know about mowls. 'And make sure you say his name right or he gets really huffy. Just remember this: "How now brown mowl".'

There was a moment's silence before Kip and Albert both burst out laughing. The mowl looked up from his enthusiastic interest in Leela's earring to stare at them sulkily.

'You better not upset him,' Leela warned, stroking the plush, black fur of the mowl's tummy. 'Half of him is cute and fluffy, but the other half can have quite a temper.'

The mowl made a lirrip noise, somewhere between a kitten's purr and a pigeon's coo, and burped.

'Its tail looks like a furry, burnt sausage!' Albert managed to splutter between giggles.

'Those eyes are nearly bigger than its head!' said Kip.

'Is that a beak?'

There was a clatter of cutlery on the next table. In response, the mowl produced a melodious rumble that could only be described as a wurble.

'Look! It has hands!' Kip said.

'They're like little otter hands!'

The mowl looked around lazily and stretched its tufty legs that ended in glinting talons. Its deft brown hands hovered for a second, some sharp claws poked out of its fingertips, and it began to comb Leela's hair.

'Where did it come from?' Albert asked.

'*He*. At least I think he's a he. Guess, and if you get it right I'll tell you,' said Leela.

'You hatched an egg you found?' said Kip.

The mowl hopped off Leela's shoulder and poked with one claw at a baked bean on Albert's plate.

'You smooshed four … no, five animals together? Baby penguin … otter … mole …? A fat blackbird? Something with giant eyes … a seal cub?'

The mowl wurbled and a long, thin orange tongue flicked out to lick the baked bean.

'Stranded alien?'

'Dinosaur?'

'Well, I suppose that's good enough,' said Leela. 'I was in the lab late, catching up on a project one night – pretty dull, dating old bones from the Quicksmiths Museum with a Time Tagger…'

Hearing his favourite subject mentioned, Albert

looked even more interested and tried to ask a question. But the Leela storytelling train had left the station.

'…anywaaaay, there was this freak electromagnetic blizzard – a weird glow came from the storage room that was full of all sorts of equipment – you know, conductors, batteries, amplifiers – that sort of stuff – before I could open the door, a huge blast blew me off my feet – and when I looked up, the bones from the museum were gone and there was the mowl – the first thing he did was burp and scratch his tummy – just like he's doing now – I swear he understands me – we still don't know *exactly* what happened – probably something to do with some faulty equipment – and we don't know exactly what he is either…'

'But you were allowed to keep him?' asked Albert, finally managing to get in a question.

'Well, of course,' said Leela. 'Someone had to look after him. And it was love at first sight.'

The mowl looked up at Leela and, when he blinked, the first pair of eyelids was trailed by a second pair coated in orange scales.

'He'll *really* start showing off if we talk about him too much. So are you getting on OK, Kip?'

Kip nodded, still staring at the mowl.

'Good. Because it turns out I'm your befriender.'

'Be-what?' said Kip.

'Befriender. Every new student at Quicksmiths gets

one. You can ask us questions about stuff and we help you settle in. Anything you want to ask me?'

Kip shrugged.

'Don't think so,' he said.

Another girl came and sat next to Leela. She wore a knitted woollen hat flecked with grey and blue. It sagged down over her ears and a stream of smooth blonde hair flowed out from underneath.

'Hello Timmi,' said Leela.

'Timmi?' Albert said. 'Isn't that a boy's name?'

'My name's Antimony,' replied Leela's friend in a soft American accent. 'Antimony Brown. So everyone calls me Timmi for short.'

'Timmi's your befriender, Albert,' said Leela. 'So you better be nice to her. Apparently, Timmi, these two already know everything there is to know about Quicksmiths, so we might as well go and talk to someone else…'

Letter from the Past

But Leela didn't finish whatever she was going to say next, as there was a sudden surge of spirited conversation in the Buttery.

'What's going on?' said Kip loudly over the hubbub.

'Didn't I tell you?' Leela said. 'Today's the day Miss Twiss reads the letter. Doctor Quicksmith's letter. Won't be long now.'

'Doctor Quicksmith?' Kip said.

'See, you do need a befriender,' said Leela, crossing her arms smugly. 'You don't even know who Doctor Quicksmith is!'

'*Doctor* Quicksmith?' repeated Kip. 'Like a making-people-better doctor?'

'I *think* so,' said Timmi. 'But you can be a doctor of other things, as well as medicine. You know, like … ah … Science, Art, Music, Philosophy.'

Timmi was quite the opposite of Leela when she spoke. She got distracted easily and paused every now and then in the middle of a sentence, her sage-green eyes not really settling on anything or anyone.

'Doctor Quicksmith mastered pretty much every subject to become the most … er … luminous thinker who ever lived. Some people think that Solomon Grittleshank was cleverer … um … but they're wrong.'

'What about Einstein?' said Albert. 'Or Newton?'

'Hah!' said Leela. 'They had nothing on Doctor Quicksmith. They'd be lab assistants, *if* they got lucky.'

'Well, I've never heard of him,' said Albert.

'*Her*,' said Timmi. 'And that's exactly why you need us!'

'In the reign of Queen Elizabeth the First,' said Leela, 'a baby wrapped in a blanket was left at the college gates – because she had been left on the bare ground, they called her Eartha – and because no one knew who her parents were, she was given the family name of Quicksmith – all this became her home.'

'Wow,' said Albert. 'She grew up here? Imagine how insane that must have been.'

'What made her so brilliant?' Kip asked.

'Eartha loved solving puzzles,' said Timmi.

'I thought we all did,' Albert said.

'We do,' said Timmi. 'But she first found out the connection between … um … quixars and Strange Energy.'

'Quixars being the receptor-cell thingies, right?' asked Albert. 'In your puzzley brain bits?'

'Oh sure,' said Timmi. '"Receptor-cell thingies in your puzzley brain bits" is the exact scientific definition.'

'Anywaaaay,' Leela went on, 'when Eartha wasn't figuring out the mysteries of the Universe and inventing amazing things – she was roaming the world – going to faraway places and talking to wise elders – hidden tribes – you know, discovery stuff – and then – suddenly – one day she stopped her research and began to build the Ark of Ideas…'

'What's the Ark of Ideas?' said Kip and Albert.

Leela leaned across the table.

'No one's ever seen the Ark of Ideas or knows what it actually is – but there's a rumour that it's a sort of knowledge bank – a giant safe where Eartha hid a load of inventions and discoveries – imagine the work of *ten*

Einsteins or *ten* Newtons – imagine a time capsule full of brain grenades that would just explode everything you thought you knew – and, the cherry on the cake – they say it contains the secret to Aeon Light…'

'Is that like neon light?' said Albert.

'Aeon Light is ultra strange and ultra-ultra mysterious,' said Timmi. 'Even Miss Twiss and Professor Mo don't know much about it.'

Albert twirled his fork at the two girls.

'So what's the big deal about this letter Miss Twiss is going to read out?'

'Well, Eartha Quicksmith disappeared in … unexplained circumstances,' said Timmi. 'And so did her Ark. The only thing she left behind was a letter and strict instructions that it wasn't allowed to be opened. Until today…'

Eight, loud, shoe-shaking notes chimed somewhere nearby. The breakfast groups began to break apart and swarm out of the Buttery.

'Come on!' said Leela.

'Where are we going?' asked Albert, grabbing the last slice of pizza.

'To Aristotle's Theatre. All the big announcements are made there.'

Kip and Albert followed their befrienders through a confusion of doors, courtyards and corridors until they popped out near an open-air theatre. It was built from stone blocks as tall as Albert, if you measured him all the way to the top of his starburst hair. Once inside, Kip peered thoughtfully at the grey sky above.

'How is it drizzling,' he asked, 'but it's warm and dry in here?'

'GENI's Easy-Breezy Weather Drones,' Timmi replied.

'Obviously,' said Albert.

Miss Twiss floated on a flat disc above the stage, facing the semi-circle of tiered stone benches that was filling up with hundreds of students and professors. She held a small wooden box in one hand.

'What are those flying-skateboard-disc things?' asked Albert.

'Skimmies,' said Timmi.

'How do they work? Can I have one?'

'Strange Energy,' whispered Timmi. 'No. And shhhhhh, it's starting!'

'Greetings, students and professors.'

Kip jumped. He had forgotten the Professor-in-Charge didn't speak like everyone else. It seemed as if she were standing at his shoulder, talking into his ear. He looked at Albert, who had also forgotten and was gazing around looking for hidden speakers.

'Welcome and welcome back to you all! I have only a few words before we begin. We are all here to understand the Strange Energies. We are here to seek science beyond science. Art beyond art. To learn the language of atoms and stars. Follow the invisible web connecting all things. Unravel mysteries. And that brings me to what you all *really* want to hear.'

Excited clamours rattled around the assembled crowd.

'Today is a very special day. Exactly four hundred years since our very own Eartha Quicksmith disappeared. And it is my honour to share with you the Letter that the great woman left to us all in her will.'

Miss Twiss broke a wax seal on the box. She opened the lid carefully, as if expecting a genie to escape, and took out the single sheet of parchment rolled up inside. When she let go of the box it just hung in the air.

Stroking her throat for a second with one finger, Miss Twiss scanned the parchment and then began to read.

"'Friends:

There is not much time. I must be brief.

Today, with the heaviest of hearts, I have burned down my Invention House.

For I have looked into the Futurescope and I have seen glimpses of what is to come.

In an unknown time and place, one of my inventions will be used to most disastrous effect.

Evildoers will corrupt it for their own selfish gain, and there shall be great death and ruin."'

Uneasy murmurs welled up and sloshed back and forth around the theatre. Miss Twiss held up her palm and when the murmurs had died down, she continued.

"'The Futurescope shows only glimpses of what may be. It is like looking through a keyhole into a room of restless birds.

I could not see for certain which invention might be the cause of such destruction, nor who might be responsible.

The risk is too great. So my life's work is gone.

Be not downcast, however, for there are two glimmers of hope.

The first hope is this: on the very day that you read this letter, a small window of possibility will open for just ten days. This is the only chance to revive my discoveries, yet avoid the disaster I have seen.

Therefore, I have created a keepsafe: the Ark of Ideas. It is hidden well.'"

'Told you! The Ark!' whispered Leela, but Kip was too absorbed in the reading to pay much attention.

"'The Futurescope has shown me how and when the Ark might be retrieved safely. There is too little time, too much to explain. The shadows are gathering – faces at windows, whispers in corridors. So we must trust my calculations.

This letter sets everything in motion. The path to the Ark is shaped by ten riddles that must be solved in sequence. Ten riddles, ten days – no more, no less.

Every time a riddle is solved, the future is changed; the path will shift subtly."

As Miss Twiss read on, Kip felt the atmosphere in the theatre change, tightening into a spine-tingling tension.

"'To answer some of my riddles you will need only your wits. For some, you will need each other. And to solve the hardest you will need to know yourselves.

Lastly, do not forget the second of my hopes, a hope I have seen standing among you in the yet-to-come; a truthseer, a defender of all that Quicksmiths stands for, who may reveal the secrets of Aeon Light to you once more, who can lead the bravest and best of you through a dark and perilous age, but not without sacrifice.'"

Miss Twiss paused to look over the top of the letter. Like her, each person was looking around at everyone else, wondering if *they* were this unnamed hero. Twiss returned to the Letter and read the last few lines.

"'Remember: there are many paths, many possibilities. Only one leads to the Ark.

Signed this tenth day of April.

In the company of myself and with my conscience as witness.

E.Q."

Miss Twiss rolled up the Letter carefully, put it back in the box and closed the lid. Lacing her fingers together, she stood for a moment and considered the many faces looking back at her, before addressing the crowd.

'This could be a turning point in history, a crucial chance to change our world for good. The Ark of Ideas could end disease, create limitless green energy. We don't yet know.'

Two professors sitting behind Kip began to whisper fervently.

'I am certain,' continued Miss Twiss, 'that here at this assembly we have all the brains we need. To assure our success, I will assign a professorial taskforce which will work day and night. And, as extra support, for the next ten days all of your usual Quixology classes will be devoted to the solving of Eartha's riddles.'

'What's Quixology?' Kip and Albert whispered at the same time.

'Puzzle-solving,' whispered back Leela and Timmi.

'But we must not go lightly into the challenges ahead,' Miss Twiss continued, with a grand sweep of her arm. 'For, if we are, as Eartha says, on the cusp of a perilous age, then we cannot afford to ignore the slightest warning. No doubt there are dark agents outside these halls who would do anything to get their hands on the Ark.'

Kip and Albert looked at each other.

'Don't like the sound of dark agents,' Albert muttered.

'I leave you with these words: be vigilant, be valorous and be victorious!' said Miss Twiss.

She ascended silently on her Skimmi and disappeared from view as the theatre flooded with applause and deafening gossip.

The Big Five

The assembly began to scatter, some people lifting into the air on Skimmies, others heading towards the exit on foot. Timmi's gaze flicked from Kip to Albert, then scanned across the faces in the crowd. And then, without a word, she just left.

Bit unfriendly, thought Kip.

'See ya!' said Leela, and started after Timmi. 'Oh wait!' she said, stopping abruptly. 'I nearly forgot. There's something else.'

Kip and Albert listened carefully, hoping for a piece of important advice.

'Would you rather have a moustache made of fingers, or a voice that says everything twice, everything twice?'

Then, with a rascally grin, Kip's new befriender was gone.

As Kip and Albert left the theatre, the Ballmoths appeared. They led the way alongside grand halls and through courtyards to a four-storey building that looked like a sprawling nest left behind by colossal extraterrestrial bees. In its many mirrored sides, a hundred white skies and trees were reflected. As they got closer, the pearly words above the Ballmoths spelled out their new location:

THE HIVE

They entered a hexagonal, glass chamber. From here they could hear the humming of many voices just as if they had walked into a busy citadel full of bee banter.

They followed the Ballmoths along a glass corridor, and past noisy classrooms to a glass door with *PROFESSOR MO* above it in glimmering letters.

The rows of seats inside weren't anything like the ones at Ledhill – those remnants from a dark age with sunken padding and splintered wood, bored carvings and inky initials. As he lowered himself into a sky-blue velvety chair, Kip realised that he would never have to sit in the Claw Chair again. The relief he felt was strong and sweet and sparkling, and he wished he could bottle it for whenever things got tough.

When Kip lifted his feet off the ground, the chair

swayed slightly. He ducked his head down to look underneath.

'They don't have legs!' he said.

'It's like sitting on a mini-cloud,' Albert replied.

One by one, the chairs around them filled up as more newcomers arrived.

'Hello,' said a girl with a rainbow of ribbons in her hair, who sat down next to Kip. 'I'm Penny and this is Em.'

A brown-eyed girl next to Penny waved. Her hands and fingers were painted with flowery red henna designs.

The boy from the car park rolled up in his wheelchair. With a lift of his strong arms and a flick of his waist, he transferred himself into a floating chair.

'I'm Badger,' he said. 'And I'm moving into this thing! A million times better than wheels.'

'My name's Maya,' said a girl with her hair in a bun so tight it pulled up her eyebrows in two steep arches above her glasses. 'I *have* to get one of these. In pink. Who do I talk to?'

'Did you all enter Brainbeard's Buried Booty then?' asked Em.

A few people giggled and Em blushed.

'What's that?' asked Kip.

'It was a puzzle in the newspaper that led to pirate treasure,' said Em. 'I worked really hard on it.

But we couldn't travel all the way to where I thought the chest was buried – it was too far from my village. So, I posted my answer. They sent me another puzzle back in the post, and that led me to the Open Day.'

'Not me,' said Badger. 'I made some optical illusions at summer camp for my art project. And the judge was a Quicksmiths scout.'

'My brother and I won an escape game,' said Penny. 'So we both got in.'

'I started feeling the Slipstream splashing on me all the time,' said Maya, with a big smile. 'So my parents took me to a doctor, who sent me to a doctor, who sent me to a brain doctor. Who sent me to Quicksmiths.'

'Ah good, you're all here,' said Professor Mo, as he entered the room.

On a scale of zero to interesting, Professor Mo probably broke the scale. The spectacles he was wearing looked like they were made out of lots of miniature magnifying glasses stuck together, and seemed to rest not on his cheeks at all, but on the very tops of the tattooed indigo brambles that sprawled up from under his jaw. Today, he was wearing a bright, jigsaw-patterned shirt. And in addition to the glasses on his face, there were four pairs on cords around his neck.

'Let's make a bit more space, shall we? I need some volunteers to sit in the top row.'

About half the class put their hands up.

'Surely he means "front row"?' whispered Em.

'Volunteers, I'd like you to feel for the buttons on each side of your Airchair. Keep them pressed down, then try to clear your mind and think "up". Don't question what's possible.'

Kip pressed the buttons, looked straight ahead and tried to think of nothing, which was harder than he expected. Then he imagined *up* things: birds taking flight, paper aeroplanes, hot air balloons. And gradually, despite his doubts, he felt the chair begin to rise.

'That's it, keep thinking. Up you go – and then think "forward". Don't worry if you accidentally release the buttons – you won't fall.'

All around Kip, Airchairs were lifting, moving into position. Badger cackled in delight. Soon, a top row of about ten chairs had formed. Kip grinned down at the ten or so faces grinning up at him from below.

'Much better,' said the Professor, pushing up his glasses with one finger. 'I'm delighted to welcome you to the First Year of Quicksmiths, you brave and brilliant souls! For those of you who haven't met me yet, I am your form teacher, Professor Mo. I also teach your Quixology class. Now, just in case you've forgotten already why you're here, I have two words for you: Strange Energies. They flow in and out of us and all around us. We have kept our ability to sense them, thanks to the quixars lighting up inside our bodies and brains.'

'Is it like a sixth sense?' Maya asked.

'You're in the right zone,' Professor Mo said. 'Only we have many more senses than just six. Quixars act like tiny aerials, picking up Strange Energies. They've always been there, hiding in plain sight. Of course, quixars haven't yet been discovered outside Quicksmiths; or it's truer to say that people might call them by another name and think they're doing something else entirely.'

Sounds like Quicksmiths is centuries ahead of the rest of the world, Kip thought.

'In your First Year you will study Quixology and Invention, alongside what we call the Big Five energies,' continued the Professor. 'Wormholes, Timeyarn, Thoughtwaves, Skycrackle and Slipstream. All of you will be able to sense the Big Five in some way – you might feel them, or see them or even taste and hear them. Any questions?'

'But how can you feel time?' asked Penny.

'Doesn't a heart beat?' said Professor Mo.

'Well, all right, but how do you … taste a thought?' she persisted.

'Everyone think of your favourite food right now – imagine how it looks, how it smells, the first spoonful. Anyone's mouth watering?'

Kip decided not to rush into asking any questions

after that. The Professor seemed to have a simple answer to everything.

'Here's the thing: many of you have sensory fusion, which means that more than one of your senses is activated by Strange Energy. Some of you will be lucky enough to tune into very rare energies, and you'll learn about these in time. And don't be surprised if you see or hear things that other people don't.'

Professor Mo paused to peer at his students through two new sets of spectacles, finally swapping the magnifying-glasses for a plainer pair.

'There is no doubt you are all talented at something,' he went on. 'But you are not expected to come first in every subject, or indeed any subject. You are here to find yourself. Strange Energy will make some of you into scientists, and some of you into inventors, poets or musicians. Some of you will be great at something we haven't even discovered yet.'

He wiggled his glasses as he looked at the class.

'And I am a thousand per cent sure that every one of you will be better than me in at least one of your subjects. You'll learn Maths and English and general knowledge too, because energy can't write and calculate for you, or have an interesting conversation with your Auntie Dave at Christmas.'

The class laughed quietly and looked around – and up and down – at each other. Kip swung his legs happily. Part of him had always known there was a place like this, a place where he belonged. This was his tribe. The Snibbug wouldn't last a day here. Professor Steampunk would baffle her with his Steampunkery and Professor Mo would probably yawn at everything she said until she shrivelled up with embarrassment.

'Now this is the bit I look forward to every year,' Professor Mo was saying. 'You'll all be pleased to hear that there are no exams at Quicksmiths.'

Kip's legs stopped in mid-swing. All around, stunned faces looked back at him. No. Exams. And then, there was a deafening uproar.

'Yes, yes, you heard correctly,' Professor Mo continued over the noise. 'We teach you things you won't learn in an ordinary school; we believe it's what you *do* with that knowledge that shows how clever you are. There are no houses either. And we don't waste time dressing in identical outfits – your Candle is your uniform.'

Kip and Albert looked at each other gleefully. So was that what it was going to be like here? All the things they hated about their old schools were going to go out of the window?

'Is that the time? Oh, cabbages and conundrums!' fussed the Professor. 'There's just a few minutes to tell you about your Candles – they connect to GENI's Strange Reality Drive which can do all sorts of useful things. For now, we'll just learn two little shortcuts – Candlelight and Threescan…'

He paused for a second to put on a pair of wraparound sunglasses.

'Where were we?' he said. 'Ah yes. Candlelight: just swipe up along your badge and keep swiping if you want brighter…'

The classroom was dazzled as everyone immediately turned their Candlelight to maximum.

'I was expecting the actual Candle to light up,' said Albert, shading his eyes. 'Not a spotlight-from-nowhere.'

'I'm starting to get a tan,' said the Professor. 'So let's try dimming your lights. Just swipe down and keep swiping to turn off. Ah, that's better. Easy, isn't it? Now for Threescan. This is short for 3-D scanning. Touch your badge with one hand and press your finger against any item you wish to replicate. GENI creates an instant copy which you can save for later.'

Kip decided to threescan the apple he had brought from breakfast. The duplicate was flawless and he was just trying to take a mouthful (it was impossible, like trying to bite water) when a ripple of laughter made him look around. Badger had somehow managed to threescan several copies of himself which were frozen in various poses. The class erupted into questions.

'Can they do my homework for me?'

'Can they walk my dog?'

'Could you make a whole football team of yourself?'

'Too. Many. Badgers,' said the Professor, dismissing the scans with a few controlled hand gestures. 'Now grab yourself a partner. Your Ballmoths are going to take you on an orientation exercise.'

Quickets

Kip and Albert landed their Airchairs and gathered around the Professor with the rest of the class.

'Each team has a different list of locations,' said Professor Mo. 'And as an optional extra, you can pick up Quickets along the way.'

'What's a Quicket?' asked Albert.

'Quicket is a game you pway in spwingtime,' said Badger.

Professor Mo looked over his sunglasses at Badger and smiled.

'Your jokes just *bowl* me over, Badger,' he said, before answering Albert. 'Quickets are the currency of Quicksmiths. And GENI is the bank.'

'Quicksmiths has its own *currency*?' said Maya. 'Surely only countries are that powerful.'

'Yes,' said Professor Mo simply. 'Instruction GENI: show us a Quicket.'

A golden Q with a double tail, about the size of a bottle cap, appeared and span slowly in the air in front of them.

116

'You can earn Quickets for doing good work and good deeds. And you can also make them by selling your inventions.'

'Where can I buy Quickets?' asked Maya. 'I've got cash.'

'You can't just buy them,' said Professor Mo. 'Everyone comes to Quicksmiths with zero Quickets, no matter how rich you might be in the outside world. But this morning, you can each earn a total of three. When you find one, just swipe it with your finger to collect it. GENI will bank it for you.'

The first place on Kip and Albert's list, the Clock Tower, was directly in the centre of the four halls of Quicksmiths: Celestial Hall, Atlas House, The Singing Mill and Quantum Quarter. The tower's four yellow clock faces looked out at each of the four halls like majestic suns.

'In. Cre. Dible!' Albert mumbled.

Together, they looked up at the ancient red brickwork. On the nearest face, a thin clock hand chased the seconds tirelessly.

'There's something not quite right about it,' said Albert, scratching his head.

'I can't see anything unusual,' Kip said, shrugging.

'You know, my mum's convinced I'm going to be a clockmaker,' Albert said, still squinting up.

'Do you want to be one?' Kip asked.

'Yes, I guess. At least I did. Now I'm here, I get the

feeling that there's something better for me. Something we don't even know about yet. It would be pretty cool to be the first person to do something. Like the first person to climb Everest or walk on the moon. Only stranger. What about you?'

'I want to be a doctor. To help my mum.'

'Is she ill?' asked Albert.

'They gave up on her years ago,' said Kip. 'But we haven't. Me and my dad.'

'Well, if there's anywhere in the world where you can find out how to help her, I bet it's here,' said Albert.

Kip looked at his new friend gratefully and nodded. Usually there was an awkward conversation when people found out about his mum. They asked questions that he didn't really want to have to answer. But Albert was different.

'Look, there's the first Quicket,' Albert said. 'You take it.'

It was sparkling in a patch of daisies. Kip bent down to touch it but the golden Q jumped away from him. Albert giggled as it hopped around the flowers.

'I see why they call them Quickets,' he said.

After a few attempts, they managed to trap it. There was a faint *drrring* as Kip swiped the Quicket with a finger and it disappeared.

The second location on their list was the Library. It stood on a hill past the workshops and laboratories and looked like an old Roman temple with huge columns. Albert found the Quicket nestled in a beanbag in the reading room. Next, they visited the Porterhouse – a small brick building with five chubby chimneypots huddled together like stone penguins on its roof. Inside, a porter was sorting letters and parcels, and the Quicket was hiding in an empty cubbyhole.

'Now we need to find Skycrackle Tower,' said Albert, as they stepped out of the Porterhouse.

It wasn't hard. The soaring white tower Kip had first seen at the Open Day was so immense that it dominated the sky, no matter where you stood. As they made their way across the large open space surrounding it, they saw that the glass tower was not white at all, but full of smoke, or cloud, which rolled restlessly. Its base was made of crossed metal bars that reminded Kip a little of electricity pylons.

'I can't even see the top of it,' said Albert.

There was a sudden red flash inside the cloud, like the breath of a dragon. Kip flinched. A word filled his mind, a feeling of rippling fear: *lightning*. Panic seemed to clutch at him from every direction. This panic was all he remembered from the day they lost Suzanna. Kip sat down, took a few slow breaths just like he'd been taught by the counsellor when he was young, and tried to picture a calming squirl.

A *drrring* shook him from his trance, as Albert collected the next Quicket.

'You OK?' Albert asked.

'Just thinking,' said Kip.

'Come on. Race you to the Portrait Gallery.'

The Ballmoths stopped outside a door in Celestial Hall which led into a quiet, unoccupied gallery. Hundreds of framed portraits were hung throughout the oval room; not on the walls, but in the air.

'Question GENI,' Kip said, remembering they could ask her anything. 'Who are all these people?'

'They are Quicksmiths' greatest thinkers, honoured here for all time.'

There was Motukōmuhumuhu Kānekeneke, beaming as he placed the final piece in a jigsaw replica of himself. And Adelaide Twiss, too – when she was much younger – doing a handstand on a Skimmi.

As Kip and Albert wandered among the picture frames, they read some more of the names out loud. Kip only recognised one or two of them.

'Hildegard of Bingen … Al-Khwarizmi … Leonardo da Vinci … Mary Anning … Satyendra Nath Bose … Alan Turing … Emmy Noether … Vera Rubin … Edward Elgar… Erwin Schrödinger … Annie Jump Cannon … Rachel Carson…'

After a while, they came across the last two Quickets, glinting like earrings on one of the portraits.

'Hey, it's Eartha Quicksmith!' said Albert.

Eartha's eyes were deep turquoise – the colour of

120

ocean sinkholes sprinkled with threads of silver sea sparkles. There were lots of fine thinking-wrinkles across her forehead, around which fell soft, short sprigs of caramel-brown hair.

'I thought all women had long hair in those days,' said Kip.

'Not Eartha,' said Albert. 'And she's not wearing a big frilly dress either. It's a funny pose for a portrait, don't you think?'

Eartha seemed completely absorbed in reading the book she held in one hand. The other hand was reaching out into mid-air. Perched on her outstretched arm was a black parrot, and tucked behind her ear was a blue buttercup.

'S'pose it is a bit,' Kip agreed.

'I've never seen a blue buttercup before.'

'Or a black parrot,' said Kip.

Chapter Six

The First Riddle

During break time Kip and Albert took a walk through the courtyards. As they strolled along the paths, snatches of conversation rose and fell from the clusters of people they passed.

'…forget the riddles, why aren't we scanning for the Ark using Strange Radiation Imaging…'

'…I bet Gorvak's the truthseer Eartha was talking about…'

'…Instruction GENI: show me a map of Quicksmiths…'

'…Aeon Light will answer some of our biggest questions…'

'What do you think Aeon Light even is?' asked Kip.

'I dunno,' said Albert. 'It sounds … wise? Galactic? How do you discover a new energy? I mean, it has to be there all along, right? And then – bam! You just know what it is and give it a name? And it's that simple?'

They sat on a bench in Clock Tower Courtyard and eavesdropped for a bit longer, but the more they heard the more they realised they didn't know. Kip closed his eyes, gazing out into the dark edges of his unseen universe. Sometimes he recognised recurring patterns in the squirls, which gave him a fuzzy, drowsy feeling, just like sunbathing.

'I feel like my brain needs to unknow everything and start again,' said Albert's voice.

'Mmm-hmmm,' said Kip, watching a meandering squirl.

'Come on,' said Albert. 'The Ballmoths are here. Break's over.'

Professor Kvörk – the Slipstream teacher – was waiting for them in The Hive. She was very tall and wore platform shoes which made her even taller. Her voice was slow and syrupy, and it sounded like she drank smoothies made of glacier moss and pine sap. In her hand was a Skimmi, folded up into a quarter-circle.

'It's a lovely morning,' she crooned. 'Let's take our lesson outside.'

'Do we get to ride on Skimmies today?' asked Em.

'Even better than that,' said Professor Kvörk. 'You get to build your very own. But it will take a few months.'

'Months,' Badger groaned.

But nobody was listening. For, as Professor Kvörk turned to leave the classroom, something waved out from a gap in the back of her tunic. Something furry and striped that snaked back and forth. At that moment, the lesson turned into a masterclass in whispering. The Professor stopped and looked around to find that everyone had their hand up.

'You're wondering what this little thing is?' she said, smiling. 'Yes, of course, it's a tail. A tiger tail, in fact. I volunteered when Professor Steampunk was testing one of his inventions.'

'Do we get tails too?' said Penny, unable to contain herself. 'I want a horse's tail.'

'Rabbit for me!' shouted Em.

'Stegosaurus!' yelled Badger.

'Only once you're old enough to go to Quicksmiths University,' said Professor Kvörk.

As she led the class outside, she twirled her tail around her hand like a thick bangle.

'Actually, having a tail is great for extra balance when you're skimmiing. Which brings me back to the lesson. All energy moves in waves and Strange Energies are no exception. Tell me something – how does a wave move?'

'It goes up and down,' someone shouted.

'Don't some go from side to side?' asked Albert.

'Or,' said Professor Kvörk, 'how about expanding

those ideas? What about waves that go *in* and *out*. Or *above* and *beyond*. Or even waves that go *now* and *then*.'

The whole class went silent with reflection until Badger held out his hands, pretending to present something in each one.

'This,' he announced, looking at this left hand, 'is my brain. And this,' he looked at his right hand, 'is rhubarb crumble. Spot the difference.'

'Me too!' sighed everyone, relieved that they weren't alone.

Professor Kvörk laughed like a bubbling spring of honey.

'You'll get used to it,' she said. 'Everyone close your eyes now and think about water. Why water? Because it can take many forms. Some Strange Energies are like mists collecting around solar systems; others are wild tsunamis; some are deep and still and take the shape of their surroundings; some even come from the cells of living things. As for the Slipstream … imagine a river of Strange Energy that encircles the whole world, and stretches between planets…'

But they didn't get to find out what the Professor was going to say next. A girl ran past, then a boy, and then a whole crowd.

'What's going on?' asked Professor Kvörk, as one of the runners stopped to tie his shoelace.

'Haven't you heard? The Egg Flower is blooming!'

Professor Kvörk's tail waved in excitement and brushed Kip softly on the shin.

'What a stroke of luck,' she said. 'The Egg Flower only blossoms every four or five centuries. Follow me!'

'I've never heard of an Egg Flower,' said Em, trotting to keep up.

'I'd be surprised if you had,' said Professor Kvörk. 'Lots of unusual plants grow here at Quicksmiths, and only here, because of the crossing of energy streams.'

At the Botanical Gardens they found a crowd was already gathered in the Tropical Flowerhouse. Albert leapt on an empty bench and pulled Kip up so they could see better.

'No one alive has ever seen what we're about to witness,' said one of the teachers.

The bud of the closed flower reminded Kip of a pineapple, resting on a bed of spiky leaves. Everyone watched wordlessly as the skin of this giant bud lowered slowly in six succulent panels, like the landing ramps of an alien craft. The newborn petals of the flower spiralled out from the folds of their long sleep.

'Why's it called an egg flowuuurrrgk?'

In the middle of this glorious moment, Kip's nostrils tried to scream. Out of the unfurling flower came a smell like egg and fish guts buried in a swamp for a month. Sleeves were held up to noses everywhere, and a few people pushed their way out through the crowd, unable to bear the stench.

When the silky, salmon-pink petals were open completely, a hard, egg-shaped sac was revealed at the flower's heart. As everyone peered closer, still covering their noses, the outer shell cracked into a pattern of fine lines. Kip wouldn't have been surprised if a hundred stink bugs had flown out. But instead, a spiral of flattened, blunt thorns gradually began to open.

'It's like a mutant pine cone,' murmured Albert.

'There are markings on them!' yelled Maya, who had somehow managed to get in front of all the people. 'Like ... letters!'

'How in Newton's name did Eartha do that?' murmured Professor Kvörk.

'What does it say?' someone shouted from the back.

After a tormenting pause, one of the professors blurted out a message:

1

Look around me

'The first riddle!' voices exclaimed from all around.

A commotion started at the back of the crowd and quickly made its way to the front as the sea of people parted. Word had got to the Professor-in-Charge that something strange was happening at the Botanical Gardens.

Holding a silk scarf to her nose, Miss Twiss stepped

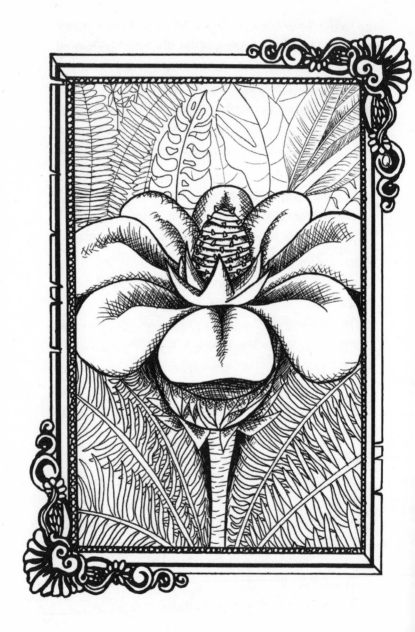

up to the flower's cone-shaped heart. She ran a finger very lightly over one of its blunt thorns, then turned around to face the crowd.

'It has begun. None of us can resist an enigma. The quixars inside you and me draw us to the enigmatic, and to Strange Energy, like moths to the light. And Eartha's Ark of Ideas is the brightest enigma we've seen for many years. If we can find it, it may contain truths that could change our world in ways we can only just imagine.'

Everyone started whispering about the Ark and Aeon Light. But Kip was thinking about what his dad had said. *What's to stop you coming back to fix Mum?*

'In the spirit of fairness,' said Miss Twiss, 'everyone shall have a chance to solve Eartha's riddle. Instruction GENI: assign time to our Riddles Taskforce first. Then create a random schedule so that everyone else can examine the flower first-hand. We will also make a Threescan, so that we can all study the flower at our leisure.'

'Can I be in your team?' asked Albert, as they returned to The Hive, gulping in the fresh air.

'I was hoping you'd say that,' Kip replied. 'We'll need a name.'

Albert snapped his fingers.

'Team Glowflyer?'

It was exactly what Kip might have said.

At lunchtime the only conversation in the Buttery was about the first riddle and the Egg Flower, and rumours spun around like dynamos. Penny and Em started a guessing game in which everyone took a turn to say where they thought Eartha's Ark of Ideas was hidden.

'It's definitely buried somewhere,' Em insisted.

'Maybe it's buried some*when*,' Albert said, stroking his chin.

'Secret panel in the Library?' suggested Maya.

'At the end of the Skycrackle rainbow,' Penny said, pretending to shade her eyes and look into the distance.

'Shhhhhhhhh!' whispered Badger dramatically, as he lifted the crust on his apple pie. 'It's hiding in here!'

Make your own Wormhole

When they got to The Hive after lunch, they found Professor Steampunk already pottering around in the classroom. He was writing an equation with one hand and with the other three he tapped on a panel and adjusted some dials.

'Goodest of afternoons to you,' he said, looking up from his tinkering.

'Are you inventing something, Professor?' asked Maya.

'I'm always inventing something,' said Steampunk.

'Even when I'm ironing my lab coat, or cutting my toenails. *Especially* when I'm cutting my toenails.'

'What will Eartha's inventions be like? When we find the Ark?' Em asked.

'Oh, Eartha's inventions are of unimaginable resplungence.'

Penny fiddled with a ribbon in her hair.

'But what will they do?'

'Well, *if* we find the Ark, and *if* we are clever enough, then I think its secrets could trigger the next revolution.'

'I'm revolting!' shouted Badger.

Professor Steampunk chortled and lifted all four hands like a weather god raising a storm.

'What critical turning points have shaped our history? Agricultural. Industrial. Internet. And what's next? The Energy Revolution! Understanding energy and knowing how it flows can fix almost any problem. Eartha knew that better than anyone.'

'How many inventions use Strange Energy, Professor?' asked Em.

'Well, for starters there are Thoughtwave Lenses, Skimmies, Timestretch Limos, Mothballs, Candles, the Great Globe and GENI. And then there are things you won't learn about just yet like ... oh ... Tetherbelts, Smell TV, the Homunculiser, Phantasm Fields, the Withinnervator, and the Large Hadron Kaleidoscope ... but you'd be at least a hundred by the time I listed them all out. Perhaps instead you might like…'

Steampunk plucked a white rat out of each of his four lab coat pockets.

'…to meet Gnawmon, Gnashley, Gnibbles and Ratfred.'

One of the rats squeaked and Steampunk held him up to one ear.

'Gnawmon here says it's time we took a trip into the Wondrous World of Whimsical Wormholes. Who's feeling brave?'

Penny's hand shot up first.

'Before we begin, I must worm you that warnholes are not for the faint of brain!' said Steampunk. 'I mean … you know what I mean.'

The Professor repocketed the rats, and selected an aluminium-coloured briefcase from a stack in the corner of the room. When he undid the clips and opened it, an empty picture frame popped up from inside. Guiding Penny eagerly, he stood her in front of the class with her back to everyone.

'Stick your face in there, my brave young adventurer!'

Penny hesitated for a second and then she thrust her face inside the picture frame. Immediately, her face appeared at the back of her own head, peering out at the class like an explorer looking through the vine-like ribbons in her hair. It took Penny a while to work out what had happened, but then her face creased into giggles and her hand appeared out of one shoulder and waved at everyone.

Steampunk wiped tears of laughter from the corner of his eye.

'You're each going to make a wormhole today. Just eeny ones to start with, nice and easy. Nothing bigger than a mouse will be able to get through. Or perhaps a rat. Now follow me, oh great thinky thinkists!'

The Professor took a gym bag off the table, put it on the floor, and opened the zips. He reached into the bag, pulled up a door frame, and clicked its two hinges into place. Turning the doorknob, he beckoned with the other three hands.

'To the Wormhole Generator!'

Following the Professor through the door-in-a-bag, the class entered a chilly vault with a high ceiling. Close to the ceiling was a large metal ring the size of a monster truck wheel. From it a chain of interlocking rings dangled down, decreasing in size towards the last ring which was as small as a bracelet.

'Splendificent, isn't it?' said Steampunk. 'The very first wormholes were made during the Renaissance, in Eartha Quicksmith's time, using sixty-three lightning attractors, twelve bathtubs full of metal ice cubes, six hundred mirrors and five magnets as big as minotaurs. Instruction GENI: activate the generator.'

The largest of the metal rings began to rotate, and

then the next largest ring, all the way down to the smallest. When the entire chain was spinning Kip felt a burst of sneezesickness, and the vault shook with a loud pop.

'Let's give that brand-new baby wormhole a splash of colour, shall we?' said the Professor.

He took a spray can from his pocket and squirted something into the last ring in the chain, revealing a smoky, purple wisp inside.

'Will someone pass me one of those cases, please? Yes, those ones.'

The Professor took the small, shiny briefcase and held it open. The tiny purple wisp coiled and curled and was sucked inside.

'Now then. Let's get making oodles of wormholes!' he said. 'Because what's the point of having these Strange Energies swirling around us if all we do is stare and gawp.'

At the end of the class, Steampunk called everyone over to the door-in-a-bag.

'Who here has ever had an idea for an invention?'

Everyone put their hand up, including Kip.

'I'll bet you didn't have exactly the right materials or tools to make it. Well, here you do. So, in our next workshop, I want you each to produce a prototype for a Strange Invention that uses the wormhole you made today. The Strangest Invention you can imagine. Something worthy of Eartha Quicksmith herself.

After all, some of our best invention ideas have come from First Years.'

The Professor held Gnawmon up to his ear again.

'One last thing, everyone. Gnawmon says that the greatest inventions are always made to help someone. It might even be someone you know.'

Ambush

Kip woke the next day with a new optimism that unsealed his dreaming eyes and curled his toes.

Albert was already up, leaning out of the window.

'Morning,' said Kip, trying to walk and stretch his stiff, still-asleep legs at the same time. 'What are you looking at?'

'Just getting some time with my favourite Clock Tower,' said Albert. 'Something's still bugging me about it.'

Kip leaned out of the window too. It was moist and misty out there.

'The clouds have sunk,' he said.

'Mystical,' replied Albert. 'Or is it *mist*ical? Hey, you know the best thing about not having a school uniform?'

'No more neck snakes?' said Kip.

'Goodbye strangle-strings forever!' grinned Albert.

They finished breakfast early and strolled out idly into the whitewashed morning. The two Ballmoths glowed eerily in the blankness like will-o'-the-wisps. In the mist above them floated the murky undersides of Skimmies.

'This must be what it's like to be a fish,' said Albert. 'Looking up at a surfing competition.'

They hadn't got far when Kip realised he had forgotten to fill Pinky's water bowl.

'You go on, I'll be there in five,' he shouted to Albert as he sprinted back towards the First Year Block.

Two figures were hanging around at the entrance. Kip caught a glimpse of a necklace made of shark teeth, and a cruel smile. Then he saw a pair of beady eyes and another smile like a split haggis.

Of all the places to lurk, Kip thought.

A boy walking ahead changed course and scurried away into the mist. But there was no time to find another way in, so Kip kept marching determinedly up to the door.

As he tried to get inside, Thag put an arm out, barring Kip's way.

'Is this Professor Mo's new fer-fer-fer-favourite?' asked Thag, putting on an irritating stutter for no reason.

'Favourite? Don't you mean feeblewit?' said Sharktooth Girl.

Her voice was sharp – sharp as the teeth around her neck, sharp enough to burst all the balloons at a party.

'You're in the way,' said Kip evenly.

136

'What an obtoid,' said Sharktooth Girl to Thag as if Kip wasn't there.

Thag ignored her and kept staring at Kip. His eyes were like tight black buttons doing up a wide, doughy face. Just like a human newt, Kip thought. His chin was about in line with Kip's eyes and there was a dribble of jam there, left from breakfast.

'We're recruiting,' said Sharktooth Girl, 'for Thag's gang.'

'Sign up and life will get much easier for you,' Thag added.

'No thanks,' said Kip. 'I'm fine.'

'Oh, OK. Well, I suppose that's your choice.'

Thag lifted up the security barrier of his arm. Kip couldn't believe he was going to escape so easily. He grabbed the door handle but Thag's arm came down again hard and fast, thumping Kip on the shoulder and forcing him back a step.

'Oh dear,' said Thag, 'you forgot to tell us the password.'

Sharktooth Girl screech-laughed. It sounded like an alien was trying to copy a human.

'We'll help you,' said Thag. 'What's the password today, Mel?'

'Today's password is "I am a loser,"' Sharktooth Girl said coldly.

Kip stared at them defiantly and said nothing.

'No password?' said Thag. 'Fine, seeing as you

decided not to join us, you have to pay for your entrance. With a wedgie. But not just any old wedgie. A Mind Wedgie.'

Thag cracked his knuckles sinisterly. Kip didn't want to try and guess what a Mind Wedgie might be. He felt his jaw clench like a bear trap. But just as he was preparing to bite and kick his way out of the ambush, a figure appeared out of the thinning mists. It was the sixth-former with the strawberry-blond hair and freckles from yesterday's Buttery queue.

'What's up?' he said.

'Get lost!' said Thag. 'I'm busy.'

'No need for that, Pythagoras,' said the other boy. 'Give him a break.'

His tone was quietly convincing, as if he were trying to persuade an escaped gorilla back into its enclosure.

Thag turned on him with a snarl.

'Worming your way into people's hearts again, Gorvak? Just because you're related to Mrs High-and-Mighty Quicksmith doesn't mean you can lord it over the rest of us.'

Gorvak stepped between Thag and Kip. Thag was taller than Gorvak and his tree-trunk arms had a powerful grip but Gorvak looked leaner and faster.

'Classic avoidance mechanism,' said Gorvak, shaking his head. 'You're the one with the real problems so you try to make everyone else think there's something wrong with them.'

Sharktooth Girl spat at Gorvak and was about to throw the first punch when Bagsworth the Porter came hurrying up. He opened a can of paint and began to brush over some black marks on the wall.

'Get yourselves off to class,' he muttered.

Thag and Sharktooth Girl clumped off angrily. When they got to the end of the block, Thag turned around and made the *I'm-watching-you* sign with two fingers, looking first at Gorvak and then Kip.

Gorvak turned to Kip and smiled. The freckles on his face and the tips of two sharp incisors gave him the look of a friendly leopard. A friendly leopard who stuck up for strangers. He took a rectangle of card out of his jacket pocket.

'Shame about that. Nice to meet you properly anyway.'

Behind the glasses were eyes the pale blue of liquid oxygen. He wiggled the business card until Kip took it.

Gorvak G. Gorvak: Genius

'So you're related to…' Kip started.

But when he looked up, Gorvak had already sauntered off, hands in his pockets. Kip clattered up to room Q10 and filled Pinky's bowl using the little sink in a corner of the room. The Ballmoth did somersaults by the door handle, as if it knew Kip was late and that there would have to be a lot more running to get to class in time.

Library

At the end of the day, Kip and Albert stopped to sit in a fragrant herb garden outside the First Year Block. It was good to have a quiet moment just to take everything in. The mint smelled strong – Kip picked a leaf and rolled it in between his fingers.

'Feels like we're at an adventure park,' he said.

'Totally,' said Albert. 'How much new stuff is it possible to learn in a single day? My head's full.'

'We're going to need a lot of spare heads,' said Kip. 'I wonder if we can use Threescan?'

'That would be great – just plug them in like a hard drive,' said Albert. 'Oh, hello, Ballmoths. What do you want?'

'Get your library card,' Kip read out loud. 'That's definitely the most normal thing I've heard all day.'

As it sank lower, the sun seemed to melt over the Library's white roof. Once they were nearly at the little green hill on which the Library stood, Albert groaned.

'Isn't that Thag? The Plasma Slug guy? And that Sharktooth Girl.'

Their new worst friend was slumped on the white steps. In his hands was a grey, whining device that he was using to attract flies. He was passing them to Sharktooth Girl, who pulled their wings off. Kip hastily told Albert about the ambush earlier.

'Could they be any nastier?' asked Albert indignantly.

Luckily, a large group was coming down the steps so Kip and Albert used them as cover to get past.

'I don't think he saw us,' said Kip.

'Let's keep it that way,' Albert replied. 'Forever.'

Inside the Library a central atrium stretched out under the spine of an arched, glass ceiling. On the right-hand side, six floors were open to the atrium, filled with bookcases the colour of red wine. On the left, the wall was formed of one continuous bookcase that went all the way up from floor to ceiling. The greens, blues, reds and yellows of the book spines formed striped patterns, as if the Library had its own genetic sequence.

Kip reached out to take a copy of *Photon Fountains and Uphill Water* off the nearest shelf, but it wouldn't budge.

'I see you are trying to select a book,' said GENI. 'You will require a library card first. I shall call a librarian.'

'Someone looking for me?' replied a voice below them.

Gazing up from a basement was a man with a steady and contemplative expression. He didn't look elderly, but he had snowy hair, which made his dark skin look even darker. The Librarian sprang up some rickety, wooden steps three at a time. He was the

141

tallest person Kip had ever seen, taller even than Professor Kvörk, and had muscly arms that bulged out of his shirt sleeves.

'Big Obi, Head Librarian, at your service,' he said with a bow.

The Librarian beckoned and walked briskly to a circular counter. A panel lifted up, allowing him to step through into the space in the middle.

'There must be millions of books in here,' Kip said absent-mindedly, looking up at the high ceiling.

'Over two hundred million actually,' replied the Librarian. 'And that's just the ones I've got round to cataloguing.'

'How many books are there about the Ark of Ideas?' asked Albert.

'Oh, thousands and thousands,' said the Librarian. 'But a lot of them are out on loan. There's been plenty of interest since Miss Twiss read Eartha Quicksmith's letter.'

Kip nodded, but he was still looking around at the huge collection of books.

'Isn't there something beautiful in the sharing of minds across time and space?' said the Librarian, following Kip's gaze. 'Thoughts and memories are transformed into marks on ancient paper, which are transformed back into thoughts and memories in your brain cells. Then, whenever you write down your own thoughts, the cycle begins again.'

'The Thought Cycle,' murmured Kip.

'You get it!' said the Librarian enthusiastically. 'New knowledge is part of a cycle that begins with old knowledge. You cannot disconnect the two. All this,' he swivelled slowly, with his mighty hands held up, 'is the heritage of the whole human race.'

He bent down behind the counter and hunted around, before standing up and handing a heavy, glossy book to Kip.

'See what you think of this,' he said, nodding encouragement.

Kip opened the book, expecting anything except the blinding light that flashed in his face.

'What *is* that?' he asked, rubbing his eyes.

'That just took your library card photo,' said the Librarian, chuckling like a pot of tickled treacle.

'But I was expecting something else!' complained Kip.

'Not all the books here are ancient. Or books,' said the Librarian mysteriously, handing over Kip's new card.

The picture showed Kip from below. His mouth was hanging open, his nose was wrinkled and one eye was shut. Albert grabbed it and laughed so much he got hiccups.

'Ha – hic – ha – hic – ha.'

The Librarian gestured to get Albert's attention. 'Just look up there for me for a second, will you?'

Albert looked up and a flash from the top of a tall bookcase caught him by surprise, right in the middle of a hiccup.

'There's no getting away from your First Year library card photo,' said the Librarian. 'It's a tradition: everyone's is terrible. I still have mine, look. Blobfish in a cardigan.'

'Hiccuppy and I would like to get some books on the Ark of Ideas,' Kip said, once he had finished laughing. 'Can you suggest the best ones that aren't already taken out?'

'Of course,' said the Librarian. 'Let me make a list for you. GENI will help you find them.'

They had collected six books when Albert's grumbling stomach started competing with his hiccups.

'My belly alarm is saying it's dinner time,' he said. 'Come on, we have enough for now.'

After dinner it was time to check on Pinky, who they found awake and scurrying about her lair. Her whole body quivered with delight to see her friends.

'Poor Pinky,' said Kip. 'Have you been bored? Let's call Dad and then we'll play Find-the-Raisin?'

'No video calls by the way,' said Albert. 'They get scrambled. Information security.'

Theo answered on the second ring and Pinky was so overjoyed to hear his voice that she tried to crawl inside the phone.

'How's everything going?' he asked.

Where did Kip start?

'Today was even better than yesterday,' he said. 'Which was awesome.'

'Best. Day. Ever!' shouted Albert.

'Is every day going to keep getting better than the last?' asked Theo. 'Until you end up in infinity awesomeness?'

After the call they played a few rounds of Find-the-Raisin, and then Lava Ground, in which everyone had to make it all the way round the room without touching the floor. Pinky didn't quite get the rules but it didn't matter.

'Do you mind if I open the window?' asked Albert, once Pinky was back in the lair gnawing at her breakfast.

'Sure,' said Kip. 'We love fresh air.'

'Hey, what's that sound?'

They craned their necks out of the window to listen to the background noise, so quiet that it flickered in and out of hearing. Kip realised after a little while that it was many layers of different sounds, like log fires crackling, rivulets trickling, the faint howling of a wind trapped in a chimney.

'It's the Strange Energies, isn't it?' said Kip. 'It must be. They almost sound alive.'

'It's kind of comforting,' said Albert. 'Makes me feel like camping.'

They listened together in silence. Kip closed his eyes and the squirls sparked up like swarms of fireflies in the distance.

'Come on,' Albert said. 'Let's make a start on those library books.'

He grabbed the first one off the pile and sat at his desk. Kip scanned the other titles until he found one that intrigued him:

Eartha Quicksmith: 100 Ways to Wonder

Flicking through the pages, he came to some hand-drawn pictures. In one, Eartha sat in a canoe, drinking tea. Her hat had been pierced by an arrow, on the end of which she had hung a teaspoon on a string. In another, she stood in front of a ziggurat, adjusting a lever on a steaming contraption with hinged legs.

'Says here that some people believe Eartha had a sort of secret study room,' mumbled Albert. 'But they searched the college and found nothing.'

Kip grunted, half-listening, and went back to the beginning to scan the chapter titles. He skipped straight to Chapter Three, which was called *Eartha the Healer*, and began to read.

Once her early schooling at Quicksmiths was complete, Eartha left to study medicine.

So, she was a doctor after all, he said to himself, and read on silently.

> After getting her medical degree, she wandered the world, seeking out shamen and wise women in remote islands, desert caves and mountain villages. Eartha returned to Quicksmiths after three long years and began to put the natural arts she had learned to good use.
>
> But it was only much later that Eartha's medical talents truly began to blossom. A number of second-hand reports confirm that she successfully used combinations of energy waves to heal illnesses of the mind.

Healing the mind? And just like that, out of the blue, the remedy to Kip's heartache was right in front of him. He could imagine his mum walking out of St Antony's, blinking in the sunshine. In no time at all, she would be doing ordinary, boring old family things, things Kip hadn't dared to hope for in a long time. Buzzing around the kitchen with his dad or playing Find-the-Raisin with them after dinner.

This is it, thought Kip. *This is why I'm here.*

'Albert,' he said, 'Eartha *was* a doctor.'

'Mmmmm. I know,' mumbled Albert.

'No, I mean she made people better.'

Albert looked up from his book. 'Like your mum,' he said, quietly.

147

'There's got to be something in the Ark that can fix her,' Kip said.

'How can we find out?' wondered Albert.

'I know,' said Kip. 'Question GENI: will the Ark of Ideas contain Eartha's experiments on energy waves and healing?'

'Hello, Kip,' said GENI. 'There is an eighty-one point six nine percent chance that the Ark will contain this information.'

'That's pretty good,' said Albert.

Kip stood up and looked out of the window again.

'We have to find it,' he said, half to himself.

Part of him wanted to call his dad back straight away. This was all happening much faster than Kip had expected. But he knew the Scrambleguard wouldn't let him say much.

All that matters is that you change your world, he reminded himself, *even if in the end no one knows who did it, or how it happened. For now, Dad just cares about you being happy. And the Scrambleguard hasn't stopped you telling him that.*

Kip stared up at the cloudless night sky. Against the darkness, the constellations were wild and brilliant.

'All those stars,' he murmured, twisting the quartz pendant under his shirt.

Tonight, the thousands of bursts of light seemed so close that Kip could reach up and touch them.

It doesn't matter where I stand, he thought. *I'm*

always looking at the past, at the memories of the Universe. But I know those stars are still alive.

'They keep on burning, don't they, Mum?' he whispered.

Egg Flower

Exactly five minutes before his appointment time, Kip parted the cascading curtain of creepers at the door to the Tropical Flowerhouse and entered. There was a short wait before a bossy porter came to fetch him.

'There are rules,' said the porter. 'No taking soil samples and no breaking the leaves or petals. Well? What are you waiting for?'

Kip walked in and sized up his huge, botanical adversary. It was just a little bit taller than him. The Egg Flower gave off a particularly smelly waft of scent in self-defence.

'Is that all you've got?' said Kip.

He started by inspecting the flattened thorns of the cone at the flower's centre. They gave up no extra information, other than the blistered letters of the first riddle.

1

Look around me

'Well, I'm looking, Eartha. Let's see what your mystery flower has to hide.'

Kip hunted under the leaves to see if the veins made any patterns. He checked the petals for any patches that felt different. The thick stem of the flower would be a good place to conceal another riddle – perhaps it was marked with zeros and ones, spelling out something in binary code.

When all else failed, Kip even tried singing to the flower – after all, weren't plants supposed to like that? When he was younger, his mum had sung to him and Suzanna all the time, but now the only song Kip could remember was *I'm Only Sleeping*. He sang a couple of verses, badly.

'One more minute!' bellowed the porter.

Come on, thought Kip. *Do something!*

But his time was up. And he wasn't even half a millimetre closer to knowing what the second riddle was.

Albert had saved Kip a seat in Quixology, and Kip slipped in quietly and sat down. Professor Mo paused to smile, then carried on talking.

'Mystery,' he said. 'Oddities. Paradox. The Universe loves to create puzzles for us to solve. And so, if we want to follow in the footsteps of Nikola Tesla, of Mercuria Sooth and Solomon Grittleshank, and of course the great Eartha Quicksmith, we must study Quixology – the art of puzzle solving. There is nothing more puzzling, after all, than Strange Energy.'

'Sisters,' Badger said quickly.

Everyone turned slowly to stare at him.

'What?' said Badger. 'I have six sisters and I don't understand any of them!'

Kip smiled and felt sad at the same time. Sisters. Suzanna. His mum. He shook away the sadness and kept the smile. He wasn't here to be sad.

'Thank you for sharing your very scientific observations on sisterly mysteries, Badger,' said Professor Mo. 'But let's get down to business. As you know, we've had an astronomically exciting revelation about the Ark of Ideas. So, for the time being, our Quixology classes will be devoted to solving Eartha's riddles.'

'What do we do if we discover something by ourselves? Outside of the class?' asked Penny.

'Well, you should do what you think is right,' replied the Professor. 'If it were me, I would share it with everyone. That way we'd all be a bit closer to the finish line. By putting our brains together, we can often get somewhere a lot faster. Now, who else is itching to solve that first riddle? Let's take a look at the Threescan GENI made. Anyone who wants to think by themselves, feel free to find a quiet corner.'

They all gathered around the Threescan of the flower.

'We should dig in the soil,' someone said. 'There could be something in the roots.'

'Whatever chemical is making that smell could be important,' said someone else.

'Maybe it's telling us to look around the Botanical Gardens?'

It felt like everyone was pulling in a different direction. Albert caught Kip's eye.

'Well?' he mouthed.

Kip motioned for Albert to follow him behind the airchairs and in a low voice told him every detail.

'Sounds like you tried everything,' Albert said.

'I can't have. Or we'd be on to the second riddle by now.'

Kip sat down and took out the Book of Squirls. It had been a while since he'd had a chance to draw anything and it felt as if a silent pressure had been building up inside. He closed his eyes. There they were, his old friends, giving shape and life and colour to the black nothingness.

'Albert,' he asked, eyes still closed. 'Have you noticed any changes since you got here?'

'Like what?'

'Well, the squirls. You know, the patterns I get when I close my eyes. They're really intense.'

'You should ask Professor Mo,' said Albert.

After the lesson, Kip waited until the room had emptied, and approached the Professor.

'Glad to see you're still drawing, Kip,' he said, tapping the Book of Squirls.

'I don't think I could stop,' said Kip. 'Even if I wanted to. It feels like they're getting sort of brighter.'

'May I look inside?' said Professor Mo.

Kip gave him the book and the Professor turned the pages thoughtfully.

'Each page is like a little mystery, isn't it?' he said.

'I recognise them sometimes,' said Kip. 'But I've never really understood them.'

'All this puzzling over Eartha's riddles is rocket fuel for the quixars in your brain,' said the Professor. 'It's not surprising that your connection to Strange Energy is getting stronger.'

'So what should I do?'

'My advice is to be patient. Keep watching. Keep drawing. These things have a way of making themselves understood.'

Chapter Seven

Look Around Me

'There,' said Albert, weaving through the busy tables in the Buttery. 'Leela and Timmi. And the mowl.'

Kip and Albert sat down and, to make a bit more room, Leela moved aside a curious-looking instrument.

'What's that?' asked Kip.

'It's my Heartsichord,' said Leela. She looked at Kip and Albert's blank faces. 'It plays music.'

'Looks like a cross between a digeridoo and bagpipes,' said Albert.

'A Baggeridoo?' said Kip.

'You can call it whatever you like,' Leela said. 'It's still the same thing.'

'Are you any good?' asked Albert.

Enthusiastically, Leela launched into one of her one-way rambles.

'A good musician can make you feel how the

composer was feeling – well, the Heartischord is the opposite – I can play how the audience is feeling – it works using Strange Energy obviously – all living things produce Thoughtwaves – even coral polyps and amoebas – but of course you need a musician – an amoeba couldn't play the Heartischord, that would be silly – note to self, maybe a coral reef could – I can play something for you now if you like – any volunteers – no one? OK, guess who this is then.'

She began to pluck the strings and blow into the mouthpiece, producing a chaotic melody with a comical, sproingy lilt. It made Kip think of circus clowns on pogo sticks, twanging rulers.

Albert snorted apple juice through his nose and began to hiccup again.

'It's the – hic – mowl!'

The mowl hop-waddled over to Albert and jumped into his spaghetti leftovers.

'You can actually see the music?' said Kip, watching a flock of yellow and pink notes float out of the instrument's pipe.

'Try tasting it,' said Timmi.

'Cheese – hic – tomato sauce!' shouted Albert, bursting a couple of notes.

'The mowl is pretty shallow,' said Leela, stopping to laugh. 'He's usually feeling something to do with food.'

The mowl made a freeping sound and flicked at

the notes with his long, forked tongue until he had popped them all. Leela put down the Heartsichord and began trying to extract him from his new pasta nest, just as Maya came to join them. Eying this newcomer inquisitively, the mowl slurped a piece of spaghetti through Leela's fingers.

'Where did you buy it from?' Maya asked, ignoring everyone else and pointing at the mowl. 'I *have* to have one.'

There was a rumour that Maya was a princess back home, but Leela wasn't the sort of girl to be impressed by a title.

'Firstly, he's a *he*. And secondly, I didn't *buy* him,' said Leela protectively, as the mowl dipped one of his claws in a purplish jam and held it up to sniff.

He seemed to know everyone was talking about him and started doing a funny, flappy dance across the table until he spilled Maya's milkshake and lirriped happily, lapping up the pink milk and all the attention.

'Hic – hee – hic – hee – hic.'

Albert's hiccupping got so bad he had to put his head under the table.

The mowl shook his feathers, sending milkshake droplets flying. When Maya took off her glasses to wipe them, he swiped them from her with a greedy wurble.

'No mowl!' said Leela, retrieving them swiftly. 'Sorry, he has a thing about glasses.'

'That's OK,' said Maya. 'What do the sounds mean?'

156

'Freep is "I'm hungry", or "yummy". Lirrip is "I'm happy", or "let's play".

Sharktooth Girl pushed past their table and the mowl made a harsh ch-chark sound.

'We can guess what that means,' said Kip. 'What about wurble?'

'Oh, wurble can mean *anything*.'

The mowl scratched an ear with his little ottery hand and began a game of tug-of-straw with Maya.

A crowd of older students walked past. Timmi shifted in her seat uncomfortably and looked around as if embarrassed to be seen with three First Years.

'We'd better go,' she said, pulling her hat down and tucking in some loose hair. 'I need to be at the Tropical Flowerhouse in ten minutes.'

'Did anyone else see the Egg Flower yet?' Leela asked.

'Hic!' said Albert, explosively.

'I did,' said Kip. 'But still no idea what "look around me" means.'

'We'll let you know when we figure it out,' Leela said. 'If you agree to change the mowl's litter box for a month.'

After Timmi and Leela had left, Kip flicked through one of the library books. But it was impossible to concentrate as Maya wouldn't shut up about how she was going to buy two mowls and make lots more baby mowls.

'What do you call the babies, I wonder? Mowlets? Mowl puppies? Mowlteenis?'

'I don't think you can – hic – buy them, Maya,' said Albert. 'There's only one of him.'

Maya stared at Albert as if he were talking a foreign language, and Kip wondered if she'd ever been told she couldn't have something.

'Kip!' said a cheery voice behind them. 'How's my favourite First Year?'

'Gorvak!' said Maya, blushing and making room for him on the bench.

'Hi,' said Kip. 'Thanks, by the way.'

'For what?'

'You know, helping me out with Thag.'

'Oh that. Don't mention it. I feel a bit sorry for him actually. He's quite lonely and hides it behind all that swagger. He's a real genius deep down, just like Solomon Grittleshank. But people who have everything get bored, even here.'

'Hic,' said Albert, unconvinced.

'Hey, try one of the vitabombs I just made,' said Gorvak. 'They taste like toffee apples and have all the vitamins and minerals you need for a day. First they're fizzy, then chewy, then they crackle, and at the end they just melt away.'

'Fizzy,' echoed Maya, gazing up at him as though she might melt away herself.

They chatted for a bit and when Gorvak left, with

a neat salute, Maya crumpled on the bench next to Kip.

'You're friends with Gorvak?' she whispered. 'You do know he's the fifteenth great-grandson of Eartha Quicksmith, right?'

'Sort of,' said Kip. 'And sort of.'

'He's *so* smart too. You know he wins the college hackathon every term. And I heard he's got an audiophonic memory.'

'What's t-hic?'

'It's like a photographic memory, only he remembers everything he *hears*. It's so sad that's he's an orphan. I'm going to go and tell Penny and Em I met him!'

They watched Maya skip off and then Kip turned on Albert suddenly with a monstrous 'ROOOOAAAAR!'

'ARRRGH!' shouted Albert. 'You know that doesn't work … oh wait, it did!'

Glad to be rid of the hiccups, he starting chewing one of Gorvak's vitabombs.

'Hey, Maya's left her library card. Oh it's baaaaaad. It's real bad. That's worse than ours. Shall we…'

Albert stopped when he saw Kip's face.

'What is it?' he said.

'Me. Look,' said Kip softly. 'Picture.'

He picked up the library card and stared at Maya's photo.

'Look around *me*. We've all assumed that *me* means the flower. But what if it doesn't?'

'I don't follow,' said Albert.

'*Me* could mean Eartha too. Ballmoth: take us to the Portrait Gallery!'

The Statue and the Mirror

It didn't take long to find the face they were looking for, captured in oil paint forever: deep turquoise eyes and fine thinking wrinkles, blue buttercup tucked behind one ear. The portrait depicted Eartha standing in a grassy courtyard, one hand extended. Perched on that outstretched arm was the strange black parrot. In her other hand she held a book with a red-and-gold chequered cover. Eartha's left eyebrow was raised and she had the kind of smile that hides an earth-shatteringly important secret.

'Maybe it's like one of those pictures that sort of moves when you move,' suggested Albert. 'That's what "look around me" means?'

They walked up and down in front of the portrait, looking at it from various angles. But the painting remained the same.

'Try crossing your eyes,' said Kip, remembering a book of stereograms he'd seen once. 'It might look different if you stare at the middle and lose your focus.'

They stood for a while with their eyes crossed until Albert broke the silence. A hiccup that had been

hiding and waiting for the right moment escaped loudly.

'Agh. I thought they'd gone. Give me a – hic – sec,' said Albert, holding his breath and wandering off.

Kip turned back to the portrait.

Look around me. I wonder if...

The wooden frame of the portrait was unusually wide. It had been carved into vines and flowers that were also painted, so it looked as if they were spilling out from the canvas. Kip looked along the frame carefully until he saw it.

'The Egg Flower!' he breathed.

Ever so gently, he moved his fingertip across the carving's surface.

'A petal's loose,' he said out loud.

When Kip pulled the petal back, a jolt coursed through his body and threw him to the floor. There was a strong smell of freshly mown grass.

'Albert!' he shouted. 'ALBERT?'

Frozen with fear, Kip thought he'd been electrocuted. All he could see was a haze of green and blue. Finding courage from somewhere, he wiggled his fingers and toes and then his arms and legs. Everything worked, so Kip sat up and things slowly came into focus. Leaves. Sky. Bushes. A bee.

Could I be...

He pushed through the bushes and walked past a

beehive and a birdbath, until he came to a figure standing on a neat lawn dotted with blue buttercups.

…*inside the painting?*

'Hello?' he said cautiously.

But Eartha didn't reply. She was just a decoration. Every little detail around her was vibrant yet still, perfect for all eternity. Even the buzz of the bees and the candyfloss fragrance of the flowers.

'KIP?' Albert's voice boomed. And then louder: **'KIP!'**

Kip spun around but he couldn't see Albert anywhere. There was only a white shimmering veil past the bushes.

That must be the border between the inside and the outside of the painting, he thought.

'WHERE D'YOU GO?' Albert's megaphone voice rumbled.

Kip went closer to the shimmering veil, through which he could see the outline of a giant Albert looking left and right, towards each end of the gallery.

'I'm here!' shouted Kip. 'I'm here – in the painting!'

He jumped up and down but giant-outside-Albert was staring right past Kip at Eartha.

'WHAT DID YOU DO WITH HIM?' Albert's voice boomed.

Kip looked around for something to get Albert's attention. It was a sunny day inside the painting, and the light winked in a large ornamental mirror by the birdbath.

'That's it!'

Luckily the mirror moved, and Kip was able to swivel it until the sunshine bounced off and streamed in Albert's direction.

It worked. Albert put up a hand as the flash blinded him. Kip turned the mirror away and Albert leaned in closer.

'KIP?'

Relieved, Kip ran over and pointed to where he hoped the Egg Flower was on the picture frame. It didn't take Albert too long to work out what to do.

His head popped up from the bushes like a meerkat's.

'They weren't kidding when they called it "Strange Energy", he said, and fist-pumped the air. 'Team Glowflyer scores.'

'Let's *look around* Eartha then,' said Kip, helping Albert up.

They circled her smiling figure, searching for anything out of the ordinary. Kip saw it first.

'There!' he pointed.

'Where?' said Albert. 'Can't see anything.'

'Try standing where I am. Do you see it yet?'

'Yes! Eartha's not alone in here.'

She was shaking hands with a statue – a statue of herself.

'Clever,' said Albert. 'You can't see it from out there and you can only see it from this exact spot once you're in the painting.'

'It's got to be a clue.'

Albert started to reply but straight away his voice hardened.

'What's that?' he said, looking over Kip's shoulder, towards the birdbath.

'What's what?'

'The mirror. Something...'

Kip followed Albert's gaze. There seemed to be a dark reflection in the mirror but it couldn't be Eartha or the statue – they were too far away. He walked closer. Was that...? Yes, it was a face – long and thin and silvery with black flecks like old, cracked leather, or the scales of dried mud.

'Was that there before?' said Albert with a shudder.

'Must have been. Anyway, this is only a painting,' said Kip.

But just as he said that, the mirror fractured with a sharp crack, and the face behind it seemed to grow larger.

'Paintings don't do that!' shouted Albert.

He was already stumbling backwards, unable to take his eyes off the broken reflection. Kip watched for a second longer too, but when the mirror burst open fully and the cracked face pushed through the

165

shards of glass, he turned and ran with Albert, his heart pounding.

Just a few steps ahead, Albert was heading straight for a keyhole-shaped opening in a hedge beyond the beehive. The leaves fluttered as he shot through it and into the shimmering veil. Kip was a second behind and, with a jolt, he was back in the gallery, hurling himself away from Eartha's portrait.

They sprinted outside without looking back. Only in the corridor, with people around, did Albert glance at Kip in fright.

'What *was* that … that … scaleface?' he managed to say, as he caught his breath.

'I don't know. But it's like it could see us,' said Kip.

'Do you think it's part of the riddle?'

'No,' said Kip. 'It felt like it was coming from outside Quicksmiths. Outside … everything. I can't explain it.'

'I don't want to go back in there, ever.'

'Me neither,' said Kip.

'Then let's get as far away from that thing as we can,' Albert said shakily.

Green Cave

As they were walking, Kip's heart gradually slowed down.

'When I was little,' he said, 'my mum used to say

166

that if you were busy you didn't have time to be scared.'

'I can live with that,' said Albert.

'We've got a good lead,' said Kip. 'Question GENI: is there a statue of Eartha Quicksmith?'

'There is,' said GENI. 'In Ptolemy Courtyard.'

Evening was approaching as the Ballmoths led them from Celestial Hall, and the songs of spring nightingales echoed from tree to pillar to windowsill.

Ptolemy Courtyard was next to the Porterhouse, and its iron gate faced the First Year Block. It was smaller than any of the other grassy squares around the college campus and had no overlooking windows.

'Why would you put a statue of the college's most famous person here?' Albert asked, saying what Kip was thinking.

'Maybe she liked to be left alone?' suggested Kip.

One side of the courtyard was formed by a long, neatly clipped hedge in which the birds ducked and flitted. The statue of Eartha stood with its back to the hedge, both feet set on a marble plinth. It was wearing a marble riding coat, down which cleverly carved raindrops were dripping. One marble hand was outstretched, fingers spread just like the statue hidden in the portrait. Its eyes were half-closed and its mouth open in merriment, as if it were eternally stuck in the moment of hearing the punchline of a particularly good joke.

'Nothing especially interesting,' said Albert, after they had hunted around for a bit. 'What about back here?'

Kip squeezed past the hedge to follow Albert around the back of the statue. He was just about to speak when Albert put his finger to his lips.

'Shh!' he whispered. 'Someone's coming.'

They peeked cautiously around the statue, to see Thag lumbering down the path towards them. Kip looked around urgently for an escape route, and spotted a gap in the hedge behind them.

'This way,' he hissed.

The gap was just big enough to crawl through and opened into a tiny, dark-green cave in the hedge. Scrunched in their leafy hiding place, Kip and Albert watched Thag's knees come to a stop in front of the statue, and held their breath.

Did he see us? Kip thought.

'What are you hiding?' asked Thag accusingly.

Kip told his legs to stay put as they surged with energy, wanting to carry him far away to a safe place. It went quiet for what felt like forever, and pins and needles started up in his left foot.

'You'll be sorry,' said Thag, 'if you don't tell me what you know. You've got no right to keep anything from ME!'

Kip wished he could see Albert's face, but they were squashed into the hedge back to back. Was a crushing hand going to reach in and drag them out, a hand that bruised everything it touched?

'Big-headed to the very end, aren't you? Even when you're dead, you've got everyone running around after you.'

That was a strange thing to say. Kip listened carefully to the scraping sound that followed. He risked twisting slightly and pulled one leaf down gently to get a better view. Thag had climbed up on to the rectangular plinth of the statue and was scratching Eartha's marble coat with a shiny pocket knife.

'Where is it you stupid, stuck-up COW?'

Thag stuck the blade under the statue's collar and tried to prise it away. When that didn't work, he put the knife away and locked his hands around the statue's neck in a stranglehold, shouting: 'TELL ME WHERE THE NEXT RIDDLE IS!'

As Thag was attempting to strangle the statue, his Ballmoth appeared. Most of the swear words that exploded out of his mouth were new to Kip. When Thag had run out of curses, he stepped back and shook a red-knuckled fist at Eartha's marble laughter.

'I'll be back. Your riddles won't stop me. And neither will Miss Twiss's community service. And when I do find your precious Ark, and your stupid Aeon Light, Pythagoras Grittleshank will become the most famous scientist that ever lived. I'll have this

169

statue pulled down and no one will even remember your name. Eartha Whosmith?'

Kip and Albert watched Thag stomp off into the twilight before they crawled out. It took a few shakes of their feet to get the blood going again.

'Do you think he's been inside the portrait?' Albert asked.

'Probably,' said Kip worriedly.

'He could be the one Eartha talked about in her letter.'

'The truthseer?' Kip asked, a bit confused.

'No. She talked about evildoers, remember? Something about corruption, selfishness.'

They looked up at the statue. The light show from the distant heights of Skycrackle Tower reflected off the marble, making the shadows around Eartha seem even darker.

The night's advance brought the face in the birdbath mirror to the front of Kip's mind. But the more he tried not to think about its horrible soul-searching eyes, the stronger the memory became.

'Any idea what we do next?' he asked a bit too loudly as he turned on the soft glow of his Candlelight.

Albert made fish lips while he looked at the statue's plinth.

'Well, isn't there normally a notice that tells you about a statue?' he asked. 'You know, a name or a date.'

'I guess,' said Kip.

'There's nothing here. Not even Eartha's initials.'

'Can't see much,' said Kip, turning up the Candlelight.

'Wait!' said Albert. 'I don't think we should draw attention to ourselves. What if people come over to see what the light is? And then Thag could come back.'

'Like a nasty bug,' said Kip. 'Agreed. We'll get a closer look tomorrow in the daytime.'

'Should we tell someone what we've found?' Albert asked as they walked back to Q10. 'Remember, Professor Mo said that if more people are working together, we can get to the Ark faster. Even if we don't win ourselves.'

'But what if we accidentally helped Thag to get to the Ark first?' said Kip. 'We can't let that happen.'

'Good point,' said Albert.

Once they were in their beds, Albert started to turn the Candlelight off, but stopped. Kip knew exactly what his friend was thinking. That dark, silvery, leathery face pushing through the mirror.

'Might leave the light on low,' said Albert. 'Just for a bit.'

The Porterhouse

Slants of brightness spilled through the curtains the next morning, reinforcing the Candlelight that had been on all night. It looked almost like a summer's day outside, but Kip's peaceful waking-up feeling suddenly cracked and the vivid memory of Scaleface burst out.

Sweating, he stayed under the covers and curled the corner of the duvet into a spyhole, through which he could safely view the room. Doorway. Wall corners. Window. Mirror above the small sink. All empty.

Once it felt safe to emerge, Kip draped himself over the side of the top bed like a giant bat, his head dangling into Albert's bunk space.

'Is the Buttery open yet?' asked Albert, through a yawn the size of a railway tunnel.

'Statue first,' said Kip.

But a whole hour spent in Ptolemy Courtyard revealed nothing new.

'We need to solve the riddles at a rate of one a day,' said Kip as they talked softly on the way to breakfast. 'And we're already way behind. It's day four today.'

'What about getting a packed lunch,' said Albert, 'then we can max out time at the statue?'

'First prize goes to Albert for today's best before-breakfast idea,' Kip said.

All that lay between them and lunch was Slipstream, Timeyarn and Wormhole Technology. But Kip couldn't concentrate in the lessons at all. In fact, he spent most of the time drawing. As he drew, all he could think about was the statue. And the more he thought about the statue, the thicker and faster the squirls came.

When they finally got out for break, Albert looked as if he was going to implode with happiness.

'I was totally right about that timeloop on my old school roof! It all makes sense: Timeyarn is like energy threads that run through time. They can stretch and fray. And make creases and knots and stitches. Timestitches!'

'Hmmm? Sewing?' said Kip. 'What's that got to do with Time?'

Albert stared at Kip.

'You didn't hear anything I just said?'

Kip made a guilty face.

'You didn't hear any of the lesson at all, did you?' said Albert.

'I can't help it. We need to find out why the statue's important.'

'We will,' said Albert. 'Not long 'til lunch. But first will you come to the Porterhouse with me really quickly? Mum's sent me a parcel.'

When they peered through the diamond-grilled window, they saw a mountainous pile of post with a white bowler hat bobbing around it.

The door gave a friendly squeak as they entered, and a kettle on a little stove started to whistle. But sullen muttering came from behind the pile of letters and boxes.

'No time for tea.'

''Scuse me,' said Albert. 'Do we get our post here?'

A waggling moustache appeared from behind the papery pile, accompanied by two scowling eyes. Bagsworth pointed a fat finger at a bank of pigeonholes.

'In there,' he said. 'But I haven't had a chance to sort through this tonne of letters. The Oddjob Drones normally do it but they've all been called to help with repairs at the Clock Tower.'

'How long…?' Albert began.

'I've NO IDEA,' snapped Bagsworth, 'how long it's going to take and if people keep interrupting me I'll NEVER finish. Mrs Fruppence has me running from here to the Botanical Gardens like a blue-bottomed fly every time she whistles.'

Kip and Albert both took a step back towards the door, but Bagsworth was now in mid-rant. He leaned against the counter and chewed on his unlit pipe.

'She calls it a visitation of voles. What does she know? Just because she's the Head Gardener. A plague of voles, if you ask me. Little beetroot burglars. You'd think in a place like this there'd be some clever ray that turns them all to vole jelly. But no, that would be *cruel*. The Grabber Drones were perfect – they dropped them far enough away so they couldn't find their way back…'

Albert inched his hand towards the door handle.

'…but then some of the Grabbers got sprayed with sprinklers accidentally and ending up taking the little blighters to the roof of the Library. So now of course that isn't *safe*. And who gets the job of trapping all these radish robbers and driving them miles away? Mrs Fruppence, whose problem it is? Professor Tuqan, the Head of Terrestrial Zoology? No. Me. That's who. Old muggins Terence Bagsworth here.'

'Thanks,' said Albert hurriedly.

'Sorry,' added Kip, and they dived back out of the door to freedom.

'Are we going to have to go in there every time we get something delivered?' moaned Albert. 'We'll have to train Pinky in the ways of the ninja and dangle her down the chimney on a wire.'

Kip felt a pang of sympathy for Bagsworth.

'I'd probably be like that too if everyone took advantage of me,' he said.

'S'pose being Chief Volecatcher all day long can't be much fun,' agreed Albert. 'But it doesn't mean you can take it out on the whole world.'

After they had walked a few steps, Kip stopped and looked back at the Porterhouse.

'I wonder if…' he said.

It was a simple and elegant idea and, as it happened, there was a Wormhole Technology workshop after break. Kip forced the statue and the squirls to the back of his mind for the next few hours, and began work on his very first Strange Invention.

The Second Riddle

Hidden from view by the hedge and walls of Ptolemy Courtyard, and surrounded by packed lunch wreckage, Kip and Albert pored over the base of the statue.

Every now and then there was a tiny contented sigh from the scarf hammock, which Kip had tied into a sling across one shoulder.

'How's Pinky?' asked Albert.

'She's fine,' Kip said. 'Sometimes she likes company during the day, even if she's asleep.'

'Pinktastic,' said Albert.

'Whatever we're looking for can't be too obvious,' said Kip. 'Maybe there's a button round here somewhere?'

But the marble plinth was as smooth as an old sea stone. It was just wide enough for Albert to climb up and stand next to the statue. He copied its pose – one hand reaching out, fingertips spread slightly. Kip stood below and looked up, eyes narrowed against the afternoon sunlight.

'What was Eartha doing in the portrait?' asked Albert.

'Shaking hands!' they both yelled.

Pinky peered out groggily from her hammock to see what all the shouting was about.

Albert faced the statue and gripped its marble hand in his.

'Is anything happening?' he asked, trying to look behind him.

'Don't move a muscle,' said Kip. 'Let me have a look.'

Encouraging squeaks came from the scarf while Kip circled the statue, looking for anything that hadn't been there before. And as he saw the black words on the white marble, it was like his birthday and Christmas had come all at once.

'It's here!' he spluttered.

'Where?' said Albert, leaping off the plinth.

The writing faded before Kip's eyes.

'Can you do it again while I take a Threescan?' said Kip. 'Ready? Don't move … done!'

Albert high-fived the statue awkwardly and then jumped back down to high-five Kip.

'We. Are. On. Fire,' he sang. 'So, what does it say?'

//

My 1st is TRUTH
My 2th is WISDOM
My 3rd is AMBITION
My 4th is DETERMINATION
My 5th is TOLERANCE
My 6th is ORGANISATION
My 7th is CHEERFULNESS
My 8th is KINDNESS

'D'you think it's one of those poems where you take the first letter from each word?' asked Kip.

'But that spells… TWADTOCK. Is that supposed to mean something?'

'Haaaang on,' said Kip. 'There's a spelling mistake in the second line.'

'Eartha's not as amazing as everyone thinks then,' said Albert, sounding disappointed.

'Unless…' Kip said.

A shadow fell across the statue as a group of boys skimmied overhead.

'Instruction GENI: close Threescan. We've got what we need, Albert. Let's get out of here. Stay under the radar.'

'Under-the-radar is my middle name,' said Albert.

'Why do you want to stay under the radar?' asked a familiar voice.

Leela and Timmi were hovering just above the hedge, looking down over the statue's head.

'We're robbing a bank,' mumbled Kip.

'Practising ninja moves,' squeaked Albert.

'Hmmm,' said Timmi, looking at the statue. 'Sounds more like you're practising your fibbing.'

The two girls cleared the hedge and descended noiselessly into the courtyard on their Skimmies. Leela's was covered in peacock eyespots and Timmi's was yellow with a black swirl in the middle like a liquorice allsort.

'Well, whatever your ikky boy secrets are, we were just about to go racing around Aristotle's Theatre,' said Leela. 'We thought because you're newbs and you don't have Skimmies of your own yet, and because we're so generous and such brilliant befrienders, that you might like to join in? Girls against boys?'

Kip looked at Albert, who raised his eyebrows as if to say, 'There's no escape, they have us cornered.'

It wasn't really what Kip wanted to be doing with his time right now. Leela was all right, if a little weird. But it was hard to warm to Timmi. She was much too jittery and, whenever she thought no one was watching, she would take out a folding pocket mirror and adjust her hat.

We don't want to make them suspicious though, Kip thought. *They're nosy enough already.*

'OK,' he said. 'You're on. But only if Pinky can come.'

Hearing her name, Pinky looked out from the scarf, nose twitching. Leela and Timmi exploded with so many squeals there was hardly any room left for breathing.

'FLUFFY ALERT! FLUFFY ALERT!'

'It's a CUTESPLOSION!'

'Where's the mowl?' asked Kip, looking around. 'Will he be a problem?'

'Oh, he's watching Bagsworth try to catch voles,' said Leela, tickling Pinky's ears. 'He'll be busy for ages. Jump up on the back – it's quicker if we Skimmi there.'

As soon as they were flying through the air, the breeze whisked away Pinky's drowsiness and she watched alertly as the scenery went by until they reached the theatre.

Once they had landed, a game of rock-paper-scissors decided who would race first: Albert and Leela.

'The Skimmi uses two Strange Energies: Slipstream and Thoughtwaves,' said Leela. 'Put your feet on the circuit connectors and just think where you want to go. If you're having trouble, pointing helps.'

'Are they sort of like Airchairs?' asked Albert.

'Yup,' Timmi replied. 'But much faster when they get going.'

'Look at me flyyyyyy,' Albert cried out, as his Skimmi lifted up fitfully.

Pinky watched from her hammock, transfixed, as Leela soared swiftly to the top of the stone theatre.

'Come on, slowpants,' Leela called down.

Albert inched up beside her and before he was quite ready she yelled 'OnetwothreeGO!'

Leela was already a dot in the distance while Albert lurched forwards for a few metres and then somehow went into reverse. She came back to fly in a loop over his head. Painted on the bottom of her Skimmi were the words 'Eat my dust'.

'Imagine you're airsurfing,' her voice drifted down from above. 'The Slipstream is always moving, like water.'

'Oh yeah, just like surfing – backwards!' grumbled Albert. 'How do you go faster?'

'Think of fast things – like a cheetah that's just eaten a falcon on rocket skates.'

It was Kip's turn next.

Leela's Skimmi trembled under his feet as if it were anchored in a current, and he could feel the Slipstream lapping at his ankles.

'Ready, Furball?' he said.

Pinky scurried out of the scarf and down Kip's trouser leg so she could look over the Skimmi's edge. Timmi counted down from five and when she got to one, Kip stepped on the diamond-shaped connectors and pointed forwards.

Jet fighters, he thought. *Comets. Neutrinos.*

The Skimmi crawled forward, speeded up, and then slowed down again.

'It does feel like water,' he shouted. 'But it's hard to make it go where you want. It keeps drifting.'

The Skimmi sped up again as Kip concentrated on keeping up with Timmi. Unable to resist, Pinky launched herself from the edge of his Skimmi and stretched out her wing membranes, soaring over to Timmi like a furry frisbee. After a second's pause, she leapt off again and glided back to Kip. Back and forth she went, as if she couldn't quite decide which Skimmi made the best launchpad.

'Pinky gets first prize!' Leela shouted up.

After a few more races, all of which Pinky won, four Ballmoths popped up. Not quite believing her luck, Pinky sprang about playfully and tried to pounce on them but the Ballmoths always slipped aside at the last second.

'I better take her back before class starts,' said Kip, wrapping Pinky up in the hammock again. 'Give us a lift?'

They were back at the First Year Block in two shakes of a flyer's tail. There, Timmi checked in her vanity mirror, said the briefest of goodbyes and skimmied away sharpish.

Leela readied herself to take off in pursuit, but then hesitated.

'Silly me!' she said. 'I just thought of something else I definitely need to ask you!'

Kip and Albert both looked up.

Her eyes glinted impishly. 'Would you rather have ticklish teeth or creaky eyelids?' she said, and soared away before they could reply.

Chapter Eight

Great Globe

Professor Steampunk waltzed himself along the corridors of Atlas House, hand in hand in hand in hand, humming softly.

'Here we are!' he said, turning back to the students. 'The Hall of Maps.'

Ancient maps were painted all over the walls and ceiling of the long hall – aquamarine seas guarded by lurking long-necked monsters, deserts and oases dotted with palm trees, and mountain ranges like the spines of sleeping dinosaurs.

Two flights of stairs curled up the far side of the hall. At the bottom of this double staircase loomed a gigantic globe, as big as an elephant that had just eaten another elephant. Professor Steampunk waltzed to a stop in front of it and they all stood gazing up at the piano-sized continents.

'Biggity-big bigness,' said Badger philosophically.

'Bigxactly,' replied Steampunk. 'I cordially invite you to feast your eyes on the gurglingly grandificent Great Globe. We don't know exactly who designed and built this big old ball but we do think it was created some time during the Renaissance.'

'But this is a modern map,' said Penny, 'with modern names like Iraq and Thailand. Wouldn't an old map look different?'

'Ah-hah! I see you're wearing your best detectiving brain,' said Steampunk. 'Look closer.'

Kip leaned in with the others. The surface of the globe was covered in tiny tiles.

'Over the years,' said the Professor, 'the tiles have been rearranged to reflect our changing world. It used to take a team of cartographers so long to reorder them that they had to get up before they went to bed. But these days, GENI and I do it every Tuesday before breakfast.'

Badger picked out a tiny sea tile and swapped it with a forest tile.

'So, does it actually *do* anything?' he asked. 'Except be big?'

'The Great Globe,' said Steampunk, swapping Badger's sea tile for a desert tile, 'uses an early version of the Wormhole Positioning System to find any location on Earth. To test this, I'm going to put you in teams of more than one and less than three. Each team will have ten minutes to find the town with the oddest name they can. Kip and Albert, you're first. Just ask the globe "Where is...?". The rest of you – follow me and shout if you see a sea dragon. I can't promise it won't jump off the wall.'

'What about ... Wagga Wagga?' asked Albert straight away. 'What? It's a place. Where is Wagga Wagga?'

The globe swivelled and a green dot appeared in Australia.

'Told you!' he said triumphantly. 'Let's see, world's oddest places. Where is um ... um ... No Name?'

The countries of the world rolled past until the globe stopped and the green dot lit up in America.

'No way is No Name a place!' Albert spluttered. 'I made that up!'

They shouted out question after question, each trying to think of the most ridiculous place name and hooting uncontrollably when some of them turned out to be real. Gorvak walked past on his way up the grand staircase. He laughed as he heard Albert yelling 'Llamallamallama!'

'Professor Steampunk's class?' he called down.

Kip nodded, still laughing, while Albert carried on shouting out names.

'Where is Scratchy Bottom?'

'Where is Why?'

'Where is Monster?'

'Where is Elephant Butt?

'Where is Scratchy Monster Butt?'

And then Albert reached breaking point. The laughter dam cracked and he collapsed on the floor, gasping for breath like a gigglefish out of water.

'What if it knows where *things* are as well?' said Kip, suddenly serious.

A thought had exploded into his head. A huge, thrilling thought. Kip faced the Great Globe and crossed the fingers of both hands. Could he be the first one to have thought of this? Eartha Quicksmith had travelled the world after all. They were all assuming that the Ark was at Quicksmiths but…

'Where is the Ark of Ideas?' he said solemnly.

Albert stopped giggling and leapt up immediately, as if someone had turned the key to cut off an engine. He stood alongside Kip, willing something to happen. Sometimes hope can move worlds, but on this occasion the Great Globe remained still.

'You thinky thinkist,' said Albert. 'That would have put Team Glowflyer well in the lead.'

The Third Riddle

All through the afternoon Kip took surreptitious looks at the Threescan of Eartha's second riddle whenever he could. By dinnertime he could recite the whole thing from memory.

'It has to be something to do with the spelling

mistake,' he said to Albert, as they sat down with their meals. 'It has to. But why does Eartha want us to think about wisdom?'

'Cheeeeeeeeese!'

Leela's trill interrupted his train of thought and there was a smell of unwashed socks as she placed a large wedge of blue-veined Stilton on the table. The mowl's eyelids drew back and his enormous orange eyes almost doubled in size.

'Skunk burps!' shouted Badger.

'Peeee-yu!' said Albert, sticking his nose under his shirt. 'That's almost as bad as the Egg Flower.'

The mowl hop-waddled across the table and started to dig out all the smelly blue bits, leaving piles of discarded yellow cheese in between the plates and cutlery.

Kip ate slowly while conversation volleyed around the table. But it was mostly background noise as the second riddle played over and over in his head.

As Albert put his knife and fork down, the mowl bounded over to lick the plate. He stopped to gag a few times and spat out something like a cherry stone, which he rolled over to Kip before returning to his cheese stash.

'Aw, look, he likes you,' Leela said.

Kip looked down at the stone, covered in slobber and bits of half-digested cheese.

'I'm not so sure,' he said, pushing it away with a fork handle.

'Riddle me this,' said Albert. 'How come the mowl is chewing when he has a beak? Has he got teeth as well?'

'I dunno actually,' said Leela. 'Are you hiding toothies in there, mowl?'

'Tooth? That's it!' Kip cried out, grabbing his books. 'Come on!'

The others looked at him curiously.

'Just Albert. It's a homework thing. You know, Albert: Team Glowflyer.'

It was a short run to Ptolemy Courtyard, with Albert close behind, clutching his abdomen.

'My dinner hates you,' he groaned.

Kip was already scrambling up on the plinth to bring his head level with Eartha's marble elbow. Next, he was pulling himself up using the statue's arm.

Down below, Albert circled the plinth impatiently.

'What are you doing?' he called up.

'Read the second line out loud,' Kip called back down. 'The one with the spelling mistake.'

'My two-th… my *tooth*?' said Albert. 'MY TOOTH IS WISDOM!'

'Exactly,' murmured Kip.

There was only one wisdom tooth inside the statue's grinning mouth, at the top. When Kip reached in and pressed it, there was an instant sound of stone grinding on stone and the mouth began to open wider.

Albert clambered up next to him and they both

stared, wide-eyed, as a marble tongue poked out from the statue's mouth. And though it couldn't speak, the tongue told them something, for the next riddle was carved into its surface.

///

Time to find my coat

As he savoured the words, Kip felt like he was expanding to stand as tall and unbreakable as the statue.

'How did Eartha do all this four hundred years ago?' said Albert. 'And it still works!'

The marble tongue began to retreat back into its mouth and, after just a few seconds, the statue laughed down at them again as if nothing had happened.

'I know what it's time for!' said Albert, jumping off the plinth. 'Victory silent disco!'

He broke into an uncoordinated whole-body wobble and Kip jumped down to join him.

'Four days, three riddles,' said Albert, his voice shaking as he danced. 'We're catching up.'

That night, Kip stayed awake long after Albert had fallen asleep and soft snoring had begun to drift up from the bottom bunk. He turned the Candlelight on low and opened the Book of Squirls at the back, where the pages were blank. It felt important to make a record of all their progress so far: the Egg Flower, the portrait, and now the statue.

After half an hour or so, his head dropped back on the pillow and he fell asleep with the book over his chest like a breastplate of blue armour.

Skycrackle Tower

'Time to find my breakfast,' chanted Albert softly.

Before Kip could reply, a loud commotion spread through the Buttery. All around, people abandoned their meals and began to leave hastily. Even Chef Garibaldi was hanging up his apron.

'What's going on?' Albert asked Em.

'Miss Twiss found a clue,' she said enthusiastically. 'In the Portrait Gallery.'

'Did she find anything ... weird?' asked Albert.

'Nope. Just a lovely little clue,' said Em.

She hurried after the others, and soon there were only a handful of people left.

'Hope they haven't disturbed Scaleface again,' muttered Albert.

Kip needed something to push that idea out of his head.

'Let's not get distracted,' he said. 'Question GENI: there's a museum at Quicksmiths, isn't there?'

'There is,' said GENI.

'Is there a coat in there? That belonged to Eartha Quicksmith?'

'There is not,' replied GENI.

'Well, if we're asking GENI questions,' said Albert in a low voice. 'How about this? Question GENI: can you solve this riddle? "Time to find my coat."'

'I do not have enough information to answer your question, Albert.'

'Worth a try,' he said.

They chewed their food for a while, thinking.

'Can you have a coat of armour?' said Albert, through a mouthful of pancake.

'Think it's a suit of armour,' Kip replied.

'What about a coat of paint?'

'I guess we could take another look at the portrait,' Kip said.

'We won't get near it now,' said Albert. 'Besides, that gallery is high on my list of never-go-in-there-again places.'

They both looked at their breakfasts thoughtfully.

'Ooo! Ooo!' Albert poked a forkful of pancake in the air. 'Animals have coats, right? Question GENI: are there any what's it called … taxibarmy … animals here?'

'The word is taxidermy,' replied GENI. 'But we do not have that at Quicksmiths.'

'So what sort of coat is Eartha …' said Kip.

'Careful!' interrupted Albert. 'We've got company.'

Thag and Sharktooth Girl clumped up to the table next to them and spread out noisily.

Thag leaned towards them so far that Kip could smell eggs on his breath.

'Solved any riddles yet?'

Albert stood up.

'Let's go,' he said. 'We're finished anyway.'

'What does he know?' said Kip, when they were out of earshot.

'Ignore him,' said Albert. 'He's messing with us. If he'd known we were hiding behind the statue he would've grabbed us there and then. We should just focus on finding Eartha's coat, whatever that is.'

The rest of the day was a blur of facts and questions and answers, while the third riddle chimed in Kip's head like a soft alarm trying to wake something up. Every time he closed his eyes, the squirls pulsed along in time – not solid nor still, more like glimpses from the window of a train.

For their last lesson, the Ballmoths brought them to Skycrackle Tower. Kip lagged behind and gazed up warily through the crisscross bars that formed the enormous base of the glass spire. A flare of green light lit up the clouds inside the tower, and it was as if a heavy clamp squeezed his chest. It took all his resolve not to curl up into a ball.

'I wonder if the tower actually makes Skycrackle?' he heard someone say.

'There are Skycrackle storms in the upper atmosphere,' Maya replied. 'The tower is like a conductor. My befriender told me. But Skycrackle isn't actually electricity. It's a kind of Strange Energy plasma.'

A star-shaped, many-eyed drone sailed past, followed by one that looked a bit like a lionfish.

'Why are all the drones swarming around it?' Albert asked.

'They're charging,' said Maya, delighted to be the source of all knowledge. 'They run on Skycrackle.'

Badger pointed at some floating symbols forming a ring around the tower above them – human figures on Skimmies with a black line through them.

'What are they for then?'

'This is a No Flying Zone,' explained Maya, trying to sound teachery. 'Combinations of Strange Energies sometimes cause interference – especially Skycrackle and Slipstream – so it's not safe to skimmi here.'

She looked round the group, hoping for more questions, but then her face fell. Professor Chiaki, the real Skycrackle teacher, was approaching and Maya's short reign of wisdom was over.

When the lesson was finished, the class tramped back towards the First Year Block. Kip was out in front, still feeling uneasy. Professor Chiaki had spent much of the lesson explaining the difference between Strange Energy plasma and lightning. But this hadn't dispelled Kip's fear of the Skycrackle – it squirmed inside him like a swallowed centipede.

A few drops of rain landed on the Book of Squirls and Kip wiped them away gently. As he looked up at the sheet of gloomy grey rainclouds overhead, there was a savage shout.

'Oi!'

Kip knew that voice. He turned to see Thag hovering a few metres away on his Skimmi, waving something with grey and blue flecks. Surely he wasn't going to try to start a fight again with all these witnesses about? Kip opened his mouth to speak but Thag looked right past him.

'Princess Chimp! You must be able to hear me with those massive flapping hearing aids. You! Spocky! Dumbo! Missy Wingnut!'

Kip followed Thag's gaze and saw Timmi walking as fast as she could. She was hunched over, trying to make herself smaller. There was something different about her: she wasn't wearing her hat and large mousey ears stuck out from her loose blond hair.

Suddenly it all made sense. That was Timmi's hat Thag had stolen. She wasn't vain: she was always checking in the mirror to make sure her sticky-out ears were hidden from the likes of Thag. And she wasn't embarrassed to be seen with Kip and Albert: all that aloofness and looking around was because she was afraid.

Albert ran to catch up with Timmi, so she wasn't alone. Kip stood in the way, staring hard at Thag. But Thag kept looking straight past him.

'Come on everyone! Ten points if you hit one of those giant head-handles.'

Thag dropped the hat, took out a catapult and aimed at Timmi. She unfolded her Skimmi, using it for cover, and started to run.

'Stop it!' Kip yelled. 'Leave her alone!'

Kip had no idea what he was going to do if Thag turned on him; he hadn't thought that far ahead. So it felt like a lucky break when Thag just shrugged his shoulders and began to glide away. Kip made his way quickly to the others, carrying the rescued hat.

'Are you OK?' he asked Timmi, who nodded gratefully. 'Where's Leela? HEY!'

Kip gave an angry shout as the Book of Squirls was yanked out of his hand. He swung around and tried to grab it back from Thag, but he was too slow.

How could I have been so stupid, he thought. *I should have known. Someone like that doesn't just walk away.*

Thag hovered out of reach, a sneer peeling back the wide slit of his mouth.

'The Book of Squirls,' he read in a mocking tone. 'Hahaha! Look!'

Sharktooth Girl skimmied up beside him.

'It's a wittle colouring book,' she said viciously.

Kip jumped up and tried to grab Thag's ankles, without success.

'I-like-draw-ing,' said Thag in a toddler voice, 'in-my-big-blue-book.'

He laughed like a seagull and Sharktooth Girl joined in with an eardrum-piercing whinny.

'Shall we let the baby have its wittle colouring book back?'

Thag looked down with beady eyes at Kip, who stared back angrily. There was a crowd forming now, including most of his class. He had never felt so embarrassed and enraged in his whole life.

'Nah,' said Sharktooth Girl.

Kip ignored her and looked at Thag. Perhaps an insult would bring him back down for another fight and there'd be a chance to snatch the book back.

'Are you called Thag because you're a thug and you can't spell?' Kip said loudly.

'No,' spat Thag violently. 'It's short for Pythagoras, you mork.'

'Uh-oh!' said Sharktooth Girl. 'Now you've done it.'

Kip's heart sank as he realised his plan had failed spectacularly. Thag did not return to earth. Instead he pointed towards Skycrackle Tower and skimmied straight through the no-flying symbols, which shimmered and reformed behind him.

'No!' Kip whispered to Albert. 'I wrote down everything about the statue and the three riddles. Last night.'

Albert looked up helplessly. But Kip was spurred onwards by a bolt of anger that was even stronger than his fear of the Skycrackle storms. He grabbed

Timmi's Skimmi and broke into a run. Before she could stop him, he had jumped on and was bumpily following Thag's flight path.

'Kip, wait!' she shouted. 'You can get your book later.'

What, and give Thag a chance to read everything? he thought.

'Kip!' Timmi yelled again.

The Skimmi was accelerating upwards now and her words trailed away as it lurched through the ring of warning symbols.

Kip felt the hair on his arms stand up as he neared the tower. Ahead, a cluster of iridescent dragonfly drones parted and, just past them, he could see Thag waiting. As Kip closed in, Thag jetted up again and looked down with a contemptuous smirk.

The Skimmi was drifting to the right, but Kip managed to ease it upwards until finally he was eye to eye with the book thief. Skycrackle raged in the spire above them, lighting up Thag's skin with a violet glow. Kip pushed down the panic that came with every sudden flash and instead focused his anger on Thag.

'Think you're pretty clever, don't you?' Thag said.

There were white crusts in the corners of his mouth, as if he hadn't washed the toothpaste away properly. Kip tried to remember what Gorvak had said about Thag being a genius. Could he be reasoned with?

'We're wasting time. We could be looking for the Ark,' Kip said.

Thag's eyes lasered through the air. He glanced down at the Book of Squirls and looked up slyly as he tossed it backwards over his shoulder.

'Good idea,' he said. 'I can. But not you.'

With a flicking of flapping pages, the book bounced down through the crisscross metal bars under the glass tower. Kip watched in dismay as it got wedged in an intersection at the height of about two Chess Nut trees. A loose page fluttered away.

Sharktooth Girl's cackle rose up from below and Thag sank away to join her, his parting words floating behind him.

'Not so clever now, are you?'

Fresh anger hit Kip like a cannonball and his stomach muscles tensed. He closed his eyes, breathed in and out a few times, and swallowed. An irrational reaction was just what Thag wanted.

Opening his eyes, Kip considered his options. The bars were too close together to get the Skimmi through.

But that makes them easier to climb, he thought.

Kip skimmied down until he was level with the book, and took his time planning the safest climbing route. Every now and then there were large gaps, big enough to fall through.

Once you go in, it's just you. No safety ropes. No harness.

He tested the nearest bar. It was just the right diameter to hold on to, but wet and slippery. Further along was a gap, so Kip skimmied sideways and reached in. It wasn't that windy and the rain hadn't been blown too far inside the forest of metal. Once he had a firm grip, he stepped off the Skimmi and it stayed hovering in place.

'Don't go anywhere,' he said.

On the lawn below, word had spread about the confrontation at Skycrackle Tower. Shouts, dampened and distorted, rose from the crowd.

Ignoring the noise, Kip climbed his way along the lattice of bars. He began to notice his left shoe was a bit loose and his palms were sweating. Gnawing doubts eroded his focus.

Wish I had climbing shoes. And chalk powder.

He stopped, looking out to the horizon, until his confidence returned and he could resume the climb. The book was almost within reaching distance, but it was important not to rush as he closed in.

'Nearly,' he said, slowly extending his arm. 'Nearly.'

There was an unexpected squeak of rubber and Kip felt his foot slip. Then his whole body was sliding through the gaps in the bars, painfully bumping straight towards a large opening a few metres away. Gasps and screams exploded from below.

Kip's reflexes kicked in and he just managed to lock one elbow around a bar, bringing him to a hard stop that slammed his jaw against metal. The drones drifting around the tower beeped and clicked and settled back to sleep.

It was a while before his body stopped shaking and he could pull himself back up, trying not to think about what had nearly happened.

Got you, he thought, as his fingers closed around the book.

Kip allowed himself a small moment of congratulation. It was the same thrill he'd got when he'd first made it to the top of the climbing wall, and the Chess Nut Tree. Escaping the everyday world below, he had felt like he could do anything, be anyone. Just like now.

Same way back. Keep it steady.

Both hands were needed for the return climb, so he tucked the book into the front of his cargo trousers. It felt quicker on the way back and the crowd cheered as Kip made it to the waiting Skimmi with his prize. He stepped on and pulled the book out of his belt, relieving the pressure where it had been digging into his ribs.

Out of the No Flying Zone and straight back to the ground, he thought, clutching the book tightly. *Nice and slow.*

The rain was falling heavily now and it dripped into his eyes as the Skimmi began to pull away from the tower. It wasn't far to the edge of the No Flying Zone, and all this would be in the past.

But then there was a sound – a sound that came from inside the tower – like a whip cracking. And before it was over, Kip knew it wasn't good. Maya's words came back to him.

Combinations of Strange Energies sometimes cause interference – especially Skycrackle and Slipstream.

Almost instantly, he felt that rollercoaster feeling, when your stomach's suddenly in the wrong place. The Skimmi dropped violently, as if a lift cable had snapped, and lurched to the side.

The force of it nearly lifted Kip into the air. For a few seconds he teetered, and the book slipped from his hand while he tried to catch his balance. He grasped around desperately but his fingers found nothing and in the next moment he was falling.

A hundred eyes stared up in horror.

Froglash

Everything that Kip experienced next was in super … … slow … … motion. His brain remembered reading something once. What was it? During survival situations, things around you seem to slow down as your thoughts speed up.

There was an eerie, whistling sound, like a lonely mountaintop calling to another mountaintop. Kip realised it was the wind in his ears as he sped towards the ground. The Book of Squirls had already landed on the rain-soaked grass. It looked like a broken kite abandoned by the wind, surrounded by a litter of loose pages. But it didn't matter now. People in the crowd turned away, unable to watch. And then…

And then … he felt a split second of sneezesickness and sank into something springy that stretched underneath him, shoving the air out of his lungs.

He rolled over on one side, winded.

'What…?' he managed to say eventually. 'Where?'

He should be dead by now, or at least have countless shattered bones. The crowd of people and wet grass had gone and he was in an empty room – empty except for the wall-to-wall safety net.

Kip balanced on the fine fabric and wobbled on his hands and knees over to a door halfway up the wall.

There was no one in the corridor outside. He turned back to the safety-net room and saw some shimmering words above the door:

FROGLASH TEST ROOM

Timmi burst in at the end of the corridor, with Albert following close behind.

'Are you OK?' she shouted as she got closer.

Kip nodded, suddenly realising he was covered in bruises.

'Are you sure?' asked Albert. 'You've gone very pale. Nothing broken?'

'I thought I was going to … I wasn't expecting … I just feel a bit weird, that's all.'

'You might be in shock,' said Timmi.

Albert took a water bottle out of his backpack and handed it to Kip. Then Timmi made him sit down and felt his forehead.

The anger began to rise again – pure, cold fury pulling all his organs into a tight knot.

What gives Thag the right…? He could have killed me. Was he just trying to impress Sharktooth Girl? Or has he guessed that we've found the third riddle already?

Kip kept sipping the water and it soon began to have a calming effect.

'What in whattery just happened?' asked Albert.

'What just happened,' Timmi said, 'is Kip got Froglashed.'

'Frogs have eyelashes?' asked Albert.

Timmi pouted.

'Not that kind of lash.'

She took a device out of her pocket – a thick triangle made of layers of black mesh. At its point, a purple light flashed steadily. On its side was a logo of a purple frog, its tongue fully extended.

'*You* saved me?' Kip said in bemusement. 'I thought it must have been GENI.'

'GENI isn't allowed to spy on what we're doing,' said Timmi. 'That wouldn't be right.'

203

'How does Froglash work, then?' asked Albert.

'Just point at your target and press the frog. Then you're set. If any sudden movement straight down is detected, the main engine over in the Wormhole Generator building projects a specialised wormhole. It grabs the target, just like a frog grabbing a fly with its tongue, and drops you here. The porters are letting me use this old storage room for testing.'

'But how did it know exactly where I was?' said Kip.

'Froglash uses WPS – you know, the Wormhole Positioning System. I set it to track you when you nabbed my Skimmi and went into the No Flying Zone after Thag…'

'Sorry,' mumbled Kip.

'S'alright,' said Timmi. 'I couldn't let anything bad happen. Thag only picked on you because you were standing up for me.'

'High-one!' said Albert, holding up his forefinger for Timmi to tap. 'You saved Kip!'

She passed the high-one on to Kip.

'Thanks for trying to help me,' she said shyly.

'That's nothing. You saved my life,' said Kip.

The anger began to ebb away as he recalled what Thag had been doing in the first place.

Poor Timmi must be feeling terrible.

Albert handed over the Book of Squirls, rescued from the lawn. There was a deep gash down the front, and the page edges were soggy. Kip turned to the back urgently until he saw his notes from the night before, and closed the book with relief.

'Found you!' Leela gasped as she ran towards them. 'Was in music practice … saw everything from the window.'

'What are you going to do?' asked Albert. 'Thag may as well have pushed you off the Skimmi.'

'Dunno,' replied Kip, looking at the remnants of his notebook. 'Don't really want to make a big thing about it. Guess I'll tell Professor Mo later.'

As they walked along, Leela hung back and pulled Kip's sleeve. While Albert and Timmi chatted about how Froglash worked, Leela whispered anxiously. She looked ashen and her usual cheeky smile was absent.

'I saw something,' she said, 'in the trees. While you were falling at Skycrackle Tower.'

'What?' said Kip, chilled by Leela's tone.

'It was a face. I saw this weird, long face looking through the branches. It had a kind of scaly black-and-silvery skin. One big eye and one small eye. It wasn't … human.'

She was trying not to let it show, but Leela was scared – hunched up and picking at her fingernails.

'I've seen it too,' Kip said. 'Before. What do you think it is?'

'Could be some sort of horrible Thag invention, like the Plasma Slug, but worse? Or something else … should we tell Miss Twiss?'

'I don't know. Let's just keep an eye on Thag for now, while we try and figure it out.'

Human Remotes

Realising that Leela and Kip were hanging back, Albert and Timmi stopped talking. No one said anything for a while until they left the building.

'Hey, stay here for a second,' Timmi said.

'Where are you going?' Leela asked.

'The Quicket Market,' Timmi shouted back.

'What's the Quicket Market?' asked Albert.

'It's where you spend your Quickets, silly,' Leela said, less cheerful than usual but still hiding it well. 'You know Timmi is an amazing inventor – Smile Magnets, Video Tattoos, Double Vision Armour – Froglash, obviously – I mean she practically invents something new every week – and she's got loads of things in the market – she makes Quickets every time one gets sold – she's almost a Quillionnaire.'

'Is that true?' asked Kip, as Timmi came jogging back. 'Are you a Quillionnaire?'

'Well that's a bit of an exaggeration,' she said, 'but I'm doing OK.'

'We've only got three Quickets each,' said Albert. 'There's no word for that. Oh wait, yes there is: poor.'

'Don't worry. You'll go from three to ch-ching in

no time,' said Leela. 'I bought this peacock hair at the end of my first term.'

They started walking towards the First Year Block.

'You must have loads of epic stuff, Timmi,' said Kip.

'A few things,' she said. 'And now I've bought a few more.'

Two grey remotes were resting snugly in the palms of her hands. They each had a single large red button.

'What are they?' asked Kip. 'Did you invent them?'

'Human Remotes,' Timmi answered. 'I wish.'

'Do they do what I think they can do?' asked Albert longingly.

'They can pause people for up to two minutes,' Leela said. 'For real.'

'But how do you breathe, then?' asked Kip.

'Well, obviously you don't stop breathing. Otherwise it would be called a Human *Death* Remote.'

'So. Jealous,' said Albert. 'Can't. Speak.'

'Well, you needn't be,' said Timmi, 'they're for you.'

She handed one remote to Kip and one to Albert. They stared down at their new possessions and back at Timmi and at each other.

'Really?' said Kip.

'Yes,' said Timmi. 'To say thank you. For sticking up for me.'

'Super ... psych!' yelled Albert.

Before Leela realised what was happening, he had

paused her with the big red button on the remote and bounded away.

Face frozen in outrage, Leela gradually slowed down as if her battery had run flat.

'Thank yoooooooou, Timmi,' Albert's voice trailed across the lawn.

Kip grinned at Timmi.

'It's the best present anyone's ever given me,' he said. 'Thanks.'

Kip followed Albert to Q10, his new gift in one hand and the bedraggled Book of Squirls in the other.

When he got back to the room, he tore out the pages where he had written about Eartha's riddles.

'I paused Leela so good,' said Albert, who was staring out at the Clock Tower again. 'She's going to be fur-i-ous.'

He put his head on one side.

'I wonder what it's like to be paused. Does time stop? Can you feel your heartbeat?'

Kip turned on the sink tap and Albert looked over. 'What are you doing?'

'Making sure these don't fall into the wrong hands,' Kip replied.

He threw the soaked and illegible pages in the bin. Now that was done, his thoughts returned to the face Leela had seen. Bad things were piling up like leaves ready for a bonfire.

'Albert,' he said, 'there's something you need to

know. Leela saw Scaleface too, at Skycrackle Tower today.'

As Albert put down the Human Remote, his hand shook just a little.

'It was watching us?'

Kip nodded, although he didn't want to.

'Have we released it somehow?' Albert asked.

'But how?'

'I dunno.'

Albert sat down at his desk and Kip joined him. Silence hung over the room until Albert spoke again.

'Didn't Eartha write something about shadows in her letter? The one Miss Twiss read out?'

When they asked GENI to repeat Eartha's words, a shudder snaked down Kip's spine.

'"The shadows are gathering – faces at windows, whispers in corridors."'

'Whoever – or whatever – that face belonged to, they must be after the Ark,' said Albert. 'Maybe they have something to do with the disaster Eartha was trying to avoid.'

'If they're after the Ark, does that mean they're after us too?'

As soon as the question had left his lips, Kip wished he hadn't asked it.

'Do we need to tell a professor?' he wondered, doubtfully.

'Then we'd have to tell them everything else. And that still might help Thag,' said Albert. 'Too risky.'

It was a relief to hear Pinky chirrup, awake and playful, and Kip and Albert threw themselves gladly into a lively game of Find-the-Raisin. After a hot meal, two desserts each, and some reading, the thought of Scaleface had receded enough for them to fall asleep surrounded once more by the soft, safe glow of GENI's Candlelight.

Chapter Nine

A Stitch in Time

'Saturday,' Kip said, throwing off the duvet. 'Know what time it is?'

'Time to find my coat,' said Albert, jumping out of bed.

'I've been thinking,' said Kip. 'Eartha's statue is wearing a coat. Maybe that's where we should start?'

'Wasn't Thag trying to get under the statue's collar with a knife?'

Kip felt an uncomfortable knot tighten in his stomach. Albert was right. Was Thag already ahead of them? And if so, how far ahead?

There was no one around when they got to Ptolemy Courtyard. The hours passed swiftly as they explored every inch of Eartha's marble coat, but they found themselves no closer to cracking the riddle.

Kip sat on the edge of the plinth and looked down at the grass.

'What could it be?' he mumbled.

'There!' spluttered Albert. 'It's doing it again.'

'What?' said Kip, looking up.

'The Clock Tower. You know how it's been bugging me. I know what it is now. Watch. Every time one of the hands goes past the four, it sort of jumps.'

Kip faced the Clock Tower with Albert.

'Nope. Can't see anything.'

They stared up together.

'Maybe it's more something you feel,' said Albert.

'Could it just be broken?' said Kip. 'The Clock Tower must be very old.'

'No. It's something else. I know it.'

Kip wasn't sure why it was so important. But he stayed quiet until Albert clicked his fingers.

'Of course!' said Albert. 'It must be a stitch!'

'A what?'

'You were away with the fairies in our first Timeyarn lesson,' said Albert. 'Ages ago, some really clever guy worked out how to make these things called stitches … they sort of tie time up. Hold on. What riddle are we on now?'

'Number three,' said Kip.

'That adds up. We're looking for riddle number four,' said Albert. 'And there just happens to be a Timestitch making the clock hand jump at number four. Coincidence? I think not. It's a clue. From Eartha. And it's been there all along.'

'I don't quite…' Kip started.

'The fourth riddle. It's *time* to find my coat. It's in the Clock Tower. That's where we look next.'

The door to the Clock Tower was decorated with four bronze panels showing the passing of the seasons. Flowers curled out from the summer section, and icicles dripped from the winter one; spring was scattered with buds and autumn with falling leaves.

Kip and Albert knocked together and the door produced a satisfying *clang*. After a short while it opened a crack.

'What is it?' said a voice.

Kip tried to squint into the dim interior.

'We, er, just wanted to have a look around,' he said.

'Interested in clocks, are you?' asked the voice suspiciously.

'Yes, actually,' said Albert.

A shrivelled porter stepped out. He was not much taller than Albert or Kip, and so old that he wouldn't have looked out of place next to a museum mummy. On his white bowler hat was the name **Dimbleby**.

'The Clock Tower is a special building, with lots of sensitive equipment. And it's closed for repairs,' he said. 'Students aren't allowed in.'

'How long is it closed for?' asked Kip.

He leaned over slightly, trying to see past the porter. But the old man pulled the door nearly shut, thwarting any attempts to peer inside.

"Til the Tuesday after next," replied Dimbleby. 'Now beat it! Clocks don't look after themselves.'

The old man retreated into his Clock Tower like a wrinkled snail into its shell, and the door slammed shut.

'That's more than a week away,' said Kip. 'By then, the hunt for the Ark will be over.'

'We could send in Ninja Pinky to look for clues,' said Albert.

Kip gave Albert a you're-not-helping look.

'Maybe it has a cellar we could get into?' suggested Albert, a bit more sensibly. 'At night time?'

'Not a terrible idea. Instruction GENI: can you show us a plan of the Clock Tower?'

'It would be my pleasure,' said GENI.

'No cellar,' said Kip, examining the Threescan plan. 'Just one door to get in and out.'

Albert made his thinking fish lips.

'This is a tough one,' he said. 'No windows either. It's like a fortress.'

They spent the whole day observing the Clock Tower from every angle and thinking of ways to get in, each one more imaginative than the last.

'How can we have so many great ideas,' sighed Albert, 'but when we try them out, not a single one will work?'

'My mind felt so full,' Kip said. 'And now it's empty. Like the plug's been pulled.'

'It's time for dinner anyway. Let's take a break?'

On their way back from the Buttery, Albert took his Human Remote out of a pocket.

'Fancy finding out what it feels like?'

'You go first,' Kip said.

'Is that what I think it is?' said Maya's voice. 'You know those things are worth like a thousand Quickets?'

She was with Em and Penny and a couple of other girls Kip didn't know so well. They crowded around.

'Can we have a go?' asked Penny.

'Pleeeeeease?' said Em.

'Sure,' said Albert, pausing all of them before they could say anything else.

'I don't think that's what they meant,' said Kip, smiling.

'Come on,' Albert said. 'Let's go hide in our room before they snap out of it. We need to finish those library books anyway.'

After half an hour of reading, Albert grew restless and tried pausing a fly that was buzzing around. When that didn't work, he sat back down at his desk and spun the remote on the smooth wood. As it began to slow down, he followed the direction in which it pointed with growing interest.

'I've got it!'

Outside, the moon's belly was bulging like it had eaten too many stars. In the milky light, the Clock Tower cast a long moon shadow across the lawn.

Albert knocked on the door and Kip knocked again. They had their hands raised to knock a third time when Dimbleby's wavering voice called out from inside its brick-and-bronze fortress.

'Who's making all that noise?'

'We just need to ask you a question,' said Albert. 'It's really urgent.'

There was a shuffling on the other side of the door. A glint of light appeared at a peephole and then disappeared.

'You again!' Dimbleby wheezed through the door. 'Don't you know it's nearly nine o'clock?'

'Would you come out for just a second?' Albert said, finger poised over the Human Remote.

'I'm counting to three,' said Dimbleby. 'And if you're not gone by the time I get to one, I'm calling Miss Twiss.'

Albert and Kip jumped back from the door and made a hasty departure.

'I was sure that would work,' said Albert flatly, as they walked back to the room.

'It's a brilliant idea,' said Kip. 'I don't think we should give up on it yet. Maybe we'll get a better chance tomorrow.'

After a game of Find-the-Raisin, Kip gave Pinky her breakfast and stood in his pyjamas looking at the wall calendar. He took a marker pen and crossed out day six. Four days left. And still seven riddles left to find.

Kip leaned out of the window and listened for the swish and click of the Strange Energies out there in the night. Moonlight reflected off the edge of one of the Clock Tower's four faces like a silver dagger.

'You're not going to beat us,' he said. 'Right, Albert?'

But Albert was in bed and asleep already. He snurcked and rolled over. Kip thought he heard footsteps outside and looked out again, but there was no one on the pathways. After closing the window he kept Pinky company for a little longer, his mind brimming with shoals of glittering thoughts, all of them pointing in one direction.

Voler Hat

It was a glorious April sunrise. From the window of Q10, Kip watched the dark-grey sky lighten into a fluorescent pink. Gradually, it turned to greyish yellow and then pale blue, and another day at Quicksmiths uncurled.

With shoulders hunched and hat angled to block out the colours of the dawn, a small, angry figure strode in the direction of the Botanical Gardens.

Poor Bagsworth, thought Kip.

He went over to his desk, opened the drawer and took out the invention he had made in Professor Steampunk's workshop.

Albert stretched and yawned and stretched.

'I love Sundays,' he mumbled, peering out of his duvet cocoon. 'What's that? Is it a porter's hat?'

'Yes and no,' said Kip.

When Kip told him how it worked, Albert rolled out of bed.

'We *have* to test it out,' he said. 'Come on, it's really early. There'll still be time to stop at the Clock Tower on the way to breakfast.'

Outside, spring was getting ready for summer and insects were stirring among the blades and the branches everywhere, testing wings and smoothing antennae.

Kip and Albert found Bagsworth in the Giant Vegetable House. On a table was a hutch with three voles in it. Bagsworth was chasing after a fourth frisky vole, which disappeared into a burrow. A fifth vole ran mockingly through his legs and, in his attempt to grab it, Bagsworth overbalanced and landed on his bottom.

He pulled himself up with the help of a giant squash stem, and scowled to see that he had an audience. There were a few aphids trapped in his bushy moustache, but Kip didn't want to be the one who pointed them out.

'What do *you* want?' Bagsworth said, wiping a handkerchief across the sweat that was streaming into his eyes.

'I've come to give you this,' said Kip. 'I got the measurements from GENI so it should be exactly the same as your old one.'

He held out the white bowler hat. **Bagsworth** was printed in black letters around the rim.

'But I've already got one,' the porter said, pointing at his head irritably. 'I don't need a new one.'

'Ah, but this isn't any ordinary hat,' Kip persisted. 'It's a *Voler* Hat.'

'A what now?' said Bagsworth, scratching his earlobe.

'It's a Voler Hat. There's a wormhole inside it that goes all the way to a meadow five kilometres away. That's too far for a vole to find its way back, I've checked. Mrs Fruppence won't complain – it's cruelty-free.'

Bagsworth took the hat from Kip and looked inside.

'There's something in there,' he said.

'That's the Vole Portal,' said Kip, 'It has a lock for when you're not using it, so they don't accidentally find their way back through the wormhole and run around on your head. And it's covered in felt so it won't scratch you.'

'You've certainly considered everything,' said Bagsworth.

Setting a trap didn't take long. They had waited only a few minutes when a vole began to follow the trail of seeds, its whiskers trembling hungrily. It gobbled up all the bait and stuck its head inside the hat – hairy backside wiggling as it hunted around for more.

'Keep going,' whispered Kip, 'just one more step.'

And then the vole was gone in a purple shimmer.

'Gotcha, you broccoli bandit!' grunted Bagsworth. 'One down, one hundred to go.'

As he jumped across and closed the vole portal, something began to happen to his face. His eyebrows were letting go of their permanent frown. His cheeks turned a rosy hue and then his moustache started to twitch. A couple of aphids fell out of the bushy hair and, finally, the corners of his mouth crawled upwards towards the sunshine. Bagsworth was smiling!

'Do you know...' Bagsworth started, and paused to wipe his face with the handkerchief again, '...do you know, I think this is the nicest thing anyone's ever done for me.'

Kip beamed and bristled all over with a kind of helper's happiness. His first invention didn't just work, it had brought a smile to the unhappiest person at Quicksmiths.

'This calls for a celebration,' Bagsworth said.

'Thanks Mister Bagsworth, but we'll come and see you later,' said Kip. 'We've got loads to get done today.'

'Ah! Hunting for the Ark, are we? Well, good luck,' said Bagsworth. 'Fingers crossed and all that.'

Kip and Albert set off for Clock Tower Courtyard and Bagsworth called after them, waving his new hat.

'Come and visit me any time! Anything you need, anything at all I can help with...'

The Room that Wasn't There

'Actually,' said Albert, doing a U-turn and heading back to Bagsworth. 'We do need your help.'

'What is it?' said Bagsworth, squaring his shoulders and chewing on his empty pipe. 'Whatever it is, old Bagsworth will make it happen.'

It was a simple request. The porter took the pipe out of his mouth and tapped it on the side of his new Voler Hat.

'Is that all? We'll fix that in no time!'

Bagsworth led the way to the Clock Tower door with his short, swift steps. Kip and Albert waited out of sight on the sidelines as their new ally rapped on the door with the bowl of his pipe and Dimbleby appeared.

'Bagsworth,' he said curtly.

'Dimbleby. I'm calling in my favour from last Christmas,' said Bagsworth. 'You know, the Snowball Cannon incident.'

'Yes, yes,' said Dimbleby hurriedly, 'best forgotten.'

'Well,' said Bagsworth. 'My favour is this: I'd like my two friends here to have as much time as they need inside the Clock Tower. Just to look around.'

Kip and Albert poked their heads around the sides of the door frame and smiled their most well-behaved smiles.

'Fine,' Dimbleby grumbled and held the door open. 'Favour granted. We're even now, Bagsworth.'

'Thank you,' Kip said to Bagsworth, trying to find the right words to match how he felt. 'I … I … you're really kind, I mean…'

'One good deed deserves another,' said Bagsworth, his face full of the warmth that only friendship brings.

Kip and Albert stepped past the porters and walked towards the shafts of early afternoon light that were streaming in through cracks between the bricks. Clangs and creaks echoed around the room, like a ballroom full of robots bumping into each other.

'Is that the clock mechanism?' asked Albert.

Dimbleby grunted.

As Kip's eyes got used to the dim light, he saw a spiral staircase that twisted up through a hole in the ceiling. Albert already had his foot on the first step.

'Here we come, number four!' he said, clattering upwards.

'Don't touch anything!' Dimbleby croaked up the stairwell after them.

Albert stopped in his tracks, looking around at the assembly of moving parts that filled the entire first level: squeaking cogs, grinding wheels, whirring gears, and scraping levers. He shouted over this industrious orchestra of time.

'Clock. Heaven.'

Kip had never seen anything like this before. It was a masterpiece of engineering: thousands of clock parts all moving precisely in time. But the most wonderful thing was that every now and then these pieces of machinery swapped places – all vanishing and reappearing elsewhere.

The drones that weaved deftly in between the clock parts must have been Oddjob Drones, their multiple extensions busy testing, repositioning, winding, loosening, fastening. When the machinery swapped around, the drones simply adjusted their extensions and carried on tirelessly.

'Is this what it's like to be in *your* head, Albert?' Kip shouted with a grin.

As they climbed the dimly lit staircase, Kip counted six storeys of machinery. At the top of the tower they came to the belfry, where the mighty bells hung from wooden beams. It was just about quiet enough to speak normally as they hunted around.

'So, what are we looking for?' asked Albert.

With his finger, Kip outlined the shape of a squirl on the surface of the nearest bell.

'We'll know it when we see it,' he said.

They began to retrace their steps, moving carefully through the whimsical machinery to search each storey thoroughly by bright Candlelight. Every cog, every cobweb seemed to gain new significance. By the time they were about halfway down the tower, Kip began to worry that perhaps Eartha's next clue had been too well hidden. But then Albert came to a stop beneath a series of large rolling wheels suspended in the air. He pointed at the wall behind Kip compellingly.

'It's… it's…'

Kip jumped one hundred and eighty degrees, expecting to see Eartha Quicksmith walking through the wall.

'…it's a different colour,' Albert spat out finally.

There *was* a patch of different-coloured bricks – about a metre across and two metres high.

'It could be a doorway that's been filled in,' Albert said.

'How can there be a room here?' Kip wondered aloud. 'Isn't this the outer wall of the building?'

'I think you're right,' said Albert. 'But nothing surprises me any more.'

Hoping to trigger a reaction, Kip and Albert began to tap, poke and swipe each brick within the door-shaped patch.

'Up here!' said Albert. 'This one isn't the same as the others: it's smooth. Can you feel it?'

Kip stood on tiptoe and extended his arm as far as it would go, fumbling along the rough clay until he came to the same discovery.

'Maybe it's a hint,' said Albert.

'Like what?'

Albert made fish lips for a moment and clicked his fingers.

'Like … what do you do to make something smooth?'

'Give it a bath? Moisturiser?'

'Or polish it?' said Albert.

Pulling his sleeve over his hand, Albert reached up and began to rub the odd-brick-out.

'Keep going,' Kip urged him on. 'Something's happening.'

He watched incredulously as a square of bricks in the door-shaped patch slowly transformed to glass.

'A window! Can't see much though,' said Kip, pressing his nose up against the glass bricks.

Albert did the same. 'It *is* a hidden room! Wait, could it be the secret study?'

'What secret study?'

'Eartha's. Remember? I read about it in one of the library books. It's sort of a legend. No one really believes it.'

'But how do we get inside? No handle. No lever.'

'Wormhole?' suggested Albert.

'That won't work,' said Kip. 'The wormholes we made will only let small things through. And I don't think we can use the Wormhole Positioning System without someone knowing. Eartha must have left a way in...'

'What was that?' said Albert harshly, pushing away from the wall.

'What was what?'

'Just watch.'

Kip ducked as something walked past the glass-brick window.

'Someone's inside already?'

It was just possible to make out a figure slinking up and down in the hidden room. As they watched, it paused and slowly turned, until it was looking straight at them.

Kip couldn't even whisper.

Scaleface.

It was almost within touching distance, if there hadn't been a wall in the way.

Kip felt his skin go cold. As he watched – unable to move like a fly in a web – Scaleface reached out with a spindly black arm.

'Run!' yelled Albert.

They pelted back down the spiral staircase, all the way to the ground floor. Dimbleby looked up from his work desk and grunted.

'Finished? Once you go, you're not getting back in again.'

But Kip and Albert were already out of the door and panting in the afternoon sunshine.

'What *is* it?' said Albert, shivering.

Kip tried to keep his thoughts calm, but all he could see was that terrifying face.

'At least we know where the fourth riddle is now,' was all he could say.

Chapter Ten

Busted

Albert's elbow jabbed Kip's ribs. There were two figures waiting at the First Year Block. Miss Twiss hovered on a Skimmi above the herb garden, her expression set in that wistful smile which never faded. Leaning on the garden gate was Tamara Okpik, the Head of Security. She was not smiling. Her long fringe was pinned back severely, and her black jumpsuit and dark sunglasses made her look like some kind of special agent. Both women had their arms folded.

'Skycrackle Tower,' said Albert under his breath. 'Thag.'

Dread filled Kip from the legs up like fast-setting concrete.

'Kip Bramley.' Miss Twiss's voice appeared in his head. 'A word with you, if we may.'

'Am I in trouble?' he asked quietly, as he followed Twiss and Okpik.

'By using a Skimmi in the No Flying Zone, you disregarded one of our most important laws,' the Head of Security replied gravely. 'Laws that are in place to keep us all safe. So yes. You are in trouble.'

Now it felt as if Kip's heart had turned to concrete too.

'But there was a Froglash,' he said.

Tamara raised an eyebrow.

'It's like a Wormhole lasso,' he explained, hopefully.

'What if there hadn't been one?' said the Professor-in-Charge.

Kip had no answer.

'However,' continued Twiss, 'we know that you were provoked in a very dangerous and irresponsible way. And this must be taken into account. We've spent the weekend checking the facts and interviewing the witnesses. The Quicksmiths Council has decided there will need to be a College Vote.'

'Vote?' said Kip in horror. 'Can't I get detention?'

'We don't have detention at Quicksmiths,' said Tamara Okpik.

A cloud passed in front of the sun and a light drizzle began to fall.

'Whenever we have an important decision at the college, all the students are included,' said Miss Twiss. 'That way we make sure that it's fair, and if there is a price to be paid then everyone has had a chance to agree or disagree.'

Price to be paid? Kip felt ill. Would he be expected to speak in front of the whole college? Him against Thag?

'So what do I do now?' he asked.

'You will be informed when the vote is scheduled,' said Tamara.

'Go about your daily life as usual,' Twiss added. 'Think of how you might have done things differently, perhaps. Just attend your classes and carry on as normal.'

The Professor-in-Charge might as well have told Kip not to feel hunger or breathe oxygen.

After they left, he walked around in the drizzle for a bit, trying to process the bad news. An uncomfortable sense of being followed dragged his gaze backwards occasionally, but there was nothing and no one there. As he reached the corner of Celestial Hall his phone rang. It was perfect timing – just who Kip needed to help him straighten things out in his head.

'Dad?' he said, hearing the relief in his own voice.

'Kip. How are you doing?'

But as soon as he heard his dad's tone, everything started to fall away. Something was wrong.

'How's Mum?' said Kip, forgetting Thag and the vote.

'She's OK, Kip.'

'But what happened?' Kip persisted.

His dad hesitated.

'She was up on the rooftop of St Antony's this morning. Looking for your sister.'

Kip felt a thousand tiny scars opening in his heart. He knew he and his dad were thinking the same thing. What if she had slipped and broken her leg up there and no one had found her? Or if she had walked off the edge, following a trick of her mind?

'But like I say, she's OK now,' continued his dad. 'They're going to keep a closer eye on her, but the staff are very busy. They might have to lock her door sometimes.'

Locked door? That made it a prison, not a care home.

Can't get thrown out, thought Kip desperately. *I'm Mum's only chance.*

'Is Professor Mo still your favourite teacher?' his dad was saying, trying to change the subject. 'Still crushing that puzzles class?'

'Everything's amazing,' was all Kip could manage.

It was like a different kind of Scrambleguard had taken over. He couldn't bring himself to tell his dad that he'd broken the college rules and might be back home in a few days. How could everything be going so wrong so fast?

After the call, Kip found Albert sitting under a tree outside the First Year Block, waiting for him.

'What happened? Why were you gone so long?'

'My dad called to tell me my mum's worse. And Miss Twiss said there's going to be a College Vote. To decide if I get punished for climbing Skycrackle Tower.'

'But, but that's not fair,' spluttered Albert, scrambling to his feet. 'It wasn't your fault.'

'They said that I broke the rules. Which is true.'

'When is it?' asked Albert.

'Don't know. Hey, Albert, can we walk around for a bit? Just walk?'

They did a couple of laps of the Library. After a while, Kip started to feel a little better so they headed back. On the way they passed Ptolemy Courtyard, where Professor Kvörk was standing on the statue's plinth. Several other professors they didn't recognise were gathered below, shouting up suggestions. Kip and Albert smiled politely and kept on walking.

'Everyone has the Ark fever,' whispered Albert.

'Can't quite believe we're ahead of the professors,' Kip murmured back.

'And Thag is too,' said Albert.

As they continued along the path, echoing freeps rolled out of Confucius Courtyard. They followed the sounds to find the mowl swooping above the old oak, and Leela looking up at him. With his feathery wings fanned in flight, glittering orange scales underneath flashed into view.

It was warmer after the drizzle and the sky was full

of May bugs that had arrived early. The mowl dived and twisted from one tasty treat to another, freeping gleefully and giving an occasional excited wurble-urble.

'I wonder what he dreams of,' said Leela, not taking her eyes off the mowl.

'Whole mountains of cheese probably,' said Kip, glad to have a distraction. 'Or a giant Leela with hair he can fly through.'

'A Jacuzzi full of glasses and shiny things,' said Leela.

'Maybe he dreams of finding a lost city of mowls,' Albert said. 'It must be a bit lonely being the only one of your kind.'

Kip nodded. That was how he had felt at Ledhill, before Quicksmiths had come along and rescued him.

'If I have to leave,' he said sadly, 'we'll never be able to talk about Eartha's riddles or the Ark. But I won't forget you, will I?'

'I don't think so,' said Albert. 'And we would never, ever forget you.'

'Why? What's happened?' asked Leela, looking down sharply.

'There's going to be a vote,' said Albert. 'Because of Thag and what happened at Skycrackle Tower.'

'That Thag,' she snapped furiously. 'He always gets away with it. It's because he's a Grittleshank.'

'You're not helping, Leela,' said Albert.

'Sorry.' She bit her lip. 'I'm sure you won't get voted out, Kip.'

'It's OK,' Kip heard himself saying.

But it was like Quicksmiths was already pulling away from him, a boat leaving the shore. Waiting in the gloom left behind were the sneering Snibbug and the Claw Chair and there was nothing Kip could do about it. This all still felt like a dream, only the dream had turned bad.

'Will you promise me something?' Kip said, as he and Albert climbed the stairs to Q10.

'Anything,' said Albert.

'If the vote doesn't go well, find the Ark and then come and find me? So we can make my mum better?'

'Of course, I'll do everything I can,' replied Albert. 'But two heads are better than one. Tomorrow we'll just have to get past Scaleface and find the next riddle.'

A Friend in Need

Kip fell asleep, still dressed, before the minty taste of toothpaste had disappeared from his mouth. Halfway through the night, his alarm went off. He sat up in bed and turned his Candlelight on low.

The College Vote was rumbling ever closer, imposing and inescapable. Tonight could be his last night at Quicksmiths. And it was the seventh night of the hunt for the Ark. Seven nights out of ten.

As Kip got up, he caught a glimpse of himself in the dark mirror above the sink. His reflection gleamed with shreds of moonlight that broke through the curtain and clutched at the blue quartz around his neck.

'Change your world,' he whispered, and tucked the crystal back into his T-shirt.

He knelt down and shook Albert's shoulder. But he was so deep, deep down in a sleepdrift that he didn't wake even when Kip said his name loudly a few times. It didn't feel right going without Albert, but time was running out. Kip scribbled a note and left it next to the bed.

Seeing that he was up and awake, Pinky flitted around in her lair. Kip posted a green bean to her through the mesh.

'Sorry, Pinky,' he said, 'not now. I'll be back soon.'

After a last quick inventory of his rucksack (bottle of water, cheese sandwich, handtowel and fingerless climbing gloves), he sneaked out alone.

Quicksmiths was so still you could have heard an atom bounce. Kip crept his creepiest creep under the hushed archways of Clock Tower Courtyard, trying to think strong thoughts, thoughts that would help him climb a tower at night.

If I get caught, the vote won't matter anymore.

He pushed the thought of the Professor-in-Charge's disappointed eyes and The Snibbug's gloating face out of his mind.

A twig cracked somewhere and Kip froze. If anyone else was awake it would be better if he spotted them first, so he could keep out of sight until they had gone. He was out in the open now, so he took a step back towards cover and immediately bumped into someone backing up the other way.

'What?' he yelped.

'Who?' Leela squealed.

'What are you doing?' he hissed. 'Why are you sneaking around so late?'

Leela's skin looked grey in the moonlight and there was none of the usual impishness in her eyes.

'Professor Mo's glasses,' she said. 'He must have left his window open – because the mowl stole three pairs – he's such a magpie – I caught him playing with them under the bed – but he flew off before I could catch him – now he's hiding in one of his burrows…'

'He has burrows? I thought he was a house pet?'

'He's a free-range mowl – and he likes digging almost as much as flying – I'll be in such trouble if I can't get those glasses back – and so will he – he's already had two warnings – what if they say I'm not doing a good job of looking after him – what if they won't let me keep him?'

Kip thought for a second.

'Mowls love cheese, right…'

'Can't resist it,' said Leela, finally sounding less flustered. 'What are you thinking?'

'A trap,' said Kip. 'Cheesy, cheesy, catchy mowly.'

The idea worked perfectly. They took the cheese out of the sandwich in Kip's rucksack and arranged it temptingly outside the mowl's favourite burrow. Gradually a clawed hand appeared and then the tops of two huge orange eyes, and then a round, furry black body.

'Got you!' said Leela.

'Three pairs of glasses,' Kip said, reaching a hand into the burrow. 'All here.'

'I owe you big time,' said Leela, cuddling the mowl, who seemed to have forgotten all about his hoard and was nibbling cheese from under her fingernails.

'Where's Timmi by the way?' Kip asked.

'In bed with tummyache. She ate about a hundred green mangoes. What about Albert?'

'Couldn't wake him up,' said Kip.

And then Leela's eyes narrowed. 'Wait a minute. You never said why *you* were out this late?'

Kip looked down at the Skimmi folded up and tucked under Leela's arm. It would be much easier than climbing. She poked him on the arm.

'Come on. Tell me and I'll let you win in the next Skimmi race.'

Her eyes were clear and bright in the moonlight.

What did Albert say? thought Kip. *Two heads are better than one.*

'Actually, seeing as you're here,' he muttered, 'I could do with some help...'

'We'll help! What is it?'

'Swear not to tell anyone. On the mowl's life.'

'I swear!'

In a whisper Kip told her everything they'd discovered and how it all led to the hidden room in the Clock Tower.

'You're the cleverest on Everest!' she said. 'Can't believe you and Albert have kept all that a secret.'

Leela coaxed the mowl out of her arms until he flapped off lazily and disappeared into the night.

'All aboard,' she said, opening her Skimmi.

Kip jumped on behind her and in moments they were hovering halfway up the tower.

War of Words

'We saw the hidden room through a secret window on the other side of this wall,' explained Kip, putting a hand on the cool bricks. 'I think this is about the right place.'

'So what next?' asked Leela, turning up her Candlelight slightly.

'We couldn't find anything else inside,' said Kip. 'So I thought there might be a clue out here. Eartha must have left some way in.'

They hunted around in the soft light for some time

until the mowl ch-charked out of the darkness. Almost immediately, they heard a voice below.

Leela switched off her Candlelight and they froze, floating four storeys up. Kip chanced a look over the side of the Skimmi to see the tops of two heads almost directly beneath them. Gorvak's rusty-gold hair was unmistakable even in the half-light. And so was the outline of Thag's crushing frame.

'Of course I don't think Eartha's talking about me in her letter,' snapped Gorvak.

'Captain Gorvak to the rescue!' jeered Thag. 'Anyway, Eartha – *sorry*, your fifteenth-great-grandmama – stole all her ideas from Solomon.'

'That's a lie. They worked together,' Gorvak retorted, his voice laced with cold rage.

'It's all irrelevant actually. When I find the Ark, whatever's inside is going to the Grittleshank Collective. And I'll get all the glory.'

'I won't let you!' said Gorvak.

'Finders keepers,' said Thag, shoving Gorvak.

Gorvak shoved him back.

'Dream on, Thag. GENI won't let anyone take it out of Quicksmiths. The Scrambleguard…'

'There's always a loophole,' said Thag, with a snort.

'I don't believe you,' Gorvak said, talking faster and louder. 'No one can get past it. But that doesn't matter. You aren't anywhere near clever enough to solve all of Eartha's riddles.'

Thag held his thumb and forefinger together, an inch away from Gorvak's face.

'I'm this close to number four.'

'Maybe you are. Maybe you aren't,' said Gorvak, icily. 'Either way, this is war.'

Up above, Kip heard a faint click from the Clock Tower's face as the hands reached the hour. One of the gigantic bells inside pealed, and he cringed away from the deafening sound. Beside him, Leela flinched too.

When they looked down again, Thag and Gorvak were gone.

'Close to number four,' Kip whispered.

'That means you're in a tie,' whispered Leela firmly. 'Which means you're not losing. Aaaaaand ... maybe you're even in the lead. What's that down there?'

By the light of the moon, Kip could just make out two initials chipped into the side of a brick.

E. Q.

He was barely able to contain his excitement in a whisper.

'You looky lookist!'

The Skimmi drifted slowly down and stopped.

'So how do we...'

Without finishing her question, Leela reached out and placed her forefinger over the first full stop. She looked at Kip, and he copied her, pressing his finger into the round dip of the second.

They both pulled back sharply as a crack began to spread noiselessly from the tail of the Q. It branched out below the chipped letters and the bricks it touched revolved and disappeared one by one, creating a crooked entrance.

'How did you guess?' asked Kip.

'Just a hunchy old hunch,' Leela said, with a grin.

Before she could point the Skimmi forwards, Kip stopped her.

'You should know. We saw Scaleface in there.'

She must have understood exactly who he meant because she went quiet and still, and Kip thought for a second that she might change her mind. But then the mowl wurbled from the roof of the Clock Tower.

'You helped me,' Leela said. 'Now it's my turn. Engage stealth mode.'

The darkness in the hidden room seemed to spill out, making the night around the entrance inkier. Leela edged the Skimmi forward and the moonlight seeped in behind them, revealing a large, circular chamber. It was just bright enough to see a chain of shadowy outlines which followed the curve of the wall.

'Looks like giant teeth,' whispered Leela.

A muffled clank came from the far side of the chamber and she grabbed Kip's arm. The mowl

241

freeped loudly behind them and before Leela could do anything, he had dived into the room.

They waited but all they could hear was the occasional dull bang and lots of freeping and clicking.

'I don't think Scaleface is here,' Leela whispered. 'The mowl has great night vision. And smell. He'd sense any danger.'

She gradually restored the Candlelight until they could see the mowl flapping around the ceiling, chasing a frantic bat.

'All that banging must be the tower's machinery,' she said. 'So, what exactly are we looking for? Is it something to do with those shields?'

The light from her Candle had dispelled the illusion of giant shadowy teeth. What remained in their place was a display of knights' shields hanging all the way around the otherwise empty room. The nearest one was decorated with a roaring lion and a rearing unicorn. Kip felt the sudden thrill of realisation, like icy water down his back.

'Coat-of-arms! That's what Eartha meant by coat!'

It was hard to believe that the riddle was finally unravelling.

'How do we know which one is hers?' asked Leela.

They walked alongside the shields, looking carefully at each image. A phoenix and an orchid. A mouse and a dragon. A mammoth and an oak. A double-headed swan and a rose.

'Trying looking for a buttercup,' said Kip. 'That's Eartha's flower.'

They had almost walked a full circle when Leela yelped and ran towards one of the shields.

'Blue buttercup,' said Kip, close behind her. 'Black parrot.'

'The buttercup sticks out,' Leela said. 'And it turns – it's a wheel!'

She twisted the buttercup-wheel until a loud mechanical sound started up behind them. Kip turned around to find a white line was materialising at their feet, forming a large circle that went all the way around the chamber about a metre in from the curved wall. A square hole had appeared at the centre of this circle, in the middle of the bare, stone floor. Rising up from this hole was a stone pedestal topped by a silver lever. When the pedestal had come to a stop, four trapdoors sprang open from the floor around it, and four looming metal figures ascended.

The Fourth Riddle

'What are they?' whispered Leela, her breathing shallow.

Each metal figure was roughly the shape of a human and nearly reached the ceiling. They were completely built of rolling clockwork parts – from their heads all the way to their feet, which were made of toothed wheels. And each one had a different weapon: a sword, a spear, a bow, and an axe.

'Clockwork soldiers?' whispered Kip.

When he spoke, the soldiers turned to face them. Their eyes were like deep black pits; their mouths were metal grilles.

'It's just machinery,' said Kip, trying to stay calm. 'They're not alive.'

A metal banner slowly descended from the ceiling and stopped just above the pedestal.

N

The missing piece faces forwards

But goes backwards.

Undo the Stitch.

Reverse Time's Arrow.

'Look, they're moving!' shrieked Leela. 'They're coming towards us.'

Kip felt hot prickles on the back of his neck, and suddenly the spacious chamber seemed much smaller.

'Back on the Skimmi,' he said quickly. 'Outside!'

It was just a few steps to the crooked opening where they had entered. But there was no moonlight visible. Leela turned back to Kip in despair.

'The way out – it's closed.'

Hoping for another escape route, Kip scanned the

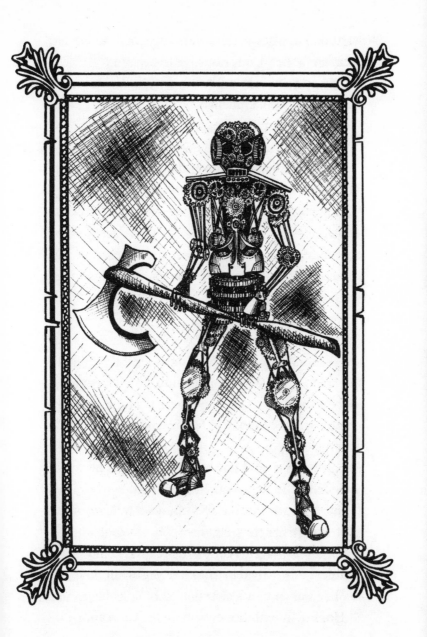

wall for the glass-brick window he and Albert had discovered. But it was nowhere to be seen.

The clockwork soldiers advanced, weapons gleaming in the Candlelight.

'Grab a shield,' he shouted.

'Won't … come off … the wall,' gasped Leela.

She started hammering at the bricks with her fist. The mowl landed next to her and spread his wings, hissing and scratching alongside her.

Behind them, the sound of a single, squeaky wheel got louder and louder as the soldiers closed in. Kip tugged in vain at one of the shields, expecting to feel the point of a spear in his back at any second. But it never came.

He chanced a look over his shoulder and saw that the soldiers were now spinning around the pedestal in a sinister dance. Just as Kip didn't think it could get much worse, long spurts of flame shot out from the mouth-grille of each one. Four metal guardians, four whirling weapons, four spouts of flame. All moving in deadly clockwork harmony.

'So, what do we do now?' said Leela.

'We have to find a way to move that lever – and hope it switches the soldiers off.'

Leela rummaged in Kip's rucksack and took out a glove. As she went to stand at the white line, the swordsman spun towards her, jabbing its blade, and she backed away hastily.

'Don't get too close,' she muttered.

She took aim at the silver lever, and threw. Four jets of flame intercepted the glove in mid-air, and it fell, smouldering, to the ground.

'Looks like we're trapped then,' she said. 'Can't go forwards, can't go back.'

'Sorry I got you into this,' said Kip.

'Don't worry,' Leela said, forcing a smile. 'We won't give up.'

She looked at Kip, eyes like black jewels in the firelight. Then her smile changed to alarm, and she jumped as the wall at their backs moved. The crooked entrance in the outer wall was opening again.

'Honestly,' said Albert's voice, 'I fall asleep for a few little minutes and you get yourself into all kinds of trouble.'

Albert and Timmi looked through the opening, the flames from the clockwork soldiers reflecting on their faces. Leela tried to hug them both together and then stepped back, confused.

'But how did you…?'

'One: Kip left a note. Two: I woke up. Three: I read the note. Four: Timmi has a Skimmi.'

Kip took a deep breath and the freshness of the night air spread through his arteries along with a cool wave of relief.

'Five,' he said. 'Albert and Timmi saved us from being toast.'

'Doesn't look like a secret study,' Albert said, clambering into the room. 'Guess I was wrong.'

'Jam my rucksack in the entranceway,' said Kip. 'So it doesn't close again.'

'What are those things?' asked Timmi. 'They look violent.'

'They're part of the riddle,' Leela explained. 'We think we have to pull that lever.'

Albert stepped forward, his shoe touching the white line.

'Careful!' yelled Leela.

The archer approached, belching a flame that singed Albert's eyebrows.

'FIRE!' he shouted, jumping back. 'I mean, thanks.'

'We're only safe behind the line,' Kip said.

'Can't the mowl fly in and pull the lever?' asked Albert.

The mowl ch-charked.

'He won't get past the flames,' said Leela.

'What do you think about the riddle, Albert?' Kip asked. 'This is kind of your thing. Clockwork. Time.'

'No winding up, after all these years? Amazing,' Albert replied.

He said little after that, occasionally crouching down or standing on tiptoe to see better, watching the soldiers' motions like a bird watches its prey. The mowl observed Albert and mimicked his movements, as if learning from him.

'It's almost like Eartha didn't want anyone to find the Ark,' complained Timmi.

'She didn't want the *wrong* people to find it,' said Kip. 'Don't forget she had a Futurescope.'

'There are no skeletons lying around,' Leela added. 'Suppose that means the soldiers can't have stabbed anyone. Yet.'

'Unless they tidy up the bodies afterwards,' said Timmi.

'Shhh, you lot,' said Albert. 'Focus.'

'The stitch in the riddle,' Kip said. 'Is it the same Timestitch you saw before? Making the clock hands jump?'

'I'm not sure,' Albert replied. 'But there's definitely something funny going on in here. Feels like time has been sort of fenced off.'

'Well, let's start at the beginning,' said Leela. 'Of the riddle, not time.'

'"The missing piece". Must be a bit of clockwork, right?' said Timmi.

'Or it could be the arrow,' said Leela. 'Look, the archer doesn't have one.'

'Whatever it is,' said Albert, 'it has to be in here somewhere.'

'Let's check the shields,' Kip suggested. 'Maybe one of them is hiding something else.'

Keeping to the safe zone in the outer perimeter, they pored over every shield in the room: every unusual beast and every strange symbol.

'Nothing,' said Timmi, hugging herself. 'Shall we start again?'

'Missing piece,' muttered Albert, staring at the soldiers. 'Wait…'

'What do you see?' said Leela.

'A gap.'

'A what?'

'A gap. A hole. A space. It's almost like there should be five soldiers.'

'The missing piece is an entire soldier?' groaned Leela. 'But we can't just build another one.'

'No,' said Albert. 'The missing piece isn't another soldier. Timmi, do you have that foldy mirror? The one you check your hair in?'

Kip could see Timmi blushing, even in the orange glow of the flames. But she took the mirror out of her pocket and handed it to Albert.

'It was already in my jeans,' she explained hastily.

Albert put his hands together around the mirror and looked up as if he were offering a prayer of thanks. Keeping the mirror in one fist, he stepped up to the edge of the white line and turned around to face the others.

'Don't follow me!' he ordered.

He opened the mirror, counted to three quickly and walked backwards – over the line and straight towards a flashing axe blade.

'What are you *doing*?' yelled Leela.

She grabbed Timmi's hand and then Kip's and they watched as Albert kept walking backwards towards the pedestal, straight into the soldiers' deadly warpath. Kip held his breath as a spear shaved the very top of Albert's hair, and realised Leela and Timmi weren't breathing either. But the soldiers didn't attack.

'They're avoiding him,' said Leela.

'The missing piece,' murmured Timmi. 'Albert's the missing piece.'

'He's going backwards,' said Kip. 'But he's still looking forwards.'

Just one more calculated step and Albert had reached the pedestal. He pulled the lever and the clockwork soldiers slowly wound down, their weapons coming to a stop and their fiery breath fading away.

'I say "Al", you say "Bert",' Leela shouted, bouncing forward. 'Al...'

'Wait,' said Albert, and his tone was deathly serious. 'Stay there!'

'He's right,' said Kip. 'That was only the first half of the riddle. He has to undo the stitch.'

Albert's eyes hunted around. He leaned forward and ran his fingers along the bowstring pulled back by the archer.

'There's a knot here. Seems out of place. I'm going to try untying it.'

As he loosened the knot the air began to thrum,

and rust started to spread over the clockwork soldiers like a rash. An arrow faded into being, notched in the archer's bow.

'Time's Arrow!' said Timmi.

'That's what the Timestitch was hiding,' Kip murmured.

Albert reached out and took hold of the arrow. It must have been sharper than he expected, as he winced but held firm.

'Careful!' Leela cried out, gripping Kip's hand tightly.

'It swivels,' Albert said in relief, 'I can move it.'

Very slowly, he rotated the arrow upwards and away from him to face its soldier. Once it was fully reversed, there was a sound of whirring wheels, the trapdoors opened and the pedestal and guardians began to descend again.

'Now it's safe,' said Albert, breaking into a smile.

Leela let go of Kip and ran with Timmi across the room to Albert where they both fussed over the cut on his hand.

'It's not bad,' he mumbled.

Kip felt his respect for Albert turned up, as if someone had added extra batteries.

'Albert, you fixed everything,' he said. 'We could never have done this without you.'

'That was really brave,' said Timmi.

'You're welcome,' said Albert, a bit awkwardly.

'Look!' said Leela. 'Eartha's shield – it's opening!'

The shield was slowly swinging up, exposing a dark gap in the wall about a foot wide. It went far too deep for the Candlelight to reach the end of it.

'Number five must be down there then?' said Albert.

'But we're not Alice in Wonderland,' Timmi said. 'That rabbit hole's too small to crawl down.'

'Maybe *we* don't have to,' said Leela, grinning.

Chapter Eleven

The Fifth Riddle

Leela whistled loudly. After a few seconds, the mowl landed at her feet, looking up at her for instructions.

'Seek, mowl!' she said, pointing down the tunnel.

In a flurry of fur, scales and feathers, the mowl was gone. A minute passed and Leela whistled again. A faint freep floated back.

'He's probably chasing spiders,' Leela said. 'Faster mowl, hurry up!'

A wurble echoed out of the tunnel. The mowl appeared after another minute, clutching a brass tube.

'Good mowl,' said Kip.

When the mowl had hop-waddled out of the tunnel's mouth, the shield swung slowly back into place. He sat on the floor and began to beak-nibble the lid of the tube.

'No eating the riddle, mowl!' said Leela.

The mowl shrugged and shook cobwebs from his feathers. Leela handed the tube to Kip, who prised off the lid and pulled out a roll of thick parchment.

'A map of the world,' Timmi whispered.

They all stared at the writing of the fifth riddle, as Kip read aloud.

V

Seek your answer in the study of secrets

As the last word left his mouth, an almighty thump shook the walls.

'What was that?' Leela hissed. 'Doesn't sound like machinery.'

Then there was another, even louder thump that made them all jump, even the mowl, who made an unfamiliar clacking sound. Dust sprinkled from the ceiling.

'Could be someone inside the Clock Tower,' whispered Kip. 'Looking for this room.'

'Scaleface?' gasped Leela, her eyes as wide as the mowl's.

'I don't think walls stop Scaleface,' said Albert.

'Who's Scaleface?' asked Timmi.

'Tell you later,' Leela said.

'It must be Thag,' said Kip, 'trying to find a way in.'

'We have to go – now!' Albert said. 'It won't be long before he realises there's a hidden window.'

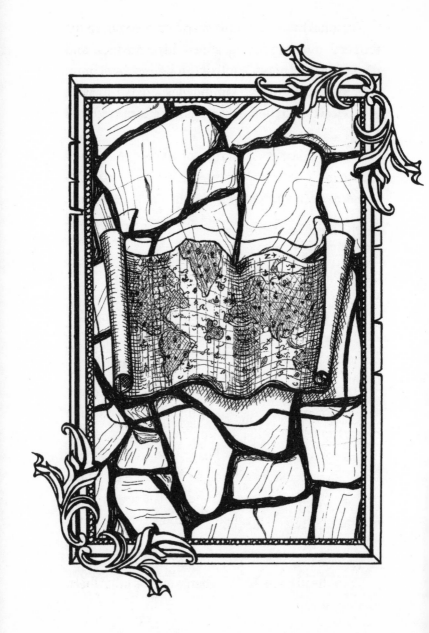

Kip quickly rolled up the map and they ran to the crooked opening. He grabbed his rucksack and ducked as the mowl shot out, followed by Timmi and Albert sharing a Skimmi. Leela and Kip were last to leave, and the bricks began to close up behind them.

As they coasted down, out of the night sky, and landed in Confucius Courtyard, Kip looked back. No one was following them. Safely on the ground, everyone bounced around in the shadow of the old oak like excited electrons.

'We've got the map! We've got the map!' Leela and Timmi whisper-sang.

Overhead, the mowl wurble-urbled gleefully.

'Wait,' said Albert, coming to a standstill. 'If we have the map that means Thag's stuck. He can't get to the next riddle.'

Leela and Timmi grabbed each other and jumped up and down even more wildly than before. Watching them, Kip felt his smile lighting up the darkness. The College Vote, Scaleface, Thag, they were all just obstacles on a mountain trail he had to climb. At the peak, his mum was waving. And his friends were like his safety ropes. With them around he could never fall.

'Can we help you solve the map?' asked Timmi.

'Four heads are better than two?' said Albert, looking at Kip.

'Welcome to Team Glowflyer,' Kip said.

Leela and Timmi twirled together victoriously. But, as they came to a stop, Leela tried to stifle a yawn and soon the others had caught it.

'We should do our map-reading tomorrow,' she said. 'The mowl needs his beauty sleep.'

As the girls inched into the air, Kip could just make out the words on the underside of Leela's Skimmi.

'Eat our dust, Thag!' he said.

'Hey guys,' yawned Leela's voice, out of the darkness.

'Yes?' said Albert.

'Would you rather have an army of one T-Rex-sized mowl, or a thousand teacup mini-mowls?'

And then she was gone.

'She never even gives you a chance to answer her weirdoid questions,' Albert grumbled.

Safely back in Q10, Kip and Albert sat together in a pool of golden Candlelight and took the map out of its tube. Ships sailed across its oceans and wagons explored its lands. Strange markings, like alchemical symbols, were inked here and there.

'"Seek your answer in the study of secrets",' murmured Kip.

'Are the symbols coded directions?' Albert wondered. 'Could the Ark be buried somewhere at Quicksmiths?'

'Maybe,' said Kip. 'Guess it's up to us to find out.'

'We need a hiding place,' said Albert, rolling up the map again.

Kip pushed it back in the brass tube and opened the lair door. While he hid the map inside the scarf hammock, Pinky scuttled up Kip's arm and hugged his neck.

'It's our secret,' he said. 'Just you, me, and Albert.'

Team Glowflyer

It was only a couple of hours until the alarm burst Kip's bubble of sleep. He'd been dreaming about a squirl – so real it felt as if he could reach out and touch its edges.

His thoughts immediately went to his mum. She might still be vulnerable and confused, but there were no new messages from his dad.

We found Eartha's map, he remembered with a thrill.

And then with a sickening lurch he remembered something else: the vote that hung over him – the gloom bomb that could go off at any second.

'Don't dolphins sleep with half of their brain at a time?' groaned Albert from the lower bunk. 'I'm doing that today.'

Kip splashed cold water on his face at the sink and the murky, unslept feeling evaporated a little.

'Let's find the others,' he said.

At the Buttery, Albert spotted Timmi's hat in the crowd and quickly navigated to the two girls who had saved a table. Kip and Albert sat down and the four of them huddled together, talking in whispers.

'Leela wouldn't tell me who Scaleface is until you got here,' complained Timmi, folding her arms.

'It's a … a thing,' said Albert, 'that's following us.'

'You've seen it too?' Leela asked.

'Wish I hadn't,' said Albert. 'We think it's after the Ark. But we don't want to tell anyone, in case we have to explain everything else we know. And that might give Thag a chance to overtake us.'

'What sort of *thing*?' asked Timmi.

'Well, it's silver and black and leathery…' said Leela.

'And scaly…' Albert added.

'It's sort of shaped like a tall tree stump,' continued Leela. 'Hard to describe its body … like a creepy cloak. And it has weird eyes you can't look away from.'

'It's basically a monster,' said Albert.

'A monster?' said Timmi. 'Seriously?'

'Dead serious,' said Albert.

'Only "monster" sounds a bit furry and fun,' Leela said. 'This isn't.'

'Listen everyone,' Kip interrupted. 'This is turning into a battle. And we're right in the middle of it. I understand if none of you wants to carry on. But I'm going to find the Ark before Thag. I have to.'

The mowl wurbled softly and pecked gently at Kip's forearm with his felty beak.

'There's no way I'm dropping out,' said Albert firmly.

'Me neither,' said Timmi. 'You stuck up for me, didn't you?'

They all looked at Leela.

'We'll come to your room at break time,' she said. 'Make a start on the map-reading.'

Kip gazed around the table. He had never had a group of friends like this: willing to stick with him to the end, despite the danger.

He started to say just that, but Timmi spoke first.

'Why are the Ballmoths here? It's not time for lessons yet.'

All around the Buttery, the small glowing spheres were floating towards the ceiling-window, like spores from a coral reef. Once they were swarming there in their hundreds, they shifted and churned and formed a message that shimmered in the morning sunlight:

College Vote
Aristotle's Theatre 11:00
Compulsory Attendance

Kip's mouth went dry. A vision of The Snibbug's I-told-you-so face floated in his imagination and he tried to swat it away. Lowering his eyes, he stabbed his toast angrily with a teaspoon.

'Is there a machine that can change things?' he mumbled.

Anything would help: a swallowing-up machine or a turn-back-time machine. Then he'd do things differently at Skycrackle Tower. As if sensing Kip's frustration, the mowl dug at the table with the claws of his little ottery hands until Leela shushed him.

'You'll be OK,' said Penny, coming over, followed by Badger and Em and lots of others.

'We'll all vote for you,' added Badger. 'Everyone will – no one likes Thag.'

Kip nodded gratefully but speaking seemed like the hardest thing in the world. When all his well-wishers had gone, Team Glowflyer huddled together again to finish their plans.

'So what happens now?' asked Albert.

Kip looked at the three trusting faces and the mowl, all expecting a decision from him. He curled a finger around the leather cord at his neck.

'We're going to team up with Gorvak,' he said finally. 'He'll be a good ally. That way if the vote goes badly, if I have to leave, he can help you stand up to Thag. Plus, he is Eartha Quicksmith's fifteenth great-grandson. I think he'll know what to do.'

'We've got just enough time before lessons,' said Timmi. 'Ballmoth: take us to Gorvak G. Gorvak.'

When they reached the lawn outside the Sixth Form Block, they found a large, jostling crowd in the way. To follow the Ballmoth, they had to push through all the people. But soon Kip wished they hadn't.

Thag was at the centre of the crowd, like a grinning parasite inside a willing host, chatting pleasantly and telling jokes. Sharktooth Girl was wearing lots of dark eyeliner and had her hair done up in ringlets. Two other boys and a girl, with pasted-on smiles, were flicking Quickets into the crowd.

'You're buying votes,' yelled Leela. 'That's not fair!'

'Buying? Votes?' said Thag, putting his head on one side innocently. 'Not at all. I just have so many Quickets I don't know what to do with them. I might as well give them to my friends.'

'Would you like some free Quickets?' asked Sharktooth Girl sweetly, batting her eyelids.

'You can't bribe us,' said Timmi. 'Nothing on Earth would make me vote for you.'

Sharktooth Girl's docile gaze dissolved into a spiteful glare.

'Let's go,' said Leela in disgust. 'I suddenly feel sick to my stomach.'

'Vote-stealing beastoid,' muttered Albert. 'Cheating newt-face.'

'Forget them,' said Kip. 'Stick to the plan.'

Timmi's Ballmoth weaved through the crowd, leading the way into the building and up to one of the bedrooms. Kip knocked and opened the door.

Gorvak was sitting with his back to them, reciting something aloud, quite softly, so that Kip only caught snatches of it.

'… to answer … my riddles you will need … your wits … each other … to know yourselves … a defender of all that Quicksmiths stands for … the secrets of Aeon Light … a dark and perilous age…'

Leela coughed and Gorvak swivelled in his chair.

'Kip! Didn't hear you come in. Good to see you.'

'Why are you learning Eartha's letter?' asked Timmi.

'I'm not learning it,' said Gorvak, sliding off the chair. 'It's just a knack I have, to remember everything I hear. I recite the letter every morning after breakfast, just in case Eartha left another clue in there somewhere, something I've missed until now. Just trying to make sense of it all really.'

He ran a hand through his hair and, just for a second, Kip thought he looked a little desperate.

'I have to get to the Ark first,' Gorvak explained. 'The race just got pretty serious…'

'Don't worry,' said Kip. 'We know Thag's planning to steal the Ark. We accidentally overheard you talking last night. Sorry, but it wasn't on purpose. We've come to suggest joining forces. You and us.'

Gorvak looked stunned. Then he smiled and put a hand on Kip's shoulder.

'Listen, thanks,' Gorvak said. 'I appreciate the offer, I really do, but sometimes being in a group can slow you down a bit. I need to be fast and agile in this race. You've seen for yourself how Thag will stop at nothing.'

'We've got the fifth riddle,' Albert blurted out.

'It's a map,' added Leela.

The look on Gorvak's face showed how deeply he had underestimated the four young friends who stood before him.

'So, are you in?' asked Kip.

Gorvak stayed silent for a moment, thinking things over.

'I think I'd be an idiot to turn you down,' he said eventually.

'There's only one thing,' said Kip. 'If I get voted out of college, you have to find a way to help me on the outside.'

'Why?' asked Gorvak.

'I need something in the Ark … for…' Kip hesitated.

Only Albert knew about his mum. But the team needed to know everything if they were going to be stronger together.

Gorvak raised his eyebrows.

'…my mum,' said Kip finally. 'She's ill.'

'Deal,' said Gorvak. 'I'll come to your room after classes this evening. Oh, and Kip – good luck with the vote.'

Democracy

As the morning wore on, exhaustion climbed deep into every muscle in Kip's body. He started drifting off to sleep in Professor Kvörk's class and Albert had to poke him twice. Then Albert fell asleep and it was Kip's turn to rescue him from a telling-off.

When they got to Q10 at breaktime, Kip was surprised to find Pinky wide awake and waiting. Normally so tidy, she had been throwing seeds through the mesh of her lair.

'What's got into you?' asked Kip.

Pinky leapt frantically from side to side of the lair, tapped her cymbal and scurried in and out of her hammock.

'Too many bananas?' suggested Albert. 'Too many nuts?'

While they were collecting up the seeds, there was a knock at the door and the little flying squirrel froze. Timmi entered and then Leela, the mowl perched on her shoulder. He looked up from delving in her hair, and locked eyes with Pinky.

'Freep,' went the mowl finally.

Pinky vaulted to the topmost platform of her lair, and chittered angrily.

'Bad mowl,' said Leela, tapping the mowl on his beak. 'Pinky's not a snack. You'll have to make friends.'

Kip scooped Pinky out of the lair and held her up to meet the mowl, who ruffled his crown feathers and crept closer along Leela's arm, under her watchful eye. His long, thin orange tongue unrolled and slurped Pinky's forehead.

'Friends, mowl,' Leela reminded him sternly.

The mowl shrugged, lirriped, jumped across to the bunk bed and rolled over, exposing his well-fed belly. Pinky seemed to know it was safe then, and glided out of Kip's hand on to the duvet. She cuddled up to the mowl and began to lick her paws and smooth down his black fur.

'Well that was easy,' Timmi said. 'Now they're in love, let's look at the map!'

But just as Kip reached his hand inside the lair, the bells of the Clock Tower began to ring. Leela and Timmi exchanged a knowing look, and he knew it was calling them all to the vote. He put Pinky in her coconut bed and set off with the others in a solemn mood.

The bells sounded deep and sombre, as if announcing a funeral. And the closer they came to Aristotle's Theatre, the heavier Kip's feet felt. Still, being surrounded by Team Glowflyer gave him a bit of strength. Albert was on his left, and Timmi on his right, and Leela led the way like a fearsome warrior with the mowl on her arm.

When they arrived Kip was directed to the stage, where he had to sit on a scratched wooden chair, just like the ones from his old classroom at Ledhill.

'Be sure to make eye contact with people,' Leela had said. 'Otherwise they'll assume you're hiding something.'

The first few tiers of theatre benches were taken up

by the professors. Behind them were the porters, Chef Garibaldi and the other kitchen staff, Tamara Okpik, Big Obi and the librarians. And behind them were the students. Kip did his best to stare out calmly from the stage, trying to project his thoughts into the crowd and hoping that his face looked innocent.

It was all Thag's fault, he said in his head.

Everyone Kip had begun to look up to looked back at him severely – even Professor Steampunk and Professor Mo.

Thag bounded up on stage as if he were collecting an award, waving at people he recognised. He settled down on a second chair a few metres away from Kip, as the Professor-in-Charge came and stood between them. She looked first at Kip and then at Thag and then addressed the crowd, her words tolling inside Kip's head like the bells of the Clock Tower.

'Democracy. We are all here today because of our right to democracy. When I look out at your faces, I see the greatest scholars of our time. And yet most of you are children. Outside Quicksmiths, you have no say in how the world is run. But here, things are different. Here, you have a voice. Treat it with respect and with responsibility.'

Thag looked across at Kip and grinned. Kip looked away and clenched his teeth so hard he thought they might break.

'We are here today following an incident involving

Pythagoras Grittleshank and Kip Bramley. I will ask Pythagoras and Kip to leave the stage while GENI recalls for you all the facts of the event. You will be asked to decide whether you would have acted the same way, had you been in their shoes. And we shall agree on what steps the college will take next.'

Kip followed his Ballmoth off the stage, in the opposite direction from Thag. It led him to a soundproof cubicle, where he waited for everyone to cast their votes. All he could hear was the sound of his own breathing. In. Out. In. Out. Was he in the college or out?

Sitting on the swivel stool, Kip was reminded of the photo booth in *Undersea Emporium*. But things were so different now. Dread dragged down his bones. Every limb of his body screamed out for sleep. He closed his eyes; at least the squirls were there, near and far, their steady pulse a comfort to him.

I'll be glad when this is over.

Part of him knew that wasn't true. Being here, in this state of uncertainty, there could always be hope. But if the vote went against him...

The Ballmoth appeared to call him back. Thag arrived first and practically skipped in front of Miss Twiss for the results.

'Pythagoras Grittleshank. You are a brilliant and gifted student. You are the descendant of one of our greatest scientists.'

Thag smirked.

'But that is not enough. You must be courteous as well as clever, cooperative as well as capable. Buying votes? Do you really think that's how a democracy should work?'

The smirk melted away.

'And, most importantly, another person could have died due to your recklessness. The students and teachers at Quicksmiths have grown tired of your antisocial behaviour. I'm afraid you are out of luck and we are out of patience. Pack your bags. Quicksmiths is no longer your home.'

Thag lost his composure completely and spewed out a string of swear words. Then he turned on the audience.

'You maggots were quite happy to take my Quickets,' he screeched, spittle flying from his mouth.

Tamara Okpik rose from her seat and sprang up the stairs to the stage. She said something to Thag, too quietly for anyone else to hear, and he suddenly stopped swearing and shouting.

He gave Miss Twiss a long, vengeful stare.

'You'll be sorry,' he said.

As he was escorted by Okpik off the stage, Thag flashed over a last look; a look that said he wanted to make a drinking cup out of Kip's skull.

But that was low on Kip's list of things to worry about right now. He stood facing the Professor-in-

Charge, his back to the audience, feeling thousands of eyes boring into him. His legs felt unsteady, as if the stage might slip away underneath him, just like the Skimmi at Skycrackle Tower. He would be falling again, only this time there would be no one to save him. No one to save his mum.

Please, he thought, over and over. *Please don't send me away.*

'Kip Bramley. You acted foolishly and could have been seriously injured by your actions. But we agree, by a large majority, that you were unfairly provoked. You will have all your Quickets deducted and do community work every weekend from now until the end of term.'

Word by word, it sank in: he'd been given a second chance. The dread in his bones began to melt away.

As the theatre emptied, Leela galloped out of the crowd and pounced. Kip was taken aback by the force of her hug.

'Save some for me!' shouted Timmi, close behind her.

'Stop hug-hogging him,' Penny's voice said.

Soon Kip was at the centre of an enthusiastic girlstorm. He looked around for Albert.

'Help,' he mouthed.

Unhelpfully, Albert made a kissy-kissy face and grinned.

'Come on,' he said eventually, pushing his way

through. 'No-sleep Albert is sh-tar-ving. I need at least three lunches.'

'Sorry you lost all your Quickets,' said Maya, as everyone drifted away.

'That's OK,' Kip said. 'All the Quickets in the world don't matter, as long as I'm still here.'

Chapter Twelve

The Theft

Kip had never imagined he would be wishing away the time at Quicksmiths. But each second was a second closer to the end of the last lesson, and the next chance to look at the map. He was hoping that, with fresh eyes, their newest recruit might work it out straight away.

'Brilliant news about Thag,' said Gorvak, who was waiting for them outside Q10. 'With him out of the way, we can focus on finding the Ark.'

When Pinky saw them enter, she rattled around her lair until Kip opened the door to let her out.

'A flying squirrel?' said Gorvak. 'I did *not* expect that.'

Pinky's chirruping got so noisy Kip couldn't hear his own reply. When he told her off, she scrabbled up the curtain to watch silently from its rail.

In the meantime, Albert was already reaching into the lair for the map.

'Kip, where did you put it?'

'In the scarf, just there,' said Kip, turning his attention to Pinky's hammock.

They both stared in horror.

'What's wrong?' asked Gorvak.

'It's gone,' murmured Albert.

'Knock knock,' said Leela at the door. 'Team Glowflyer assemble!'

'It can't be gone,' said Kip, searching around.

'What? What's gone?' asked Timmi.

'The map,' said Albert.

He ran suddenly around the corner of the room and a desk drawer was opened noisily.

'And so are the Human Remotes,' he shouted.

Plummeting, dissolving, shrivelling. No single word could describe how Kip felt in that moment.

Albert returned and sat on the bunk-bed steps. He punched the wood listlessly.

'We should report him,' he said.

'He's already voted out. What else can anyone do?' said Leela.

She kicked the bookcase and a book fell off. No one did anything.

'Stay here,' said Gorvak, his mouth set in a harsh, straight line. 'He's not left yet. I'll go and talk to him.'

Timmi sat on the lower bunk and put her face in her hands. Kip wanted to smash the window, but instead he sat down and put his arm around her.

'We'll figure something out,' he said.

They waited for an hour, hardly speaking. Albert went to get some sandwiches and fruit from the Buttery but he was the only one who could manage more than a few mouthfuls.

'Come on, got to keep our strength up,' he said.

When Gorvak returned, they all looked up hopefully. But his expression hadn't changed.

'I'm really sorry. He denied everything of course. I watched while GENI scanned him at the gate, before he gave back his Candle. I was sure something would show up, but he doesn't have the map. At least not on him.'

'So is that it?' said Timmi, eyes filling up again.

It was as if all the happiness, all the hard work, all the hope had been sucked out of the room.

'I think we need a break,' said Gorvak. 'No offence, but you all look terrible. I'm going to head to my room. Get an early night. Ladies? Shall I walk you back?'

As soon as they'd left, Kip realised how tired he was. Sadly, he filled Pinky's food and water bowls. And then without brushing his teeth, he climbed up to the top bunk, and gave in to sleep.

Small Animal Ninjaglider

The alarm went off. Kip waved his hand to snooze it

and rolled over. The mattress felt like a soft bog into which he was slowly sinking. Why did everything feel so hollow, so dark? And then he remembered. The map had been stolen, before they'd had a chance to work out the riddle. Even Gorvak didn't have any ideas. The hunt for the Ark was over.

Why didn't I get a Threescan? Kip thought miserably. *It would have taken seconds.*

There was a buzzing sound and, without opening his eyes, Kip waved his hand to snooze the alarm again.

'Not getting up,' he mumbled, and pulled the duvet over his head.

'Kip Braaaam-leeeeeey,' said Albert, in a high-pitched voice. 'It's mee-eeeee. Pink-eeeee.'

The buzzing got louder and something bumped gently against the duvet. When Kip peeled up a corner and looked out, he saw Pinky hovering just in front of him.

'Tah-dah!' said Albert.

Kip looked out properly. Pinky was attached to a harness, hanging from a slim, bird-like drone.

'When I showed her what I was making, she pretty much put on the harness herself,' said Albert.

'A Pinky Drone?' was all Kip could say.

Albert twiddled the control box and Pinky swooped around Kip's head, spreading her arms wide.

'Actually, it's called the Small Animal Ninjaglider.

Pinky's just a test pilot really – I've been building it in Professor Steampunk's workshop, for Gnawmon. Eventually it'll hook up to the WPS.'

Pinky, who was now dangling in front of Kip's face again, reached out a paw and poked him on the nose.

'Nutjobs,' said Kip. 'Both of you.'

'It's still early,' said Albert. 'Let's take her for a flyabout round the garden. And we can try and work out what to do next.'

Kip huddled under the duvet for a second.

Albert's given you a good reason to get up. Don't spoil it.

'Give us the control box then,' he said, kicking back the duvet.

Things only got better from then on. At breakfast, Chef Garibaldi must have seen the miserable expression Kip was trying to hide and dolloped an extra mountain peak of cream and strawberries on to his waffles. As they were finishing up the meal, Gorvak came to find them. He was whistling, and saluted the professors on his way to the table as if nothing had happened.

'I've been thinking about it,' he said, plonking a mug down. 'We should follow Melinda.'

'Who?'

'Thag's girlfriend. I bet he gave her the map. If he can break the Scrambleguard, he might be in touch with her. And if we follow her closely, she'll give them both away.'

'We can do shifts,' said Leela. 'There are five of us. And the mowl.'

'He'll be a good spy,' said Gorvak. 'Let's get him started straight away. And I've got an unlocked Mothball we can use.'

'Unlocked?' said Albert.

'You can link an unlocked Mothball to anyone,' Gorvak replied. 'Technically, we're not supposed to have them. But it can track Melinda's movements and alert us to anything unusual. She'll be sneaky and hard to catch. Thag has spies everywhere too – we should keep whatever we find to ourselves.'

Gorvak programmed the Mothball; the mowl was asked to report back regularly; and then all that was left to do was watch and wait like six hungry hawks.

Sideways Thinking

After breakfast Kip couldn't shake the feeling that someone was staring at him. He looked around uneasily. One person stood rooted to the ground as the crowd flowed around her. If a look could pull someone's guts out and stamp on them, that was exactly the look she gave Kip.

'I know her real name now,' muttered Kip. 'But she'll always be Sharktooth Girl.'

'She's totally got our map,' Albert said through the side of his mouth.

'Two days left,' whispered Kip, not taking his eyes off her. 'If Gorvak's right, she'll lead us straight to the next riddle.'

'It's a good plan,' said Albert, as they made their way to The Hive for Quixology. 'But is it good enough?'

As it turned out, it didn't matter.

'I expect some of you may have been wondering why I have so many of these,' said Professor Mo.

He reached up and wiggled the square glasses on his face. Then he unfolded an orange-tinted pair that was hooked in the v-neck of his shirt and fished out some reading glasses from his top pocket.

'What I'm going to tell you now is confidential,' he said. 'I don't really need them. Not for everyday things anyway.'

The Professor went around the class and handed each person some glasses from a lucky-dip bag. Kip put his on – they were made of stiff cardboard with one red lens and one green lens.

'Are they like X-ray specs?' he asked.

'In a way,' said the Professor. 'You see, Strange Energies often don't like to be looked at. So, at Quicksmiths, we use a technique called *sideways thinking*. And this is an extremely useful method for puzzlers too.

People have all sorts of different styles of sideways thinking. But I find that putting on new pair of glasses helps me to look at a puzzle differently. Every time I change them, my perspective shifts. I'm literally seeing the world through a different lens. And every now and then in sideways corners and crannies I might just find what I'm looking for.'

Kip tried looking sideways through his glasses and saw everyone else was doing the same.

'To learn sideways thinking, you don't need to actually look sideways,' said Professor Mo. 'Although, who knows? It may help. Instruction GENI: may I have a sphere, please?'

A football-sized sphere appeared above the Professor's head.

'I like to imagine that every mystery is a shape: it might be a pyramid, or a cuboid, or a simple sphere. There is a door in the side of it, which is the answer I am seeking. A puzzle might even have several doors and several answers.'

He reached out to touch the sphere but it moved away.

'But here's the problem: you cannot control a mystery; you cannot force an enigma. It doesn't always behave the way you want it to. So, I imagine I am walking around it. *It* stays the same, but *I* am adapting in order to find the door to my answer. When we think sideways, our quixars fire up like a million electric bubbles, our connection to Strange Energy gets stronger. And we often find we already have the answer we need.'

'So, finding a different angle is the key?' asked Kip.

'Exactly,' said Professor Mo.

Something stirred in the ashes of Kip's hope and flexed its wings.

Losing the map was like a dead end, he thought, *and that made it easy to give up. But what if following Sharktooth Girl isn't the only answer. What if there's a doorway in the dead end?*

For the rest of the day, Kip tried to remember what he could about the stolen map. His mind reached out sideways into the corners and crannies of new perspectives. Squirls rose and fell like tides, rolling and churning in his head whenever he closed his eyes. But he couldn't hold on to any of them.

It was only when the night fell that it happened.

As Albert slept, Kip lay in bed with his eyes closed. He was still trying to visualise the map but it was hard to concentrate. Pinky was darting to and fro around his feet. And the squirls kept beckoning, stealing away his attention.

Eventually, when Pinky curled up with a plushie toy, Kip gave in to the squirls. It was easier to let go and just follow their lines – coil within coil, ripple after ripple. Time lost all meaning until he realised with a start that there was a strange sensation – a gentle sizzling – moving around his body like an itch. His eyes were open, not closed. And the squirls had broken free.

It's like they're evolving. Becoming more real.

All the squirls he'd ever drawn twinkled before him, like light on the surface of the sea. And there were new ones he'd never seen before. One of them pulsed to the foreground, stronger and brighter than the others – strands of lingering light like electric blue silk.

The squirl summoned him out of bed and pulled him in a trance towards the door. Pinky leapt across and caught on to the back of his dressing gown, climbing up to tuck herself into his pocket, but he hardly noticed.

Down stairways and along cold corridors he followed the squirl, over dewy lawns and through courtyards, all the way to the Hall of Maps. It was quiet in there, quieter than the space between planets. The colours of the Great Globe had faded into night greys. Around it the squirl flowed like a living atmosphere, lighting up the hall.

'It's coming from inside!' Kip whispered.

And then, everything fell into place. A question bubbled up in him so strongly that it felt like a breath.

'Where is the Study of Secrets?' he said.

The hall echoed with a mechanical wheeze as the moon-splashed continents of the Great Globe slowly turned. When it came to a stop, the outline of Africa cracked and gently swung upwards. A puff of smoke fanned out and wooden stairs descended dramatically from within, spilling out electric blue tendrils.

Kip felt something indescribable – a zero-gravity

moment, in which everything seemed to drift and then resettle.

Pinky chirped and scampered up to his shoulder.

'It was here the whole time, Pinky.'

He climbed the stairs, following the path of the squirl. Around him, the night air was cold and he could see his breath swirling at the border between light and darkness.

The inside of the Great Globe was lit in a soft golden glow that seemed to come from nowhere. All around was an Aladdin's cave of curious contraptions, glittering gadgets and ancient artefacts, but Kip couldn't think of anything except tracing the squirl to its source. Soon he was kneeling at a plain, wooden chest, too plain to be otherwise noticed among all the treasures.

The chest was not locked and there, inside, at the very heart of the squirl, was an ancient book with a metal clasp. Two words glimmered on the cover.

Aeon Light

As Kip picked up the book, the squirl faded. Not daring to imagine what was inside, he clicked open the clasp and began to turn the pages. When he realised what was drawn there, he felt for the floor with his free hand and sat down. Pinky's furry body pressed closer against his neck.

'How is that possible?' he whispered.

The pages were full of squirls.

A loose leaf of paper fell from the notebook. Kip picked it up and began to read, each new sentence like a shot from a stun gun.

To the boy I have seen but not met:

I know your bravery. I know your heartache. I know why you seek the Ark.

You are like me. You see Aeon Light. And as far as I know, we are the only two of our kind.

Aeon Light radiates from the future, shining out from beyond the end of the Universe. It is the strangest of all the Strange Energies.

Even the greatest among us are too busy looking backwards. Ah! If only they knew. To see Aeon Light is to see so many hidden things.

We are at the shore, you and I. The sand on which we stand is the past. The waves rolling in are the future. And the shoreline is the present, the Inbetween, where you step into the swirling foam, where anything is possible. Here, where the surf of each moment breaks, you and I can see bright things. These things reflect Aeon Light because they express enormous potential, the possibility to change many paths and many worlds.

Listen to the light. This is just the beginning. Things will never be the same again.

The Sixth Riddle

Kip's bare feet thumped dully as he ran down the dark corridors, over cold wet grass and up the stairs to Q10, holding Pinky carefully against his chest.

'Albert. Albert. Albert. Albert. Albert. Albert. ALBERT!'

'Hmmph,' said Albert.

'We don't need the map – Pinky and I found the answer!'

Albert sat up so suddenly that he banged his head on the wood of the bunk bed.

'Ow!' he said. 'What?'

'Come on,' said Kip, grabbing his slippers. 'I'll show you.'

On the way there, he tried to explain what had happened.

'I followed a squirl,' the words tumbled out. 'I was trying to see sideways, you know, and then it just sort of appeared. With my eyes open. And then I realised the answer to the riddle. And there's a letter, and a notebook. Eartha's notebook. It's … it's full of squirls.'

'Slowwww down,' said Albert. 'Where did you find this stuff?'

'We're here,' said Kip. 'The Hall of Maps.'

For the second time that night, he asked the question that had remained unspoken for hundreds of years. The words felt as though they belonged to him now.

In the light of the moon, Albert's pupils grew as big as pennies. His eyebrows went up so high it looked as if they might launch off his face and flap away in astonishment.

'Un. Be. Liev. Able!' he whispered.

Kip led Albert inside the Great Globe, taking the steps two at a time, with Pinky keeping watch from a dressing-gown pocket. Africa closed behind them with a gentle hiss and Kip allowed his eyes to roam, slowly this time, taking in all the artefacts.

'The Study of Secrets?' said Albert. 'It's Eartha's secret study!'

'Look – there's the letter and the notebook,' said Kip, pointing to the wooden chest.

Albert leafed through the drawings and read the letter. There was a new kind of light in his eyes when he finally looked up.

'You're the one, aren't you? *You're* the one Eartha talked about!'

'I dunno,' was all Kip could say. 'We've got this far together. Leela and Timmi helped us.'

'Every truthseer needs his friends,' said Albert.

'Someone else can be the truthseer,' said Kip. 'I just want to find the Ark so I can help my mum.'

Albert closed the lid of the chest and sat down on top of it.

'If Eartha's looked in the Futurescope and she wrote you this letter, she must know that we win, right?'

'I don't think the future is fixed like that,' Kip said. 'What did Eartha say? "A window of possibility." Finding the Ark is just one possible path. But she's probably done her best to help us.'

He ran his fingers over a chess set made of precious stones.

'Have you noticed the air's really fresh,' Albert said, inhaling deeply. 'And there's no dust. But there wasn't any on the clockwork soldiers either.'

Kip only half heard him. The secret study, squirls, Aeon Light: it was a lot to take in. Only a short time ago he had never heard the name Eartha Quicksmith, and now here he was, inside the great woman's refuge.

He found that Eartha's chair was exceedingly comfortable as he sat down at her desk. Taking up one corner of the workspace was a large model globe with hand-sized blue continents and green seas and he gave it a spin. Pinky's head swayed as she watched it, hypnotised. Next to them, Albert picked up a brilliant-purple quill pen from the desk clutter and tried to write on his arm.

'It would take a year to tidy this up,' Kip said, 'it looks just like *yours*.'

'Messy desk, tidy mind,' retorted Albert. 'But you do kind of have a point. It won't be easy to find the sixth riddle. I mean, it could be any one of these mad things.'

Pinky shook herself and dived across to an embroidered bench. From there she parkoured to the top of a bookcase and began to shimmy up a thick copper cable that curved along the wall towards the centre of the domed ceiling.

Kip leaned back in the chair and let his gaze follow her progress upwards. He squinted and smiled.

'Actually, it might be easier than you think, Albert.'

There, in the very centre of the ceiling, was painted the sixth riddle.

VI

Within a sphere within a sphere

Albert held up a high-five for Kip and grin-yawned.

'Don't get me wrong,' he said. 'I'm way more excited than I look. Even more excited than when we found the first five riddles, if that's possible. But can you hear that? That's my bed ringing on the Comfyphone. It misses me. And it has loads more sleep waiting. Buckets of sleep. Swimming pools of sleep. Oceans.'

Once Albert said that, Kip felt an overwhelming urge to get back to his own cosy bunk.

'The Great Globe isn't going anywhere,' he said, calling Pinky back down. 'Let's come back tomorrow with the others. With five of us we should be able to work much faster.'

'This is where we came in, right?' said Albert, heading over to the wall.

'Right,' said Kip, close behind. 'There's a door handle on this side.'

Albert had already grasped it. Africa's outline lifted with a hiss and the wooden steps extended downwards.

Ghost Town

Excitement lifted Kip clear out of bed the next morning, flooding into his chest with his first waking breath. Albert was already up, buzzing around the room.

'I was just about to wake you,' he said. 'Miss Twiss has cancelled lessons today. So everyone can work on the riddles.'

He pointed out of the window.

'There's a load of Skimmies around the Clock Tower. I think people are catching up. You get dressed and I'll send a message to the others to meet us at the Great Globe.'

The Buttery was almost empty. They shovelled down their breakfasts in record time and then it was just a short run to Atlas House.

'It's like a ghost town in here,' said Kip.

'Good,' said Albert. 'Makes sneaking around much easier.'

Leela and Timmi were already waiting at the foot

of the double staircase in the Hall of Maps. The mowl was pluck-plucking idly at the tufty red carpet like a cat with oversized claws.

'Where's Pinky?' asked Timmi.

'Sleeping beauty,' Kip replied. 'She wouldn't come out of her coconut today.'

'I have a question,' said Leela, looking up at the Great Globe. 'If Turkey and Hungary are countries, where are Chicken and Thirsty?'

'You won't care in a second,' said Albert. 'We're going to show you something that will make your brain jump out of your eyes to see for itself.'

'My brain is going to strangle you in a second if you don't tell us what's going on,' said Leela.

'No Gorvak?' asked Kip, looking around.

'I don't know, should we wait?' said Albert.

'No time,' said Kip. 'Go on. It's your turn.'

Albert double-checked the hall was empty and cleared his throat.

'Where is The Study of Secrets?'

Leela and Timmi watched in amazement as the continent of Africa lifted up and the steps came down.

'No ... mowling ... way!' said Leela.

She strode fearlessly up the steps, followed closely by the others, and the door hissed shut behind them. Once inside, Kip felt his wonder burst its boundaries again as he gazed around at the thousands of trinkets in Eartha's treasure trove.

Timmi stopped to admire a jewelled birdcage, and Leela ran her fingers over the keys of a glass piano.

'Look at all these beautiful things,' murmured Timmi. 'Do you think Eartha collected them on her travels?'

The mowl went crazy, flitting around from one shiny thing to another. He stopped at a silver bonsai tree that had sparkling stars and a single crescent moon dangling from its branches. One by one, he tapped them, making them dance about on the ends of their chains.

'Don't break anything, mowl!' said Leela.

'Where do we even begin?' Timmi asked.

The mowl rolled over on his back under the tree and stared up at the dancing stars.

'He has the right idea,' said Albert.

'It's in the tree? Seriously?'

'Think bigger.'

Leela's eyes lifted to the ceiling.

'You found it already!' she protested. 'Without us?'

'Last night,' said Albert. 'Pinky found it actually.'

'"Within a sphere within a sphere",' said Timmi. 'Could be about atoms? Subatomic particles?'

'Or a snowglobe?' suggested Kip.

'A frog's egg? A pearl? An onion?' Albert added.

'Well, what are we waiting for then?' said Leela. 'Albert does the bookcase, Timmi and I will check out those cabinets and wooden chests, and Kip takes the desk.'

The mowl wurbled.

'Mowl, you be in charge of spider-hunting.'

Kip sat down in Eartha's chair and breathed in deeply through his nose. There was a pleasant smell of leather, moss and autumn. He had a vague sense of Albert reading out book titles, and the mowl scrabbling around under a table.

Eartha's desk was an obstacle course of curiosities: rolled-up astronomical charts; a stone wheel covered in strange letters; an abacus made from shells; painted masks. But before Kip could look at anything more closely, a squirl seized his attention. It was a strange, twisted ripple that seemed to emerge from a large box with a slanted lid. Kip pushed and pulled but the lid of the box remained closed. There was no keyhole, nor a latch, only the squirl pulsing over and over. Following an irresistible impulse, he traced the shape of it on the sloping wood.

Creeeeeak. Perhaps it was just the pressure of his finger – or somehow the pattern of the squirl – that unlocked the lid, causing it to open a centimetre. Kip leaned forward excitedly and pulled it up. Inside, a wooden framework held dozens of metal cylinders of varying sizes – the smallest ones were like thimbles and the largest was nearly as big as an ostrich egg. They had engravings but Kip couldn't read any of

them, because the squirl was too dazzling now –
pulsating around a small, squat cylinder made of
bluish metal.

If squirls are Aeon Light, thought Kip, *and if important
things reflect Aeon Light, then this must be important.*

The rippling light faded as he picked up the
cylinder. It fitted neatly in the palm of his hand and,
with the squirl gone, he could read the engraving on
its side.

Grandfather Clock

Danger

Handle with care

Kip knew what a Grandfather Clock was and this
wasn't anything like one. A hooked clasp held a
hinged lid in place but, looking at the engraving
again, Kip decided not to open it. Instead, he held it
up to one ear and listened for ticking. There was
none.

Whatever it is, Albert will love this.

A quick look around the room revealed that
everyone else was completely absorbed in searching
for the next clue.

*I should be looking for the riddle too. I'll show them
all later.*

Taking the advice of the engraving, he put Eartha's
strange Grandfather Clock gently into his pocket.

WITHIN A SPHERE
WITHIN A SPHERE

Then, still leaning forward on the desk, he looked past the open box and spun the model globe gently, watching its raised light-blue continents blur into the deep-green seas.

Globe, he thought. *Little. Big. Sphere.*

'Hey guys…' he said.

Everyone followed Kip's gaze to the desk globe, as it gradually began to slow.

'A sphere within a sphere!' shouted Leela.

They gathered around and Albert gave the globe a tentative tap.

'It's hollow.'

'Where is the seventh riddle?' asked Timmi.

The globe ignored her.

'Maybe it doesn't open,' said Albert. 'What if *we* have to get inside it, like we did in the portrait? Or…'

His eyes widened, and he started polishing a bit of ocean with his sleeve.

'Why are you cleaning it?' asked Timmi. 'It's not dirty.'

'That's how we found the hidden room in the Clock Tower,' Kip explained. 'The bricks turned to glass.'

'Mmmmm. I don't think it's working,' said Leela.

Refusing to admit defeat, Albert began to polish even harder. But then he froze as a rolling creak slowly grew and shuddered around them like the groans of a wooden sailboat in a storm.

'The Great Globe moved!' Timmi yelped.

'Did I do that?' said Albert, stepping back hastily from the desk globe. 'Is the little one connected to the big one?'

'No,' whispered Kip. 'Someone must be outside, asking questions.'

'Won't we fall over when it turns?' whispered Leela. 'Or would Eartha have thought of that?'

'I think we'll be OK,' Timmi whispered back. 'There must be something keeping the inside upright. Some sort of gyroscope. Otherwise everything would be broken.'

'It might be Gorvak outside?' whispered Leela.

'But he doesn't know how to get in,' Kip muttered.

'It could be Sharktooth Girl,' hissed Albert, eyes fixed on the entrance. 'She does have the map.'

The knuckles of Kip's fingers whitened as he gripped the desk tightly, hoping the door wouldn't open.

Chapter Thirteen

The Seventh Riddle

The creaking of the Great Globe grew slower and slower, quieter and quieter, as though it were a sailboat drifting into calmer waters.

'I think we're OK,' whispered Albert. 'The door isn't opening.'

'Whoever was outside asked the wrong question,' Kip whispered back.

'That was close,' said Timmi. 'We'd better hurry up before they come back with the right question.'

'Here's a question,' said Leela thoughtfully. 'Would you rather have chopsticks instead of hands or mousetraps instead of feet?'

Timmi rolled her eyes at Leela and put her hands around the desk globe as though it were an oversized crystal ball.

'What are you hiding?'

It squatted stubbornly, refusing to give up its secret.

'Africa is the way into the big globe, right?' said Albert. 'So, we should start there on the little one.'

'But it doesn't have an Africa,' said Kip. 'Look, the continents aren't shaped like ours.'

'Weird,' said Albert.

'They each have a sort of belly button,' said Timmi. 'Right in the middle.'

Kip put his finger in one of the dimples and felt the light-blue continent shift slightly. Giving it a cautious push, he felt it move a bit more.

'If you press down, you can slide the land across the top of the ocean,' he said.

'What if…' Timmi started.

'… the continents fit together?' finished Leela.

'Boom!' said Albert.

'That ziggy-outy bit matches this zaggy-inny bit,' said Leela.

'And there's an island that would fit into this coastline,' Timmi added.

Kip steered his jagged piece of land towards a corresponding bay in the polar cap. There was a slight magnetic pull as a peninsula on one piece approached a deep inlet on the other, and then a soft, satisfying click as they came together.

As each continent docked snugly into place the supercontinent turned a darker blue. When they were finished, the single landmass formed a familiar shape.

'Eartha's buttercup!' said Leela.

With a *clunk* the dark-blue buttercup sank about a centimetre into the globe's crust. A deep quake travelled around the planet's circumference and one hemisphere swung open, exposing the inside of the hollow sphere.

'It's her,' said Kip.

A miniature Eartha Quicksmith was sitting inside a miniature study at a miniature desk. There was even a miniature globe on *that* desk.

'Do you think there's another study inside the ittle-bittle globe?' said Timmi in awe. 'A sphere within a sphere within a sphere?'

'There's probably an infinity of spheres,' said Leela.

'Look what she's holding,' Kip said quietly.

It was a miniature version of the red-and-gold book Eartha had been reading in the portrait. The double spread of pages was about the width of a Mothball's wingspan, and when Kip squinted it was just possible to make out some tiny words.

VII

Find the Sea of Silence

Kip glanced up at his three friends, and knew from their faces that they were feeling exactly what he felt: this supercharged thrill, this immense satisfaction, this shared hope. But there was no time to wallow in it.

'Another question for the Great Globe?' asked Leela.

'Can't be that easy,' said Albert.

'Well, we're already here,' said Leela. 'Won't take a minute.'

She bounced to the exit but stopped suddenly.

'What is it?' said Timmi.

'It's stuck,' Leela groaned, rattling the door handle in a panic. 'We're trapped! Just like the Clock Tower.'

'It opened before no problem,' said Albert. 'But I don't remember that red light.'

'Me neither,' agreed Kip.

'It's a *secret* study, right?' said Timmi thoughtfully. 'So Eartha wouldn't want anyone to see her leave. Maybe it lights up when there's somebody in the Hall of Maps?'

Sure enough, when the red light disappeared not long afterwards, the way out was unlocked and they piled outside.

'Where is the Sea of Silence?' Leela roared, before anyone else had a chance.

But the Great Globe didn't budge an inch.

'Any other amazing ideas?' she said.

'Aren't there places on the Moon called seas?' Timmi asked.

'Good thinking, but I'm pretty sure there's no Sea of Silence,' said Albert. 'Let's go back inside? If Eartha's reading a book, maybe we should take a closer look at that bookcase.'

In the middle of the study, the mowl had begun

collecting a pile of mowl treasure – jade beetles, lenses, geodes, medallions.

'At least you're quiet, I suppose,' said Leela. 'Fine, but everything stays in here!'

The mowl ignored her and hugged a silver goblet. They stepped around him and stood in front of Eartha's bookcase. It was tall, with twelve shelves, and was curved to fit the wall.

'You start from that end,' Albert said, 'and we'll start from here. We'll worry about the top shelves later.'

'Keep an eye open for anything that has a red-and-gold cover,' said Kip.

As they checked along the book spines, the mowl flew to the top of the bookcase to watch, parading up and down and wurbling happily. Kip knelt down to see the bottom shelf better. The titles were exactly the sort of thing he expected: *Talking with the Stones. Painting with Skycrackle. Timestitches Volume 6: Zigzags and Slips. The Galapagos Islands in the Year 500,000…*

'THERE!' shouted Albert.

He had pounced on a book bound with black leather, and was pulling it off the shelf. Large silver letters the length of a little finger spelt out the title along its spine.

SILENCE

'What's inside?' asked Leela, almost grabbing the book from him in her eagerness.

'It looks like a science textbook,' said Albert, flipping through. 'Maybe we search for the word "sea"?'

'But then we'll have to read the whole thing,' Timmi said. 'Look how thick it is. It'd take days.'

'We don't have days,' said Kip.

Albert's stomach growled so loudly it drowned out Leela's reply. She gave it a withering look.

'Stop whispering, Albert's stomach,' she said. 'I can't hear you.'

'Sorry,' he mumbled. 'I can't think properly on an empty stomach.'

Timmi checked her watch.

'It's already lunchtime,' she announced.

'Albert's stomach is right,' said Kip. 'We don't know how long we'll be here. Let's break really quickly to eat.'

They left the Book of Silence on Eartha's desk and headed out of the Great Globe.

'Mowl!' Leela called, lagging behind. And then louder: 'HEEL!'

'Leela, don't keep the door open,' said Albert. 'The study's a secret, remember?'

'The mowl's up to mowlfoolery,' she grumbled.

Kip weighed up the risks.

'We can't hang around,' he said. 'Just leave him in there. Mowl: don't break anything. Or eat anything. Unless it's a spider.'

The Watcher

As they came to Confucius Courtyard they saw Sharktooth Girl sitting up on a branch of the old oak, watching them with death-ray eyes.

'What's she doing here?' groaned Albert.

She spat down at them forcefully, missing by a few centimetres.

'Just ignore her,' Kip muttered. 'There's no time.'

They walked as fast as they could away from her. A storm was building and the world was bathed in a yellowish twilight, even though it was early afternoon. Clouds in the distance sagged with rain.

'Let's find out where Gorvak is,' Kip said. 'Maybe he didn't get Albert's message.'

Leela stopped at a fork in the pathway.

'We want to grab our Skimmies,' she said. 'Meet back at the GG?

'I'm going for a jumper,' said Albert. 'It's freezing in that study.'

Kip felt in his pocket and found the cold, metal edge of the Grandfather Clock cylinder.

'Got something to show you,' he said. 'Remind me when we get back to the Great Globe. I'll look for Gorvak. Everyone power up. Bring anything that might be useful, but be quick.'

They parted ways and Kip looked over his shoulder to check that Sharktooth Girl hadn't followed him.

'Ballmoth,' he said. 'Take me to Gorvak G. Gorvak.'

The Ballmoth appeared but didn't move. Instead, GENI spoke.

'Gorvak is not at Quicksmiths, Kip. He has been called away to a family emergency.'

Kip frowned. Family emergency. That seemed like too much of a coincidence. He hated to think what Thag might have done to lure Gorvak out of the way.

At the Buttery he grabbed a packed lunch and chewed it fiercely as he walked back across Clock Tower Courtyard to Atlas House. Looking down at his feet stepping rhythmically one in front of the other, Kip wondered how he was going to get in touch with Gorvak.

And then he sensed that unmistakable feeling.

Someone's watching me.

When he raised his eyes from the ground, they settled immediately on a staring face looking out from an arch of brickwork in the wall, not five metres away. A gargoyle. But there was something terribly wrong about it. Kip's legs stopped walking. The brickwork seemed to be moving, the face was warping, and then something came *through* the stone.

This close up, Scaleface's features were clearer. That terrifying large eye. As inescapable as a black hole. The other, smaller eye was bright: too bright. A white dwarf.

'Get away from me,' Kip shouted.

Two praying mantis arms reached out towards him.

Kip dropped his lunch and retreated, unable to unlock his eyes. But the stare was broken as something heavy meteored into the ground before him with an alarming thud. It felt like he was being ambushed from all sides. Kip gaped down in disbelief.

Thag's Plasma Slug?

Bits of it had splattered across the grass, which was starting to wilt. Some feelers sticking up from the remains of its squashed body hissed out slime-gas. Luckily none had touched Kip. He glanced up for a second. Far above, higher than the rooftops, he glimpsed the base of a Skimmi.

His eyes flicked back down to find Scaleface sliding around the archway. Its mouth opened, but only a dry rasp escaped. And somehow, although the creature didn't seem to have any fingers, it beckoned.

Kip's body finally obeyed his brain and he turned and ran as fast as he could, heading for cover behind the Clock Tower. He risked a look back as he turned a corner but, in that moment, he collided with someone. It knocked the wind out of him and he buckled over. Before he could straighten up, he heard his name, and he knew the voice.

'Are you all right?' asked Bagsworth.

Kip wheezed, still unable to speak. He looked back again, but Scaleface was gone.

'I saw it too,' said Bagworth worriedly. 'This means the Prowlers are back. That's troubling. Very troubling indeed. You're coming with me to Okpik's office.'

Prowlers? Kip thought.

'You know what that thing is?' he asked, still stunned.

'All I know is that you see Prowlers lurking around when bad things are about to happen,' said Bagsworth.

'As far as I'm aware, they've been turning up for about a year now. But the professors have no idea what they are. Or what they want. Now you know as much as I do.'

Kip nodded, but stayed put when Bagsworth headed in the direction of the security office.

'Come on,' said Bagsworth. 'We must report this.'

Kip bit his lip.

'Can you keep a secret?' he said. 'We're close, really close, to finding the Ark. But if we don't get there today, we'll lose the chance forever. And someone's depending on me.'

Unplanned and unrehearsed, the sad story of Rose and Suzanna Bramley bubbled up like the effervescence of a deep-sea vent. And then the story of how Team Glowflyer had reached the seventh riddle. At the end, when Kip was empty of words, he heaved out a big sigh.

'If I promise to come with you and report Scaleface … the Prowler later, will you help me with something now?'

Bagsworth tapped his pipe on the side of his Voler Hat.

'What do you have in mind?' he said.

'Just in case…' said Kip, and a plan spilled out.

It didn't take long, and Bagsworth nodded in all the right places.

'There's only one thing you need to remember,' said Kip, finally. 'It's a question. It's THE question: where is the Study of Secrets?'

Bagsworth gave Kip the kind of look only his dad had ever given him before.

'Be careful,' he said.

Albert, Timmi and Leela were sitting at the foot of the Great Globe. When they saw Kip coming, they ran to greet him with urgent whispers.

'Where were you?'

'What happened?'

'I ran into Bagsworth … tell you later … no time to explain now. We have to keep going.'

Skulls and Pirates

Inside the study they found the mowl roosting on the back of Eartha's chair, scratching under his wing. When he saw them, he did his flappy dance and showered them with excited wurbling.

'Oh mowl, we missed you too,' said Leela.

The mowl spread his wings and ruffled his head

crest and presented Leela with something small and shiny.

'You little magpie,' said Leela. 'What's that?'

'Looks like a crescent moon,' said Timmi.

As Leela held it up to see better, the thin horns of the silver crescent caught the light.

'That's very nice, mowl,' she said.

But when she tried to put it back with his treasure hoard, the mowl pecked and hissed and pulled at her sleeve with his little hands. Before she could react, he had grabbed back the crescent and flown to the top of the bookcase.

'Mowl!' said Leela. 'Naughty!'

'Hang on!' said Albert. 'Is he pointing at the Book of Silence?'

'What is it mowl?' said Kip. 'What are you trying to tell us?'

The mowl swooped back to Eartha's desk. A small, brown finger jabbed at the spine of the book.

'He's pointing at the letter C,' said Timmi.

They stared as the mowl gave the crescent back to Leela. It was identical to the C of Silence.

'You utter, utter genius!' said Albert.

'How could I have doubted you?' asked Leela, kissing the top of the mowl's head.

'Yay, mowl!' Timmi sang.

'I had no idea he was so clever,' said Kip.

The mowl lirriped and puffled up with pride.

'Oh riddle number eight,' called Leela, 'come out, come out, wherever you are.'

As she clicked the silver C into place on the black leather, Kip felt the floor of the study shake slightly under his feet.

'Watch out!' shouted Timmi, pulling Albert back.

Just in front of them, a square section of floor about the size of a Skimmi was beginning to lift. At first, Kip thought it was a platform but, as it kept on rising, he realised it was a large wooden cube. It levitated completely out of the floor and hovered at about chest height, while the gap left behind in the floorboards sealed itself up.

Before their eyes the cube dissolved into dust. Too amazed to speak, they simply watched as this cloud began to whirl like a swarm of tiny insects. Gradually, the dust came back together and solidified again into a giant, floating skull.

The mowl ch-charked.

Attached to the bottom of the skull, in a crossbone arrangement, were a sand timer and a glass tube. The tube had three compartments, each containing a separate fluid – oily yellow, bright red and putrid green.

'I'd say something happens if those liquids mix together,' Albert said. 'Something not good.'

'Poison gas?' asked Leela. 'Or an explosive?'

'The clockwork soldiers and now this,' said Timmi. 'Who do you think Eartha set these traps for?'

'Doesn't matter. We still have to get past them to reach the Ark,' Leela said, picking at a fingernail.

Kip stared into the skull's hollow eye sockets.

'We have to trust ourselves. We don't know what Eartha saw in her Futurescope or why she set these traps. Maybe it was to keep Scaleface away. Or Thag. But don't forget we're the good guys.'

'And we've got this far together,' said Albert, nodding.

Almost as soon as he'd spoken, the timer flipped to a vertical position. Sand started dribbling through its bottleneck and flame-red words glowed on the skull's forehead.

VIII

I have a radius but I can be many shapes

I have a tail but can't wag it

I have a collar but no shirt

I have a cap but not on my head

And something about me is funny

'A circle has a radius,' Timmi said. 'But a circle's a circle. How can it be many shapes? That just doesn't make sense.'

'Let's move to the next line,' said Leela.

'Tail and collar,' Albert blurted out. 'A dog! But why wouldn't a dog wag its tail?'

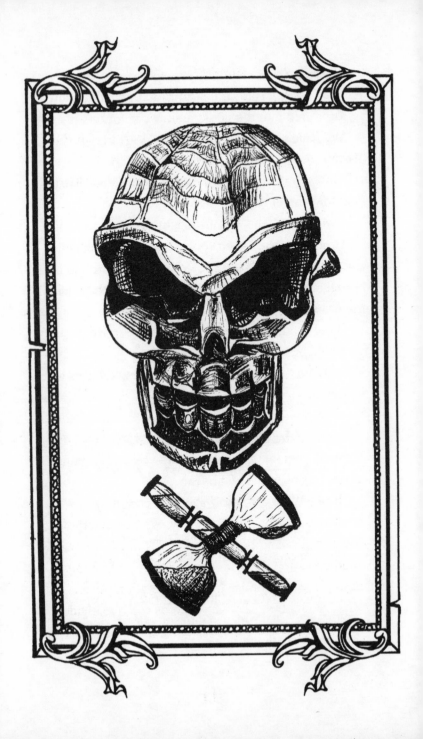

'A sad dog?' said Timmi.

'That doesn't sound like an Eartha answer,' said Leela.

'And it doesn't explain the radius,' agreed Kip. 'Or the cap.'

'How about jesters? They have caps,' said Albert. 'And they're funny.'

'A sad dog jester?' Timmi suggested.

'That can't be it,' said Leela. 'Keep trying while I look for clues.'

She paced around the skull and stopped on its left side.

'There's a kind of funnel here,' she said, 'where its ear would be.'

Before anyone could stop her, Leela put her lips to the funnel and said 'Hello?'

There was an ominous click and one of the partitions in the glass tube broke. The oily yellow and bright red liquids mingled to form an evil-looking sludge. Leela squealed with fear.

'Oh no! What did I do?' she wailed. 'I'm sorry – I got all excited – had a hunch it would do something – I was just seeing how it worked – I didn't know it would break the thingy – stupid skull – stupid me – I'm so sorry – I promise I won't do anything else…'

'It's OK. It's OK,' said Kip. 'There's still one divider left in the tube. Everyone stay calm until we're totally sure of our answer.'

Kip had never seen Leela look so angry, but he knew she wasn't angry with him. She took two steps back from the skull and stared at it furiously. Its blank grin didn't change.

'Does anyone want to leave?' Kip said. 'It's not too late.'

'Never!' said Albert, and Leela and Timmi both nodded.

'Halfway down,' said Kip, looking at the sand in the timer. 'Come on, think.'

Albert started tapping on his forehead with his knuckles as if he were trying to knock the answer out. It made a dull, thumping rhythm.

'Albert,' said Timmi. 'Your skull is really thick. And loud. And annoying.'

'My skull does have feelings you know.'

'Actually, maybe you're on to something,' replied Timmi. 'What if the skull itself is a clue?'

'Go on,' said Kip.

'Well, a skull is a type of bone...'

'Technically, yes,' said Albert.

'... and isn't there a radius bone in your leg?'

'Arm, I think,' said Leela.

'Right,' Timmi said. 'And isn't that bit at the bottom of your spine your tailbone?'

'Ooo! Ooo! Collar bone!' shouted Albert.

'Cap? *Cap*?' said Kip, mentally running through the bones in his body. 'Kneecap!'

314

'And funny bone!' said Timmi. 'That has to be it!'

She stepped up to the skull's funnel-ear, looked at the others for approval, and quietly uttered her answer: 'skeleton'.

There was a click and Leela swallowed another squeal as the sand timer slowly began to move back to its crossbone position.

'So is that it?' she gasped. 'Were you right?'

'I think so!' said Timmi, hugging Leela, and then Albert and Kip.

Like the cube before it, the skull dissolved into dust that began to spin around in a stormy blur. Little by little, this wild tornado slowed again and reformed into a new shape: a galleon.

The polished wood of the hull was almost black. On its deck were several treasure chests, spilling out their contents. At the helm was a ship's wheel and a jewelled compass edged with gold, ruby, emerald, diamond and sapphire.

Leela cradled the mowl tightly in one arm and stroked his feathers.

'No touching the shinies,' she said.

Masts began to sprout from the galleon's deck, and sails unfurled. From the very tallest mast, a pirate flag rolled down. Under its skull-and-crossbones emblem, sewn in bone-white thread on the black silk, was the ninth riddle.

IX

Set a course for Greed

As they watched, cannons thrust out from the galleon's sides. Albert took a step to his right and one of the cannons swivelled to keep him in its sights.

'Oh goody,' he muttered.

In the place of a figurehead on the ship's bow was another sand timer. It flipped around and the sand began to dribble.

'Here we go!' said Timmi. 'It has nine sails. And this is the ninth riddle. Maybe that means something?'

'Might do,' said Kip. 'Or "setting a course" could be something to do with steering. There's a wheel and a compass.'

'And there's a rudder at the back,' said Leela, keeping her distance.

'But how do you set a course for greed?' asked Albert. 'It's not a place.'

'Neither was the Sea of Silence,' said Timmi.

'Well, I'm stumped,' Albert said. 'Who votes we start with the sails?'

'Me,' said Timmi.

'What about the wheel?'

Kip and Albert raised their hands.

'That settles it.'

Albert leaned over the top of the deck.

'Keep your eyes peeled for anything,' he said, nudging the ship's wheel gently.

'Don't think that did much,' said Kip. 'Try again.'

Albert gave the wheel a forceful turn.

'Stop!' shouted Timmi, grabbing Albert's elbow and making him jerk his hand back.

'What?' he spluttered.

Timmi pointed to the sand timer.

'It sped up.'

As Kip watched the pouring grains, he realised his heart was beating fast, so fast it felt like it was trying to batter down his ribs. He took a few slow breaths and closed his eyes. A squirl immediately slipped into view, calming him down.

Timmi sucked air through her teeth sharply and Kip opened his eyes to see Albert was leaning over the deck again.

'Geez,' said Albert. 'I'm not stupid. I'm not touching anything, just looking.'

Leela muttered the riddle over and over, until it began to sound meaningless.

'Greed, greed, greed, greed,' she chanted. 'Pirates are greedy for treasure, aren't they? And there are three treasure chests.'

'What about the jewels on the compass?' said Albert. 'You would need compass directions to set a course...'

Everyone leaned in as close as they could without touching anything.

'A sapphire, an emerald, a ruby, and a diamond,' said Kip. 'And I suppose that's a nugget of gold?'

'That's five. And there are five letters in *greed*,' said Albert. 'Gold-Ruby-Emerald-Emerald-Diamond?'

'You're a diamond, Albert!' shrieked Leela.

'But we would need two emeralds,' Timmi said. 'There's only one. And what about the sapphire?'

Kip eyed the river of grains slipping away in the sand timer.

'Do what you can, Albert,' he said. 'It's our best guess. Now!'

With a steady finger, Albert touched the blue sapphire. It turned into a ruby. With another light tap, it became an emerald.

'They all change colour,' he said, trying the other gemstones. 'All except for the gold one.'

'Start from there,' said Kip. 'That's the first letter of greed.'

As the last few grains of sand were trickling out of the timer, Albert finished transforming the gemstones to spell out the answer. No one moved, or spoke, or breathed, until the cannons began to retreat inside the pirate ship with mechanical clicks and clanks.

'He's done it,' yelled Leela. 'I think I love you, Albert!'

Albert's face flushed a darker colour.

'In a mowly way,' added Leela hastily.

The pirate galleon began to spin as if it were caught in a ghostly whirlpool, and dissolved back into dust.

'You know, we're really good at this,' said Albert.

'Don't jinx it now,' Timmi murmured. 'Last one.'

The dust solidified. Before them floated a wooden cube, smaller than the first, and with one other difference: a crooked crank handle on the side.

Kip felt about ready to explode, like a shaken-up soda can; but he couldn't let himself relax yet.

'Are we ready?' he asked. 'The tenth riddle.'

The four friends looked at each other: expectant, focused, exhilarated.

'Do it,' replied Albert. 'We're ready. We have to be.'

Kip took a deep breath and turned the crank. The lid of the box sprang back and *Twinkle Twinkle Little Star* started playing. When he let go of the crank the music carried on.

'That's not creepy at all,' said Albert.

'At least it's not skully,' said Leela.

A red glass rod floated eerily out of the music box, followed by six more of different colours. Each one was twice as tall as the mowl. The rods hung in the air at about eye level, like a neat row of rainbow icicles.

'What do *they* do?' asked Timmi.

'Any clues inside the box?' Kip said.

'Yes!'

Leela reached in and picked up a small wooden hammer.

'And look!' said Timmi. 'There's the riddle on the inside of the box lid.'

The Music Box

X

Play me in time

'I've got it!' said Leela, her eyes shining. 'The glass rods are like a glockenspiel.'

'But there's no sand timer,' said Timmi, 'so how do we know when our time runs out?'

'And what do we play?' asked Albert.

'I guess *Twinkle Twinkle Little Star*, right?' said Leela.

'You do it,' said Timmi. 'You're the musician.'

Leela turned to the eerie glockenspiel, holding the hammer tightly.

'I'll do my best,' she said, 'but there are seven rods and I only need six different notes to play *Twinkle Twinkle Little Star*. One note's spare. Until I play them all, I won't know which one.'

'Whatever you do, it will be better than any of us,' said Kip.

Leela put down the mowl and began to play. Tinkling notes rang out from the hollow glass rods,

sounding over the soft melody that still came from the music box. But there was no sound when she struck the seventh rod – the red one. Instead, it began to glow and a single red bubble sailed out of the top.

'Pretty,' said Timmi.

'Not so fast,' said Leela. 'Isn't that a … skull?'

A bitter smell flooded the study. The room echoed with the foulest sound Kip had ever heard. It vibrated in his gut, making him clutch at his stomach.

Skull-shaped notes puffed out like red smoke clouds from a hellish chimney and floated up to collect under the ceiling. The mowl hissed at them and made a sound like the screeching of brakes.

'Don't touch the red one!' yelled Timmi. 'It's rotten.'

'I won't *now*,' Leela snapped back.

In the background the music box went on playing *Twinkle Twinkle Little Star* softly on repeat. It began to annoy Kip. And over it the two girls squabbled, louder and louder.

'Leela! Stop whatever you're doing!'

'I can't stop doing nothing!'

'Yes, you can. Try playing something else!'

'I wish that stupid tune would stop. It's distracting me.'

'Oh, stop whining!' barked Albert.

'YOU stop whining,' screamed Timmi, turning on him.

Kip tried to block it out. This wasn't normal, this wasn't natural, this volcanic anger he was feeling.

323

'STOP!' he shouted. 'Stop.'

The others broke off their argument mid-word and swivelled to look at him.

'Didn't Eartha say that to solve the hardest riddles we would need to know ourselves? Well, this isn't us. It's that sound, that *red* sound. It's done something to us.'

'You're right,' said Leela. 'It must be using Thoughtwaves, a bit like a Heartsichord. We have to ignore how we're feeling.'

Kip looked up at the ceiling where a legion of toxic red skulls was already gathering.

'We haven't got much time before this whole place is full,' he said. 'Leela, please, try again.'

Leela stood tall in front of the floating glockenspiel and struck the rods carefully, pausing every now and then to make sure she was going to get the next note right. At the end she stood back, looking pleased. Not a single mistake.

'Well done,' sighed Timmi.

Kip watched the music box, waiting for it to do something. But instead, the evil sound churned around the study again and the red skull notes started pouring out even faster.

'You idiot!' shouted Albert.

'Albert!' Kip snapped. 'I told you to hold it in. It's not Leela's fault.'

'Who put you in charge?' yelled Albert, with a nasty grimace.

He shoved Kip and Kip pushed him back. Albert swayed for a moment. He made a fist and it looked like he was going to punch Kip. But then he stepped away and put his hand over his mouth as if he were swallowing something disgusting.

Kip stamped down the urge to follow Albert and push him again. The skull notes had nearly filled up the top half of the study, like a loathsome red frogspawn. Soon, they would spread down to the top of the floating glockenspiel.

'Don't want to know what happens if one of them touches you,' he said.

'How much time have we got left?' moaned Timmi.

'Just hurry up!' said Albert.

'All of you SHUT UP while I think!' Leela snarled.

Timmi opened her mouth, but closed it again quickly before she could say anything else.

Leela bowed her head in thought. Then she started to tap her finger in the air.

'That's it!' she said, looking up again. '*Play me in time*. You can read it two ways.'

'What do you mean?' asked Kip.

'Play me before the time runs out. Or play me in time with the music!'

She began to strike the rods again with the hammer, following the beat of the music box. The skull notes kept streaming out of the red rod, crowding down now just inches from her hand.

It was getting harder and harder to push away the dark feelings.

She isn't good enough, thought Kip, feeling his stomach turn. *We're going to lose. We're all going to die in here. Maybe we'll actually end up killing each other.*

Timmi and Albert were crouching down at the side of the music box, jostling for space. The mowl cowered at Leela's feet. Kip knelt down and closed his eyes.

This can't be the end.

There was just him and the squirls and the music in the darkness. Leela's notes felt lonely, far apart, never touching. When the final one rang out, there was a moment's silence and then a sound like popcorn in the microwave.

'They're going!' Timmi cried out.

Above their heads the notes were bursting – one by one, and then in clusters. Inch by inch, the four friends were able to straighten up, until finally all signs of the skulls were gone and, with them, the terrible red rage.

'I could never have done that, Leela,' said Kip. 'Not in a million years.'

'Me neither,' said Timmi. 'Sorry for snapping at you.'

Leela smiled in relief and hugged Timmi, tears in her eyes.

326

'I'm sorry,' said Albert, facing Kip sheepishly. 'That was not cool.'

'Me too; we're good,' said Kip.

'Group hug!' said Timmi, pulling everyone in.

Kip sank into the safe comfort of his friends. It felt like hot chocolate on a cold day. The mowl crept between their feet and did his flappy dance inside the hug-circle.

'Um … the box,' said Leela, over Kip's shoulder. 'It's doing that thing again!'

Kip turned to see the music box spinning and collapsing.

'I'm sick of skulls,' groaned Albert.

'No, that was ten,' said Kip firmly. 'Now we get the Ark.'

The box crumbled from wood to dancing dust and gathered from dust to solid wood again. When the transformation was complete, they found themselves looking at a reading lectern. Resting on the lectern, there it was, finally: a book with a red-and-gold chequered cover.

Kip picked it up and stared at the prize.

'The Ark of Ideas is a book,' he said. 'Just an ordinary book.'

'Doesn't matter,' whispered Leela, 'we did it.'

'I knew we would,' said Albert. 'I knew from the start.'

Kip's fingers rested on the cover of the book for a

second. Every atom in his body was light, lifting, soaring. His hands trembled as if he'd climbed a five-mile peak. This was it.

Eartha, he begged silently. *You wrote in your letter that you know why I seek the Ark. Is there something in here to help her?*

Chapter Fourteen

1,001 Pages

Kip opened the cover and turned the first page carefully, expecting the paper to be old and frail. But it was thick and strong, so he turned the next page more confidently. Both were blank. He turned a few more.

'Keep going,' said Albert.

But page after page was empty: no ink, no words, no wisdom. Kip's eyes scanned hungrily for something and he turned the pages faster and faster.

'It's not possible,' he said through clenched teeth. 'Where's all the knowledge? Where are all the Strange Inventions? Where's the *cure*?'

'Is it another of Eartha's tricks?' asked Timmi.

'But she said ten riddles. That was the deal.'

Albert counted them out, from the Egg Flower to the Musical Skull Box.

'We've definitely solved them all,' said Leela. 'There has to be something in there.'

But, apart from the page numbers, all one thousand and one pages of the books were empty.

What if Sharktooth Girl somehow got here first, Kip thought, *and left a blank book just to mess with our heads? Or Prowlers sucked the words out of it?*

Life couldn't be this unfair. Kip pictured his mum, locked in her room at St Antony's. His fists clenched up but there was no anger left – only a gloomy weariness remained.

'All that work,' he said.

Thag. The clockwork soldiers. Scaleface. This empty book seemed harder to face than any of them.

'It can't all be for nothing,' murmured Leela.

'Can we look?' asked Timmi.

Kip passed a hand over his eyes and stepped back from the lectern, pulled down by his sinking heart.

'Go ahead,' he said.

Timmi felt the pages of the book, and tapped the hard cover.

'It feels too light,' she said, weighing it with both hands.

'Probably because there's nothing in there,' said Kip.

Timmi began to turn all the pages again, one by one.

'Kip already did that,' said Albert.

'Give her a minute,' said Leela. 'She's thinking.'

When Timmi got to the last page she gave a little

squeal and put the book down on the floor, still open.

'What are you doing?' asked Albert.

'Just watch!' she said.

Timmi did jazz hands above the open page but didn't seem to mind when her hands disappeared. With a big grin on her face, she danced around the book, making her hands appear and then disappear again several times.

A torrent of hope came tumbling back, lifting Kip's spirit up again.

'A wormhole? Inside the book?'

Timmi's grin got even bigger.

'How did you know it was there?' asked Albert. 'There's no purple.'

'I'm good with wormholes,' she said with a shrug. 'I just look sideways and there they are.'

'Wait. So the book isn't the Ark? Or is it?'

'Get with the programme, Albert,' said Leela, grabbing her Skimmi. 'Come on, mowl!'

Kip waited until everyone else had vanished into the wormhole, before he looked around the study.

'Where are you?' he whispered.

Then he saw what he was looking for – a mothy white flutter in the corner of his eye – all part of the plan. Satisfied, he stepped into the book, only to bump into Timmi, who had stopped directly in front of him.

'It's so beautiful,' she said, shuffling to one side.

They were standing on a wide, flat rock overlooking a frothy waterfall that tumbled into a canyon. A half-rainbow played in the mists over the spot where the river curled and hung and fell eternally. Both sides of the river were cloaked in the scarlet of a wild poppy meadow.

Albert gripped a boulder near the precipice and looked down.

'I can't see the bottom,' he said.

A wurble interrupted the enchanted scene and they all looked around for the mowl. There he was, perched on the roof of a glass summerhouse behind them.

The Summerhouse

Kip was first inside. Sand crunched underfoot as he walked to a small, ornamental tree made of polished driftwood. There was nothing else in the summerhouse, no hint that Eartha Quicksmith had been here.

'Empty,' said Timmi.

'We thought the book was empty but it wasn't,' said Albert. 'Come on, let's look around properly.'

They began to search every inch of the place – patting the tree's branches and digging in the sand.

As he inspected a windowpane, Kip saw a shimmering blob forming outside. The blob became a humanoid shape. Then the air seemed to split open, as if a shadowy seam had ripped, and someone skimmied through the wormhole book.

'Gorvak!' yelled Kip, running outside. 'Is your family OK?'

Gorvak smiled, but didn't say anything. He was carrying a small, metal box and looked exhausted.

'There's so much to tell you,' continued Kip, hurriedly.

'At first we thought the book was the Ark,' Timmi added, 'but it brought us here.'

'We can't find it,' said Albert. 'The Ark, we can't find it anywhere.'

Gorvak opened the lid of the box.

'Do you mean this?'

Everyone fell silent as Gorvak reached inside and pulled something out. A black parrot.

'May I introduce the Ark of Ideas.'

'The parrot in Eartha's portrait?' said Albert. 'And on her coat-of-arms!'

'Oh. My. Flippin. Mowl,' Leela sighed.

Kip reached up to touch it, but Gorvak pulled back and his Skimmi automatically retreated.

'It's very delicate,' he said.

A parrot couldn't possibly be alive after hundreds of years. As Kip looked closer, it moved its head slightly and whirred.

'It's mechanical!'

But something still didn't make sense.

'So, what was … how … where did you find it?' asked Kip.

'I got here before you,' said Gorvak, as if this were the most obvious thing in the world. 'It was just sitting on that tree in the summerhouse.'

'How does it work?' asked Kip, suddenly conscious of time. 'Sharktooth Girl could be here any second.'

'Melinda's not coming,' said Gorvak.

'But what if Thag's found a way round the Scrambleguard?'

'No one's coming,' Gorvak said slowly. 'Not for you.'

Kip stared back at those freezing blue eyes, feeling a chill creep across him like the shadow of a predator. He heard Albert swallow next to him, but still no one spoke until Gorvak took a Human Remote out of his jacket.

'Why do you need that?' Timmi said, taking a step back.

'Thag has never been a threat to me,' said Gorvak. 'He's got no strategy. But you, Kip. Well, you're different. Thag's temper provided the perfect smokescreen for me. While you were busy watching him, and then Melinda, I could keep tabs on you and make sure you didn't get to the Ark first.'

Kip looked at the others. This couldn't be happening.

'Haha,' said Albert. 'Bad joke. Terrible timing.'

Gorvak ignored him.

'I knew you were worth keeping an eye on, Bramley,' he said, 'from the time I heard you ask the Great Globe where the Ark of Ideas was. As it happens, you were closer than any of us thought.'

'All that stuff you said that night at the Clock Tower?' Leela said, her voice cracking. 'We heard it. You told Thag you were going to stop him stealing the Ark.'

'You stupid little oik,' said Gorvak. 'You think I wasn't following Kip's every move? I knew you were listening. And baiting Thag is like giving peanuts to a monkey. Besides did you hear me say *I* wasn't going to steal the Ark?'

'But we're a team,' pleaded Timmi.

'I'm the only person in my team,' Gorvak snarled, looking more like a leopard than ever, but not the friendly kind.

Kip's insides shuddered and shifted as he finally accepted the truth.

'At first I sat back and let you do all the grunt work,' Gorvak gloated. 'And then,' he let out a cold laugh, 'you nanobrains even told me all about the map, which you didn't hide very well. From there it was just plain sailing. But it turned out that you were harder to get rid of than I expected.'

'You dropped the Plasma Slug?' Kip asked, already knowing the answer.

'Pity you jumped about so much,' Gorvak said. 'It was meant for your head.'

'But if you solved all the riddles before us,' said Albert, 'why didn't we just find the wormhole book straight away?'

'Finally. An intelligent question. When I'd finished here, I replaced the book on the lectern in Eartha's study. That reset all the puzzles, and covered my tracks, just in case.'

Gorvak held up a shiny silver crescent.

'I thought taking this would kill the riddle trail. That you wouldn't be able to get past the Sea of Silence. But Eartha must have hidden more than one of these in her study.'

'Is your "family emergency" even real?' asked Leela acidly.

'What do you think?' sniffed Gorvak. 'Gossip and chaos provide a great distraction. Nice and easy for me to disappear.'

The sound of the waterfall poured into the stillness that followed. Then Timmi reached for something in her pocket and Albert lunged forward to try and grab the black parrot. But Gorvak was too fast for them both. With two swift button-presses of the remote, they were paused and began to wind down second by second.

Albert's eyes flicked to Kip's as he came to a final stop.

Do something, they said.

Leela clutched her Skimmi and stared fiercely at Gorvak, her face hardly recognisable behind a mask of hatred.

We still outnumber him, thought Kip, wishing he had a Thoughtwave Lens to communicate silently with Leela. *Have to find a way to distract him.*

Gorvak pointed upwards and his Skimmi drifted a few feet higher above the flat, bare rock.

'Thanks for this remote by the way,' he smiled. 'I had fun adapting it. Now it doesn't just pause you for two minutes. It pauses you. For. Ever.'

Kip's eyes darted around, looking for a weapon – a loose rock, or a stick to knock the remote from Gorvak's hand.

Can I reach that little glass house?

There was sand on the floor inside, perhaps he could throw it in Gorvak's eyes and buy himself and Leela a few seconds. But it was too far, six, seven steps at least…

'What shall I do with you all when I've paused you, I wonder? Push you off the edge?'

Gorvak sucked his teeth and wagged the remote at the lip of the canyon and the steep drop beyond.

'No,' he said, waving the parrot in the direction of Timmi and Albert. 'I think I'll just leave you all to stand around here forever. Like a sad art exhibition. That no one will ever see.'

As Kip returned Gorvak's stare, he saw movement out of the corner of his eye. Leela was slowly opening her Skimmi to rest it on the air. She raised her foot, carefully, carefully, eyes fixed on the enemy.

'You wouldn't dare,' said Kip, trying to keep Gorvak looking his way. 'Someone will come looking for us.'

'Oh, they might,' said Gorvak. 'Except no one will find the study in time. The ten days are nearly up. And just to make sure, I'll burn the wormhole book when I get back.'

'But why?' said Kip. 'You're related to Eartha Quicksmith. You're already famous. Everyone looks up to you. They all want to be like you. You don't need this.'

'Oh, but I do,' said Gorvak. 'Being liked isn't the end goal. There's something so much bigger going on here. Bigger than Eartha. Bigger even than the Earth. And now that's quite enough of that.'

Without looking at Leela, Gorvak pointed the remote at her and pressed the pause button. Instantly, an anguished roar exploded from the top of the summerhouse. Gorvak looked up as if expecting to face a mountain bear. But it was the mowl tearing towards him like a guided missile, every cell in his body aligned to defending Leela.

At exactly that moment, electric blue strands began to pull at the edges of Kip's vision. He looked down. squirls – Aeon Light – were pouring upwards

338

out of his pocket. It felt as if all the quixars in his body were sizzling with blue fire.

The mowl smashed into Gorvak. There was a clatter as the Human Remote fell to the ground and skidded away. And then Kip became aware of his shoes pounding against the rock, his body obeying a deep instinct to protect his friends. Everything faded away apart from the struggle before him. Gorvak was only two steps away, and then one.

Kip was close enough now to hear the sound of the enraged mowl's talons scratching at bare skin and then feel the force of air whip past him as Gorvak hurled the mowl into a boulder. A sickening crunch followed by a strangled yelp echoed across the canyon. Unable to fly or walk, the mowl lay hissing at the feet of the breathing statues.

It was just Kip and the enemy left now. The chaotic Aeon Light seemed to condense, becoming one pattern, one pulse, one arc of brilliant blue.

Listen to the light, thought Kip.

As he moved, it felt like his body was following the curves of the Aeon Light. His fingers had already reached into his pocket and taken out the Grandfather Clock. But then the squirls stopped dead and he hesitated, just for a fraction of a moment. Why was the engraving a warning? What did the clock do? Was he endangering all of them, and the Ark too?

Gorvak saw the hesitation and his hand shot out, snatching at the small cylinder.

'Don't!' yelled Kip.

But it was too late. The Grandfather Clock was slipping out of his hand. Kip knew he wouldn't catch it. The only thing he could do was to throw himself backwards as far away as he could.

As the blue metal cylinder hit the ground, the lid flew open. Long, powdery filaments the colour of ash spooled upwards – more than seemed possible from such a small container. Gorvak reacted quickly, shielding himself from below by urging his Skimmi forward. It took the brunt of the outpouring and patches across its surface began to disintegrate.

There was a delay of a few seconds before Gorvak screamed in agony. Kip realised that some of the powdery filaments had flowed up past the side of the Skimmi. Horror-struck, he watched Gorvak's arm and one side of his face withering like a winter branch, while the hair on that side of his head turned smoke grey.

Grandfather Clock, Kip thought. *Timeyarn. It's aging him.*

The Skimmi began to malfunction and dragged Gorvak through the air in random directions, until he fell heavily, groaning, on to the rock, still clutching black parrot in his uninjured hand.

shook himself into action and grabbed the

Human Remote that Gorvak had dropped earlier. They locked eyes as he pressed the pause button.

Gorvak blinked. Kip pressed the button again firmly.

Grimacing in pain as he stood up, Gorvak hunched over his withered arm. Then he began to laugh, tears collecting behind his glasses and rolling along the newly formed wrinkles on the left side of his face.

'Surprised? Do you really think I'd be stupid enough not to have thought of that? To risk a counterattack from my own weapon? It won't work on me.'

'I have more of those cylinders,' Kip lied. 'Give me the Ark.'

'Fine,' said Gorvak. 'You can have it. It talks, you know. And I've already listened to everything. It's all in my head now.'

He dropped the black parrot at his feet with an inviting stare.

'I'm not that stupid either,' said Kip. 'Turn around and walk away.'

Gorvak smiled, exposing his teeth. He took a step back and gave the Ark a mighty kick. It slid over the bare rock and bounced off a boulder, heading straight for the lip of the canyon.

'NO!' yelled Kip, lunging to try and stop it.

But he wasn't fast enough. As he dived after Eartha's black parrot, Kip saw it go right over the brink.

'Bye bye, Ark,' said Gorvak in the background. 'Bye bye, Eartha's little secrets. Bye bye, mummy.'

Powerless to save it, Kip lay on his stomach and watched the parrot falling away faster and faster until it was a black dot in the mists below.

'Give up,' said Gorvak, from behind. 'You've lost.'

Kip rolled over.

Dangling out of the clouds above the flat rock was a ladder made of a strange glittering silk, like woven spiderwebs. Gorvak was clinging to it, his good arm wrapped around one of the rungs. He was breathing heavily, but his eyes were triumphant.

'How does it feel? Is your heart cold? Broken?'

The gently waving ladder began to rise into the sky, lifting Gorvak with it, its source concealed by the clouds. Kip scrambled to his feet.

'Oh, and Bramley,' said Gorvak, waggling something in the dry claw of his ancient left hand, 'there were two remotes, remember?'

Kip began to run, but there was nowhere to hide. As the Human Remote started to take effect, pins and needles spread from his toes and fingers inwards. Numbness lapped at his skin. His eyelids were closing, millimetre by millimetre. Squirls and glimpses of dreams began to overwrite everything.

Beyond them, the waterfall was turning red, as thing churned up the poppy petals. Two blurry hovered above it.

'Over here!' he tried to shout, but he couldn't feel his throat or tongue or lips.

As they began to walk across the curve of the falling water, he could just make out their silver-black faces and their asymmetric eyes. They turned towards him purposefully. A slow-motion shudder cut through him like a shard of glass.

The shadows are gathering.

Kip watched, terrified, as the waterfall below started to curve up into the air, defying all natural laws. The Prowlers sped along this impossible, liquid road until it began to fork. One shadow continued upwards, to where Gorvak was being winched into the ragged clouds. The other shadow was carried towards Kip.

With one last, great effort, Kip tried to reach for the quartz crystal around his neck but his arm only moved an inch. He would never get to say goodbye. His heart was slowing down, too, but he could still feel it aching.

I tried, I really did, but I let you all down, was his last, muddled thought.

As the scenery around him faded, a black streak flashed through the sky and something landed on his outstretched arm. And then he fell into the deepest silence.

Awakening

Kip was a giant, so tall the trees were like blades of grass at his feet. Great flocks of golden eagles circled his head, but they were like midges to him.

On the blank, blue canvas of the sky he was drawing a squirl – white trails spilling out behind his finger like crushed ice. He looked up and saw the edge of the Earth's atmosphere; beyond it, the stars were clustering like glow-worms.

The squirl went on and on and Kip drew for days, months, years, decades, aeons, until the entire sky was full. And then he sat on the Earth and looked up at his masterpiece. It was a message. Something urgent, something that could save everything, stop the world from tumbling into nothingness…

'Kip Braaaam-leeeeeey,' said a high-pitched voice.

Kip frowned and kept looking up. The loops and whorls were complex but if he could see them *sideways* he knew the message would be so simple that even a small child could understand it. The Earth beneath him quaked as he shifted his weight to see the sky from a different angle. If he could just…

Something bumped against Kip's forehead. There was a pause, and there it was again.

'It's mee-eeeee. Pink-eeeee,' said the high-pitched e.

v? Am I…? So where's…

Darkness was everywhere. All the muscles in Kip's body were tensed: one arm was bent at the elbow, his head was turned, his toes gripped the inside of his shoes. Where was he? Was he running from something? Running *to* something?

Kip's eyes wanted to open, so he let them open.

It took a few moments to recognise the flat rock. The waterfall poured into the canyon. Down. It poured down, exactly as it should. The air was fresh and moist against his skin and birdsong drifted from somewhere. Kip turned his aching head to see that a fence had been built along the cliff edge. There was also a table with a jug of water. And Albert was sitting in an armchair next to the table.

The Small Animal Ninjaglider circled Kip's head, and Pinky chirped excitedly.

'Finally!' said Albert.

'Albert?'

It felt strange to talk, as though it was someone else's mouth.

'Everyone else is awake already. The professors didn't want to move you. Said it was too dangerous. They all just went for a meeting.'

He landed the Ninjaglider and unharnessed Pinky, who was wriggling with excitement.

'He's awake!' he yelled in the direction of the wormhole. 'Kip's awake!'

'Thirsty,' said Kip.

He tried to walk towards the table, but his stiff legs gave way.

'Woah,' said Albert, running over.

'Feel like I've walked a thousand miles,' Kip croaked.

'Yeah, it'll be like that for a few hours,' said Albert.

He helped Kip limp over to the armchair and fetched him a glass of water. Pinky scampered up the chair, rolled on her back in Kip's palm and stuck out her paws in joy.

'Did you miss me, Furball?'

'She's been pining,' Albert said. 'Your plan worked brilliantly by the way. When you didn't come back, Bagsworth opened the Great Globe like you'd agreed and followed your Mothball into the wormhole book. Professor Steampunk fixed the remote to unpause us, but we took a while to wake up as we'd been paused for so long.'

'Where are the others?' Kip asked.

'Leela and Timmi? They're in the study.'

Kip tried to stand, and dropped back as his leg muscles cramped.

'And the Ark. I mean the black parrot?' he said.

'It flew back to us, landed on your arm, but ... well...' said Albert, 'it's damaged. It will only say a few words. I'm sorry, Kip.'

Kip sank back in the armchair. He didn't think his heart could take any more disappointments. It felt too full and so empty at the same time. Pinky trotted up his arm and laid herself quietly on his chest.

'So, it was all for nothing,' he said.

'It wasn't all for nothing,' replied a voice inside his head.

Kip looked up as the Professor-in-Charge walked from the wormhole entrance over to the armchair. At her side was Professor Mo, wearing a brightly coloured crossword shirt.

'Congratulations!' said Miss Twiss. 'You found the Ark.'

'Thanks,' said Kip.

But I still couldn't help Mum, he thought sadly.

Hope spilled out of the Professor-in-Charge's mist-grey eyes.

'Not only did you find the Ark but you stood up to Thag and you stood up to Gorvak. And the Ark may be broken, but life is a sea of possibility, just like Strange Energy. There may be other ways to heal your mother, and if there are, you will find them. And we shall help you.'

Kip smiled, feeling his strength slowly return.

'Had I understood the danger you were in,' said Miss Twiss, 'I would have done things differently. Despite that, you have proved yourselves to be the bravest, most determined, and deserving individuals I have ever known.'

Professor Mo held up Eartha's Book of Aeon Light and Kip's Book of Squirls.

'We thought we'd find the secret to Aeon Light in the Ark. But you had it all along.'

'I didn't know,' said Kip. 'At least not until the very end. And then everything happened so fast. But why me? Why can I see it?'

'If you agree – and you don't have to say yes – then we can compare your drawings to Eartha's, to help us understand the mysteries of Aeon Light. And try to answer that very question.'

Kip took the tattered Book of Squirls.

This belongs to the old me. The me before Quicksmiths. The squirls won't fit in this book, not completely. The pages aren't big enough any more.

He flicked through it one last time, closed the cover and handed it back to Professor Mo.

'It's yours,' he said.

'Can Leela and Timmi visit now, Miss Twiss?' asked Albert.

'Certainly,' she replied. 'But then Kip will need a thorough medical check-up. And I'm sure he'll want to call his father, as soon as he's feeling up to it.'

'You're worth your weight in Quickets and more,' said Professor Mo, with the kindliest of smiles. 'All of you.'

The Professor patted Pinky, who scratched inquisitively at one of the crossword squares on his shirt. Then he walked away with a wave and left in a purple shimmer. But Miss Twiss turned at the entrance to the wormhole and said one last thing.

'How do we know this outcome isn't what Eartha planned all along?'

Kip and Albert remained quiet after she had left, listening to the birdsong.

'So, what happened to Gorvak?' asked Albert, eventually.

'Everything felt a bit unreal,' said Kip. He explained all about the Grandfather Clock and the struggle and the Timeyarn effect. 'After that I tried to pause him, but it didn't work. Someone was helping him too. A weird ladder came out of the clouds and he escaped. And there were two Scalefaces with him at the waterfall. Only they're called Prowlers. I found out before but there was no time to tell you.'

'Two?' said Albert, glancing at the horizon. 'Do you think they'll come back for the Ark?'

'I guess not, if it's broken,' Kip said.

'Happy Wakey Day, Kip!' announced Leela.

She marched over, with Timmi close behind, plonking herself and the mowl down on the rocky floor. The mowl licked Kip's hand with his long, forked tongue, and then returned to plucking at the plaster cast on his wing. Pinky jumped down from the arm of the chair and stroked the cast gently.

'So,' said Leela, 'I've been trying to work out which

famous fairytale character you are: Sleeping Ugly or the eighth dwarf, Snorey.'

Timmi knelt and took the black parrot out of its box. Its beautifully crafted mechanical feathers glistened like rainbows in oil.

'We thought you'd like to hear the Ark speak,' she said. 'Seeing as you rescued it.'

She flipped a switch under the parrot's wing. There was a whirring sound and one of its eyes winked. It cocked its head, lifted a foot, and twitched.

'The Crazy Paving…' it said, in a crackling voice. 'The Crazy Paving…'

'That's all it says,' Timmi explained. 'Over and over.'

'Apparently, the Crazy Paving was one of Eartha's inventions,' Albert said.

'Miss Twiss says it was like a doorway to a shifting labyrinth of realities, to other worlds called Myriads,' Timmi added, her green eyes sparkling. 'And the entrance is hidden somewhere at Quicksmiths.'

'But now we'll never find it,' said Leela.

'One person knows,' said Kip. 'And he's not telling.'

'At least all this flushed Gorvak out,' muttered Albert. 'Good riddance to bad rubbish.'

'The Ark might be broken,' Timmi said brightly, 'but there are loads of books and papers in Eartha's study. Who knows what we'll find in there?'

'You're right,' said Kip, switching off the black parrot and looking into its unblinking eyes. 'Ten days.

All this happened in just ten days. And we've got years ahead.'

'I s'pose this is kind of like the eleventh riddle,' said Timmi, touching the parrot's head.

'Still can't believe we did it,' Leela said. 'We were so lucky.'

Kip put down the Ark and looked at everyone gathered round. Despite the darkest dangers and the deep disappointments, these had been some of the best and most thrilling days of his life.

'Gorvak was a fake,' he said. 'He studied us and used us, and pretended to be like us, but he could never have what we have. Our friendship. Our trust. *That's* why we got the Ark, not because of luck.'

'For real,' said Albert. 'In Team Glowflyer we make our own luck.'

'You know,' said Kip. 'There was something I couldn't figure out. While I was paused.'

They all looked at him, waiting to hear what it was, even the mowl and Pinky, who had been comparing tails.

'Would you rather go flying inside a fish, or fishing inside a fly?'

Kip knew his friends so well now that he could almost hear their thoughts.

His head's messed up from being paused so long.
Maybe his Scrambleguard's broken.
Does he need a doctor?

It was impossible for Kip to keep a straight face for long. And then Leela's eyebrows tightened in realisation. She gave him a playful punch.

'I'm the one who asks the annoying questions,' she said.

Q

'It's only been a few weeks,' Kip said. 'At Quicksmiths.'

Theo had gone to get some tea and Rose was gazing dully at a bee that was bumping against the window and trying to get out. It was dark already outside and the lamps blazed brightly in the care home sitting room.

'A few weeks,' Kip repeated. 'But it feels like a lifetime. A good lifetime.'

Rose put her face up to the window and hummed along with the bee.

'We had a chance, Mum. I wanted to … to bring you back. But I couldn't get to it in time.'

Kip looked at his dim reflection next to his mum's in the window glass. Was it an illusion, or was his pendant glowing faintly? He undid the clasp and held up the blue quartz to see it better in the lamplight.

Rose reached out with a sudden clumsy motion, as if she couldn't control her hand, and touched the pendant. Kip turned to her in surprise, to find her looking straight at him.

And then she spoke to him, though it seemed as if

her voice came from a great distance, across arching mountains and deep-cut valleys and impassable ice fields.

'I'm so proud of you, Kip,' she said.

Mum?

It was the first time she seemed to know his name in seven years.

'Look how you've grown. And you've kept it safe. I knew you would.'

She opened her arms and Kip tumbled into the hug he'd been hoping for, imagining, for so long. He knew he should shout for the nurse but he couldn't shatter this moment.

'It's very important, this fragment,' said Rose. 'You mustn't...'

She smiled weakly and paused for so long that Kip thought it was over and bowed his head into the embrace that still lingered.

'The Earth turns, Kip,' she whispered. 'The night drifts away. There's a dream I've been having. A wonderful dream. I see us all back together, as clear as day.'

Then the lost look reclaimed her eyes as she turned back to the window and the moment was gone. Kip sat motionless, hoping that his mum would stir again. But she just hummed along with the bee's buzzing.

He couldn't be sure, but it sounded like the tune of *I'm Only Sleeping*.

'I won't give up,' Kip murmured, holding her hand. 'There must be a way to bring you back for good.'

Footsteps crunched on gravel outside and he looked up. Kip's mirror image in the window glass returned his gaze. Somehow, there in the halfway world between the inside and the outside, the squirls seemed to enter into the reflections and wrap around them, stirring an inkling of something else, something better to come, like gold glistening in the grass.

'We're going to change this world, I promise,' he whispered, just as Theo returned, whistling, with a tray of tea.

Acknowledgements

There are five people without whom this book wouldn't exist, at least not in its current form:

Mum, who gave me the first spark of an idea; Liam, who has read drafts and given comments probably more times than there are stars in the Milky Way, and who constantly feeds my imagination; Roland Clare, whose careful scrutiny always resulted in a much improved manuscript; Anne Clark, who gave me my first break and steered the way with ever insightful and excellent advice; and Penny Thomas, who found this book a sunny corner in the Firefly garden, pruning, sculpting and tending its leaves with a gloriously light touch.

Special thanks to: Dad for teaching me to think sideways; the charismatic Robin Bennett and all the lovely Fireflies – Simone, Janet, Meg, Rebecca and especially Leonie Lock for her bubbling enthusiasm and eagle-eyed copy-editing; Anne Glenn, Hazel Guppy and Jacqueline Maxwell for bringing the world of Quicksmiths to life so delightfully and imaginatively in the book cover, illustrations and map respectively; Chris Lewis for his astute and good-natured counsel; Philippa Donovan for guiding me through early stages; Bill McEvoy for the candid and thoughtful critique; Clare Pearson for spurring me on at the LBF; Rachel Leyshon & Clare Whitston for the gold nuggets of feedback; the very patient Elaine Sharples; Margot Edwards and Pam Woollard.

I was very lucky to have a bunch of perceptive middle grade/YA readers, who gave me some brilliant comments. They were: Sacha Baber, Darci Clare, Charlie Cronin, Kai Cronin, Cian Fincham-Cronin, Alex Hatley, Tayla Hatley, Kai Sayer.

Additional thanks to: Bristol Grammar School Year 7 English Class 2018 (Lanre, Lauren, Adam, Keira, Samuel, Izaak, Abdullahi, Nikki, Olwyn, Charlie, Louis, Jack, Archie, Sophie, Harry, Prithija, Joe, Lucy and Ollie); the Winchester Writer's Festival (now the Writers' Weekend Winchester); Dan, Jessica & Luke; Ryan Hatley; Parbati Tikhatri; Jane Wilson; Jeannie Lloyd-Jacob; Koleta Kelekolio; Te Pūtahi Whakawhiti Reo; Steven Webster; Tonya McNamee; Tosin Sanyaolu; 郑旭明 (Zheng Xu Ming); and my Zimbabwean Ladies WhatsApp group.

If I have accidentally missed anyone out, please forgive my forgetful brain.

Terry Woollard

Clare College Porter from 1984 – 1997

Always Remembered